Ander grinned. He reversed his blade, and with both hands plunged it down at the assassin.

The assassin rolled to one side, slicing his sword upward. The blade bit into the underside of Ander's arm, and a flash of pain shot down to his hand. His fingers went numb, and he dropped his sword.

The assassin smiled. "You are quite the fool," he said as he got to his feet.

Ander grasped his arm. Hot blood flowed past his elbow and dripped onto the dock. It was over. Strangely, he felt no regret. He'd lived a good life. He only wished Emma had lived. The ways of the sellsword had never suited her. She had the heart of a poet, not a swordsman.

Ander dropped to his knees and stared into the dark eyes of the foreigner. "Make it quick," he told him…

FELL'S HOLLOW

AN EPISODIC NOVEL

Bernie,
Thanks for the support
and for remembering me!! — Jim

A. J. ABBIATI

LAK Publishing
http://lakpublishing.info

For Lexi and Adrian

ACKNOWLEDGMENTS

Thanks to my family, friends, fellow students, professors, workshoppers, MNFers, and to all those who lent their support for this book. I appreciate everything you've done for me.

Thanks especially to Todd Potter, my ever-present sounding board, who played an integral part in every aspect of FELL'S HOLLOW, from inception to completion.

Thanks to Jerry Dorris at AuthorSupport.com for the awesome cover work. He's a man of much talent and even more patience.

Thanks go to my in-process proofer, Rich Kornacki, and to my post-process proofer, Mark MacKinnon. Their eagle eyes caught many a potential flub.

And finally, a huge thanks to Julia Leef, my wonderful copyeditor. I should have brought her onto the project much earlier than I did.

CONTENTS

FOREWORD

FELL'S HOLLOW BEGAN with a phone call I received in August, 2009. Randall Choat, a UCLA archaeologist I'd done business with on occasion, was in England. He had stumbled upon something that I, a somewhat renowned antiquities dealer, might be interested in. He wouldn't divulge the details over the phone; he would only reveal the names of his two colleagues: Cordell Kane, an Oxford professor of linguistics and ancient languages, and Mirco Synakowski, director of the history department at Stanford University. The three were looking for a buyer, and Choat had immediately thought of me. If I was interested, I would have to meet them in London to find out more.

As my business had slowed dreadfully over the past few years, and as I knew Choat would not waste my time, I figured the trip would be worth my while.

I was not disappointed.

I flew out of JFK that night, and the next morning I met with Choat and his two colleagues. Choat had unearthed a cache of chests that appeared to be 16th or 17th century in origin, somewhere near the ruins of an abbey in Lymington. The seams of the chests had been sealed with paraffin, and when Choat had opened them he discovered a wealth of well-preserved documents. The documents, of a crude paper also typical of the 16th or 17th century, were covered in a variety of illustrations and handwritten text. The text seemed to be penned by the same precise, meticulous hand, and, surprisingly, was in a language unfamiliar to Choat. So Choat had turned to Cordell Kane.

Kane determined the language to be a strange variant of Middle English, one he had never seen before and one which he couldn't read with any degree of certainty. This had baffled Kane, which had caused some concern in Choat. If Kane couldn't read the documents, then perhaps they were simply an elaborate hoax, a stockpile of Voynich-like manuscripts buried by a lunatic monk over four hundred years ago, and therefore essentially worthless, at least from an historical perspective. That was a distinct possibility.

According to Choat, the abbey had been abandoned in the late 1700s, but there were still rumors running around Lymington that it had housed some of the more unstable of the Benedictine order.

Kane wanted more time to study the documents, and Choat, not having much of an alternative, agreed. Two months later Kane cracked the code, so to speak, and began to translate the contents of the first chest. And that brought them to Mirco Synakowski.

It turned out the documents were a collection of transcriptions. There were copies of journals, diaries, ships' logs, merchants' records, shop manifests, personal letters, broadsides, plays, poetry, and more, all of which had one thing in common: each made reference to a port city called Fell's Hollow, a city that, as far as Choat and Kane knew, never existed.

Synakowski's task was simple: find out everything he could about Fell's Hollow. Was it a lost city? Or was Fell's Hollow perhaps a more obscure reference to Atlantis? Or to Maly Kitezh? Or, more likely, was Fell's Hollow an alias or code name for a city that still exists today, perhaps somewhere in or near Great Britain? That might explain the documents' strange relation to Middle English.

Based on information contained in some of the documents, Fell's Hollow was located on the western end of a peninsula, in a hidden, cliff-lined cove. The cove, more like a giant basin, was roughly elliptical in shape and stretched a few miles across at its longest point. It was hilly in parts, dotted with various species of trees and plant life. It had a deep harbor on one side, fed by a narrow gorge that led out to sea. On the other side, a steep, twisting ravine climbed out of the cove to the rocky bluffs of the peninsula. The city itself stretched from the shores of the harbor all the way to the base of the cliffs that surrounded the cove.

Fell's Hollow had been divided into wards, similar to London, and it had been a rough place to live, its streets littered with thieves and cutthroats. Its citizens depended on trade, most of it illegal. Enterprising captains would sail through the gorge and into the city's harbor to conduct business, avoiding the high tariffs of their own countries. As the city grew and prospered, it eventually expanded onto the surface of the harbor itself. Clever craftsmen constructed a maze of docks, buildings, and wooden structures that ran all the way out to a long, stone wharf that stretched from one side of the harbor to the other.

All this described a city unlike any medieval or Renaissance city of record. Whatever the answer, Choat and his colleagues were getting pressure from their respective universities. The dig was costing too much and producing too little. If they wanted to continue their work at the Lymington site, they would somehow have to prove Fell's Hollow was real, and therefore historically significant. So the three doubled their efforts. Kane went back to translating the contents of the first chest nearly round the clock, while Synakowski, with the help of Choat, scoured Stanford's archives for clues.

Unfortunately for the three, the upcoming weeks brought nothing but bad news. Synakowski and Choat failed to locate a single reference to Fell's Hollow. To make matters worse, Kane uncovered within the documents more previously unheard-of locations: Alar, Nyland, Thalia, Ithicar, Bosk, and others. This meant that either Fell's Hollow was part of an entire continent that had vanished from the face of the earth, not to mention history, or the documents were indeed fictional.

Their hopes faded and a few weeks later were dashed completely. As Kane wrapped up his work on the first chest, he began to encounter things that even the most open-minded would find too far-fetched to be factual: references to unknown gods, magic rituals, daemons, strange beasts, and other oddities I won't mention here.

At that point the jig was up. Disappointed, the three had decided to cut their losses and to call me. They suspected I might pay them enough for the documents to help recover some of their costs. Hoax or no hoax, the documents were certainly antiquities and therefore had to be worth something, for carbon-14 dating had confirmed them to be at least 400 years old. If the documents had no historic value, the three had hoped they might have some aesthetic value to a few of my more eccentric customers. I had agreed with that line of thinking, so I bought the documents—with a single caveat: Kane would have to finish translating the contents of all the chests (for an extra fee, of course) and provide the translations to me at a later date. A full set of translations, I knew, would make the documents far easier to sell.

A few days later I was sitting in my shop in SoHo trying to figure out how to maximize my profits. I could sell all the documents and translations as a bundle, or I could break them into lots. The latter idea sounded better, as it would take Kane more than a year, perhaps several years, to finish the rest of the translations. I could sell one lot at a time as the translations of each chest became available and start to recoup my original investment. Either way, though, I was not looking at a windfall. After paying Kane for his work, I could not expect to make more than a few thousand for my efforts. There had to be a better way, some way to suck every penny out of the deal. As a result of the floundering economy, my profits had begun to dwindle and the lease on my shop was due. For the first time in forty-seven years, I was facing the possibility of going out of business.

Frustrated, I decided to take a walk. I wandered about the city for a while, and just as I strolled past the Strand it hit me. I whipped out my cellphone and contacted one of my favorite customers, an executive at LAK Publishing, and by the end of the month I had a signed contract.

My idea was simple. I would hire a ghostwriter to take the translations from the first chest, extract from them the strangest, most intriguing characters, places, and events, and then dramatize it all into a novel. The writer would, of course, use discretion to fill in any gaps where the documents lacked detail. For this reason, finding a writer with a good dose of common sense and some insight into human nature was a must. And when done, the writer would collect a nice check, and I would collect (and continue to collect) the royalties on the novel, not to mention the money I would receive from selling the original documents and translations in the first place. In fact, I could repeat the process again and again as Kane wrapped up his work on each of the chests.

I was a happy man. My shop was saved.

But getting this new project off the ground was no easy task. The hunt for the right writer took time. Over six months, in fact. Of those that could prove themselves qualified technically, most wanted a cut of my advance and a cut of the royalties. Others wanted a cut of my advance, a cut of the royalties, and their name on the front cover. So much for being ghosts. In the end I found a reasonable fellow from Connecticut who only insisted on a one-time payment up front. We hit it off rather well, and, as it turned out, I am putting his name on the cover anyway.

And that, Dear Reader, is how this novel came to be. I hope you enjoy it as much as I enjoyed, and continue to enjoy, managing the Fell's Hollow project.

Thomas Walter Whitaker Parker
Rare Antiquities Dealer
New York, New York
November 2012

DEATH COMES ON THE WIND

"In every myth there lies a mote of truth."
Har and Iva, *Act II, Sc. 3*
—*Espare dae Kesh*

THE *DESTINY* SLICED through the chop of the Sellum Sea as stormwinds whipped from the west and stretched her sails taut. White-crested waves beat mercilessly at her sides. Behind her, dark clouds smothered the horizon. Her masts creaked under the stress, and the sound of it joined the crashing of the surf and the squawking of the gulls that followed over her wake.

She was an old ship, but she could still handle a rough sea. Originally a small Nyland frigate, she'd spent years running up and down the mainland coast chasing Ukrian pirates, spying on Kern, and harassing Alar warships with hit-and-run efficiency. But she was a private vessel now, refitted for fishnetting the deep gray waters of the Sellum, a far less glorious, though hardly less dangerous, mission.

Her crew scurried about her hundred-foot deck as she ran before the wind. Last evening they had finally finished their task. After a month at sea, the ship's hold held enough croll, haddock, and korshark to earn a hefty sum on the docks at Fell's Hollow. The haul lent the ship ballast, yet not enough to prevent it from listing far to port as it slipped suddenly down the side of a ten-foot swell.

The crew, seasoned as they were, scarcely noticed. They carried on with their work, tightening stays, battening hatches, securing topside barrels and equipment, while below deck a young fisherman new to the *Destiny*, and to life at sea, clutched the edges of a small table in a white-knuckled grip.

The ship leveled, and Chibb's ears burned with embarrassment. He was sitting down, for Ryke's sake, and still he'd almost toppled over. What would the old man think?

Across the table, Ossillard rubbed his well-weathered scalp, brown and hairless as a scrap of leather, and smiled warmly. On Chibb's first day at sea, the old man, an Alarman like himself, had taken to watching over Chibb like a kindly grandfather. He said he'd never met such a groundhugger before, and if he didn't take matters into his own gnarled hands, Chibb was bound to end up as croll chum by the end of the trip.

Chibb was only nineteen. He'd grown up an orphan on the streets of Ithicar, begging and stealing his way through life. It had been a terrible existence. He knew there had to be something better out there for him, a life he could lead with his head held high, not bent in shame as he scoured the streets for scraps of food. When Chibb had signed on to the *Destiny*, he'd known nothing of a fisherman's life. He still knew nothing, or very little, anyway. So when Ossillard spoke, Chibb made it a point to listen.

"It's your move, boy," the old man pointed out.

Chibb turned back to their game. A nine-by-nine grid of squares had been burned into the top of the table. Each square had a hole drilled at its center. Black and white pegs dotted the grid. Chibb was down to six pegs: five knobs and his king. And he was losing. Ossillard had said everyone in Fell's Hollow played taffyl. It was an obsession, enjoyed by the high- and low-born alike. If Chibb wanted to fit in when they arrived, or at least not lose all his hard-earned coin, he needed to learn the basics.

At the center of the board, Chibb's king, a

single white peg taller than the rest, was in a bad state, nearly surrounded by Ossillard's black knobs. Chibb needed to find a clear path to a corner of the board where his king could flee to safety, but he was damned if he could see one.

"Watch yourself," warned Yngot.

Yngot, Ossillard's oldest mate, was lying lazily in one of the narrow bunks built into the ship's hull. The old Nylander was missing a few front teeth, and a month of gray growth covered his cheeks. He took a candle that flickered in an iron holder nailed into the ship's frame, stuck the flame to the end of his hand-carved pipe, and puffed. The tabac's thick aroma filled the cramped cabin, mingling with the smell of salt and sweat and fish.

Ossillard glared at Yngot. "Leave off. The boy needs to learn for himself."

Yngot took a puff from his pipe and snorted. "From what I hear, he ain't been learnin' too well."

Chibb tried to ignore them both. He searched the board. There had to be an opening somewhere.

"What's that supposed to mean?" Ossillard asked his old mate. "The boy's coming along fine with his ropes."

"It means," Yngot said as he blew out a smoke ring, "there's talk he broke the first rule."

A lump of dread dropped into Chibb's belly. He hadn't been aboard ship for more than an hour when Ossillard had taught him the first rule of the *Destiny*: No one, ever, was to fraternize with Saera Gretch.

Saera was a great captain: smart, tough, experienced. Though still young, she was a legend in nearly every port town on the coast. Some said she was raised by pirates. Used to be a pirate, in fact, and knew every reef and current up and down the mainland. Saera Gretch could run a ship better than most men, men who had spent twice her time at sea. But great as she was, she was still young, and at times, still unwise. She tended to favor her favorites a little too much, and that meant unequal shares when it came time to split the coin. Sailors don't take well to being cheated. More than one of her favorites had turned up missing, not showing up on a morning when they were to set sail, or simply vanishing at sea during a dark night's watch. And now, Chibb thought, he had broken the first rule. Or at least he was about to.

"He's not that stupid," Ossillard said.

Yngot chuckled. "Oh, really?"

Ossillard stared hard at Chibb. "You're not that stupid, are you, boy?"

"Course not," Chibb lied. He kept his head down. Some seamen, he had heard, could tell a man was lying simply by looking into his eyes.

The *Destiny* dipped again, and Chibb grasped the table. Ossillard, oblivious to the sudden motion, waved a hand at Yngot, dismissing the topic. "There, see?"

As Chibb looked for a move, he hoped Yngot would drop the matter. After all, it wasn't really a problem. Not yet, anyway. And even if it became one, it wouldn't be his fault. He had been minding his own business, his concentration bent on learning the tasks Ossillard had set to him: rigging sails, manning nets, coiling anchor lines. But from the first time he'd seen Saera Gretch, hand at the ship's wheel, golden hair whipping in the sea breeze, his heart had been caught as sure as a croll in a net.

He found her the most magnificent creature, with eyes bluer than a spring sky after a storm. She seemed a serious woman and yet at the same time as carefree and reckless as any of the girls he'd chased through the dirty streets of Ithicar only months before. When she'd approached him at midnight two nights past as he stood the watch alone, leaning against the bowsprit and staring into the star-flecked sky, he'd been helpless to resist. Her kiss had tasted like honey, and her embrace had been as hot as a blacksmith's furnace. It had happened only once, just for a moment, but it ended with a promise. A promise to meet in secret when they arrived at Fell's Hollow. And that was a promise he meant to keep.

"They say the boy and the captain have been tying knots together on the late watch," Yngot went on. "They say—"

Ossillard slapped a hand on the table. "They say! They always say, you old gossip. And they're usually wrong. Talk like that could get the boy killed. You should know better."

Chibb kept his mouth shut and his eyes on the board.

Yngot puffed at his pipe and blew out another ring. "Fine," he muttered. "But there's always some truth in what people say."

Ossillard let out a grunt.

A flush of relief washed over Chibb. He was glad the dangerous conversation was over. He raked his eyes over the board one final time, and then he saw it. With a grin he moved one of his knobs. He had discovered a way to beat the old man. At last. One more turn and Chibb's beleaguered king would be free.

The ship dipped, deeper this time, and he nearly rolled out of his chair. Even Ossillard had to catch himself.

Chibb whistled. "That was some—"

The hatch above their heads opened abruptly, and a gust of sea air blasted into the cabin. A crewman peered down at them, a look of worry lining his sun-cooked face. "Captain says all hands," he called to them. "There's a storm coming, and she thinks it's a big one."

Yngot dropped from his bunk as Chibb stood and snatched a beam for support. Ossillard placed a crooked finger onto one of his knobs, a knob that Chibb had written off as harmless, and pegged it over a square, capturing his king.

"Sorry, boy," the old Alarman said.

*

"Furl all sails!"

Saera Gretch's command was nearly lost in the howl of the wind. A handful of crewmen scrabbled about the foredeck preparing the ship for the worst as Chibb held on tightly to the capstan. A heavy downpour had begun, and he was soaked to the skin. They'd been running with the wind for more than an hour trying to outrace the storm, as well as the setting sun, to Fell's Hollow. A storm at day was one thing. At night, Ossillard had told him, it was twice as dangerous. Back on the quarterdeck, Saera clutched the ship's wheel, fiercely focused on her task.

Chibb watched Ossillard as the old man wrestled with the jibsail along with Yngot and another crewman, a short, red-haired Nylander who was missing half an ear. Rain ran down their faces. Above, the skies had turned nearly black.

Ossillard shot a look at Chibb. "Help us with this sheet!" he yelled through the wind.

Chibb let go of the capstan and grabbed a handful of wet canvas. The ship dropped. Chibb staggered, and Ossillard caught him by the arm.

"Come on, boy! Heave!" the old man ordered.

Chibb helped the three men yank the soaked sail along the rolling deck. Then, with the coordination of seasoned sailors, they folded it again and again until it looked like a long, white worm. They folded it once more, lengthwise, and stowed it in a chest beside the gunnels.

"Good work!" Ossillard clapped Chibb on the back. "You're learnin'!"

Chibb smiled, feeling a rush of appreciation for the old Alarman. The half-eared Nylander muttered something unintelligible and stalked back aft, head bent against the wind.

"Now watch this!" Ossillard shouted. He skirted around the anchor housing and trudged through the rain to the bow where Yngot already stood leaning against the gunnels. Chibb stumbled along behind him.

The *Destiny* was losing speed. With no sails to catch the wind, they were now slamming through the rough swells on momentum alone. In front of the ship a short distance off loomed a length of craggy cliffs. Chibb recalled the details of the chart the old Alarman had used to teach him the basics of navigation. He figured they must be at the tip of the Harkkan peninsula, a long, nearly untraversable stretch of rocky land that jutted miles out from the mainland like the blade of a long, curved knife. On the other side of the peninsula were the calmer waters of Farstun Bay. It was his first sight of land in a month, and, with the storm threatening to smash their ship to bits, he was glad to see it.

Dead ahead a dark crack split the cliff face. It was the opening to a narrow gorge, and, Chibb realized, they were heading straight for it.

"Is she crazy!" he shouted.

Ossillard laughed. "That she is! Now, hold tight!"

Wind whipped at their wet clothes and sea spray pelted their faces as Chibb watched in horror. The *Destiny* sailed straight into the gorge. There was barely a ship's width of space on either side. Darkness fell over them, and it felt to Chibb as if they'd sailed into a cave. Sheer rock walls stretched high overhead. The gray waters turned to white foam as the ocean funneled and twisted around them. The howl of the wind, the crash of the water, the sounds of shouting seamen, exploded into a thunderous cacophony.

The *Destiny* plowed through the madness. Chibb tried to look ahead but could make out nothing beyond two roughly carved towers set into the cliff walls at the far end of the gorge. From the tops of the towers, the snouts of several cannon pointed down at their ship like black fingers. He caught a glimpse of men manning the guns. As the *Destiny* dashed between the towers, the men stared down at them, stern looks on their faces, tabards of red and black flapping about them in the wind.

Then, with a rush, the ship shot out of the gorge. Its prow plunged dangerously low, nearly submerging into the froth. It reared once and righted itself. Chibb slipped on the sea-soaked deck and lost his grip on the gunnels. Ossillard snatched a handful of his tunic, steadying him. Yngot gave a harsh laugh, and the roar of the gorge fell away in a muted hush. Deck planks creaked and masts groaned. The winds calmed. The *Destiny* pitched and rolled as it slowed its frantic pace, until, at last, it came to a settled stop.

The crewmen threw up their hands and cheered. Yngot slapped a hand on Chibb's back and gave him a toothless grin.

"Welcome to Fell's Hollow!" he said.

Slack-jawed, Chibb took in the view. They were on a small harbor tucked away in a hidden cove. The cove was enormous, a great cliff-lined basin cut from the land as if some god had scooped it out with a spade. Covered in a thin, wispy haze, it stretched north to south for perhaps three miles or more, and ran at least a mile deep. From the base of the cliffs, a series of lush, tree-lined hills spotted with spires and tiled rooftops tumbled down to a wide swatch of level land where the buildings of the main part of the city sat huddled together in the mist.

Ossillard snapped open his spyglass and handed it to Chibb, who held it to his eye for a closer look. The buildings of the city spread down to the shore and, shockingly, out onto the surface of the harbor itself. There they formed a labyrinth of tilting wooden structures set atop thick, pitch-smeared pilings. Thin lengths of dock mazed through it all. Hemming in the buildings, a massive stone wharf curved from one side of the

11

harbor to the other.

Chibb shifted the spyglass. There were ships of all sorts tied to the wharf and moored out in the deeper waters of the harbor. Sailors and dockworkers were scurrying everywhere, rolling barrels, lugging up cargo from the holds, storing sails, coiling rope. At each end of the wharf, a wooden crane stuck up like a spike. One crane was busy offloading crates from a sleek, triple-masted vessel as black as tar. The other was dangling a rope down to a low-riding trader. On the trader's deck, bare-chested men stood around an iron cage that held some winged, lizard-like beast. The beast was as big as a horse, if not bigger. Black-scaled and snarling, it bit at the bars as the men taunted it with shouts and sticks.

Fell's Hollow was nothing like the sprawl and squalor of Ithicar, Chibb thought. He blew out a long sigh. "Amazing."

"You may think so," Ossillard said, taking back the spyglass, "but it's a dangerous city. Many a lad's first visit here was his last. You stick close to me. Or to Yngot. We'll look after ya."

"Aye, we will," Yngot confirmed.

"Doesn't the king keep the peace?" Chibb asked.

"King?" Ossillard snorted and rubbed his bald head. "There's no king here, boy. Fell's Hollow's ruled by the Triad."

"The what?" Chibb asked.

"The Triad," Ossillard repeated. "The Lord

Mayor and his two advisors, the Guildmaster and the Watch Commander. The Lord Mayor runs the city. The Guildmaster looks out for the interests of the merchants and the shopowners. It's the Watch Commander who's charged with keeping the peace, along with defending the city. We passed some of his men back in the gorge. The blokes in the red and black tabards."

"Watchmen," Yngot muttered. "Stay clear of 'em. They'll as soon cut your throat as protect it."

"Fishguts!" Ossillard spat over the gunnels. "They're honest men, most of 'em. But still..." He gave Chibb's shoulder a squeeze. "It doesn't hurt to mind one's business, does it? Just don't run afoul of anyone and you'll be fine."

"Way the yawl!" the captain barked. "Chibb! I want you back here!"

Chibb turned. Saera had moved to the front of the quarterdeck to oversee the docking process. Her golden hair fluttered in the breeze as she watched him with those intense blue eyes, the most beautiful eyes he'd ever seen. She grinned slightly and beckoned to him with a cock of her head. He felt the blood rush to his face, and he smiled broadly. "Aye, aye!" he shouted, his voice cracking with excitement.

He was about to move, when Yngot snagged his arm and whispered in his ear. "She's a beauty, ain't she?" he said. "You almost couldn't blame a lad if he got carried away, you know, and forgot the first rule." Worry was plain on his stubbled face. "You sure you ain't hiding something?" he asked.

Chibb glanced over at Ossillard. The old Alarman was studying him. He got the feeling they both could read his thoughts as clearly as they could read the stars. He would have to be careful. More careful than ever. Especially after tonight. A wave of anticipation tingled down his spine. "I'm not hiding anything," he said.

"We'll talk about this later," Yngot informed him. "At the Hole."

*

The Hole reminded Chibb of his cabin on the *Destiny*, only darker and even more cramped. A handful of candles flickered on the bar and on the dozen or so tables crammed haphazardly around the room. The wooden ceiling was low, causing some of the taller visitors to stoop slightly as they made their way to and from the bar. Set into the front wall was a huge window of green glass. According to Yngot, it was the bar's namesake, a porthole salvaged from some war galley long ago, and it revealed nothing but blackness beyond. A thick odor of onions, sweat, and stale ale hung in the air.

Chibb let his gaze wander. Nearly every table held sailors, dockworkers, or common cityfolk caught up in conversation. At the other end of the bar, a rugged woman of middle years was wiping her mouth across the back of an arm. Her other arm was missing, its empty sleeve dangling loosely at her side. At a nearby table, a watchman in battered chainmail sat alone staring into the contents of a wooden tankard, the corners of his mouth turned down in deep thought or perhaps sadness. Near the back, a man and a woman were in the corner playing taffyl. They wore their tawny hair tied back with thin strips of leather. Black oilcloth cloaks covered them to their ankles. Their longswords were resting against the table, unhid and unsheathed. Chibb had seen their kind skulking about the docks of Ithicar. They were surely sellswords, dangerous folk at the best of times.

Chibb downed the last of his ale and clunked his tankard on the bar. The bar was old, oaken, and etched by a thousand knife points. Behind the bar, Morg, a well-muscled man of perhaps fifty or sixty summers, was busy rinsing a tankard in a bucket of dirty water. His head was shaven, save for a narrow strip of spiked hair that ran over the top. It was dyed a dark, bloody red. A silver skull dangled from each of his ears.

"Want another, boy?" Ossillard asked, his words slightly slurred. He, Ossillard, and Yngot had been downing ales for hours, ever since they'd docked and sold their haul on the wharf, or Stonewharf, as Yngot had called it. When Saera split the coin, Yngot had laughed and clapped Chibb on the back. She'd counted out seventeen gold troyals for Chibb, same as the rest. It was more money than he had ever seen.

Chibb set down his tankard. "I've had my fill," he announced. "I don't want to wake up with a pounder." The truth was, he wanted to keep his wits about him. It was almost midnight, and almost time to head to Madame Maara's, a small inn near the shores of Oldtowne, the oldest warde in the city, so Saera claimed. She kept a room there and would be waiting for him, as promised. He wasn't about to get drunk, stumble off a dock, and drown. Not tonight of all nights.

Yngot gave him a wide toothless grin. "The question is, what will you wake up with? Or who?" He winked at Chibb and laughed. The old Nylander drained the last of his ale. Amber sparkles dripped from his grey stubble as he slammed the tankard onto the bar. "Morg! Another!" he bellowed.

After the coin had been split, Ossillard and Yngot had seemed to drop their suspicions. When they had turned to teasing Chibb, calling him a besotted groundhugger, his worries had eased.

Ossillard slapped Yngot on the back of the head. "You still at it? We've tormented the lad enough for one night."

"Ow!" Yngot protested, but his grin remained stuck to his face.

Morg came over and set a fresh tankard in front of Yngot, taking away the empty one. "What about you two?" the barkeep asked.

Ossillard nodded. Chibb shook his head, just as a woman came up to the bar and sat next to him. She was older than him by a bit, and quite beautiful. Her eyes were chips of dark green and her hair fell in auburn curls past her shoulders. She shook the rain off her cloak and smiled at Morg.

"Hey, Morg. Where's Kretch?" she asked.

"Evening, Vara," Morg said. "Gave him the night off. The usual?"

She nodded. "Please."

Morg moved away and the woman hung her cloak on a hook under the bar. As she waited, she fingered a gleaming black rose that hung from a silver chain around her neck. It was carved from a single piece of flamite, Chibb noticed. Flamite was a rare stone not often seen in the Nine Kingdoms. The woman was no peasant.

Morg returned with two foaming tankards. The woman took one. Ossillard took the other. Morg swept a rag over the bar and then turned to the woman. "They found another one," he said. "Night before."

The woman slipped the rose beneath her tunic. "I heard." She took a slug of ale.

Morg looked around suspiciously and then continued in a low voice. "Had those marks all round his face. Found him floating down by Dredger's Dock."

"Found who?" Yngot asked.

Chibb watched Morg carefully. For such a

tough looking man, there was the glint of something in his eyes. Something Chibb recognized all too well.

Fear.

The woman turned to Yngot and gave him an appraising look.

After a moment, Morg shrugged. "I don't know who he was," the barkeep said. "A sailor, most like. But he's the second in a week."

"Someone knifed 'em?" Ossillard asked.

Morg glanced at the woman. She met his eye, and it seemed something unsaid passed between them. Morg slopped his rag back onto the bar.

"No," the barkeep answered. "Somethin' drained every drop of the poor bloke's blood. People are scared. They say there's something evil roaming the streets."

"And the docks," the woman pointed out.

"And the docks," Morg agreed.

A chill ran through Chibb. He'd never heard of such a thing. Ithicar was a deadly city, full of wicked people and wicked deeds. In his short life on the streets, he'd witnessed plenty of violence. But he'd never heard of anything like this.

Ossillard snorted. "Evil? The poor bloke probably skivved on a debt, that's all."

"Oh, I don't know," Yngot said. "I've heard there're strange creatures that walk among us. Years ago when I was down in Aegiss, the townsfolk caught something that'd been..." He paused and took a long pull from his tankard.

The old sailor's eyes filled with a faraway look.

"Been what?" Ossillard prodded.

Yngot set down the tankard. "Been eating people," he said at last. "They dragged the thing into the square and tore it to bits."

"What was it?" Chibb asked.

"Don't know," Yngot admitted. "Some said it was a daemon."

The woman laughed. Morg rolled his eyes. Ossillard shook his head. "You'll have to excuse him," the old Alarman told them. "He likes a good yarn."

Yngot smacked a hand on the bar. "Yarn my yawl, you old croll. It happened."

"Well, I don't know about daemons," the woman said, "but whatever it is, I'm not complaining. I've made a good bit of coin over the last few days escorting merchants around the city. They're petrified. All of them."

"That's not your usual line of work, Vara." Morg studied the woman. He'd given up wiping down the bar. The rag hung dripping over his shoulder.

"A woman's gotta make the most of a situation." She drained the last of her ale.

"True enough," Ossillard grunted.

"When did they find the first body?" Yngot asked the woman.

She looked at Morg, then said, "Maybe a week ago. About the time the winds started picking up."

Morg nodded. "Aye. That's about right."

Yngot gave a low whistle. "They say death comes on the wind."

Ossillard snorted.

Chibb had heard enough. He slid off his stool. "I'll catch up tomorrow," he said, faking a yawn. "Gonna head back to the ship."

"You want me to tag along?" the woman offered. "To get you there safely, that is. Do it for a silver."

Chibb mulled over the idea. That last conversation had raised the hair on his arms, no question. He hadn't been looking forward to walking across a strange city in the dead of night, in the midst of a storm no less. And now with some kind of madman on the loose, he looked forward to it even less. But he had to keep his rendezvous a secret. Saera was waiting for him, his golden-haired captain, and he didn't know what she'd do if he showed up with a stranger in tow. He wasn't about to risk changing her mind. "I can manage, thanks," Chibb told her.

"Suit yourself." The woman turned back to the bar and gestured to Morg for another ale.

Chibb was about to leave when Ossillard put a hand on his shoulder. "Be careful," the old Alarman warned. "I'll see you on the morrow."

Chibb smiled. "Plan on it."

*

Saera Gretch held open the door. "You coming

in?" she asked with a smile. Her blue eyes sparkled, and her hair, mussed and wild, gleamed like the sun. A long white tunic, untied to the middle, hung down to her bare thighs.

Chibb's heart thudded in his chest. He was late. He'd left the Hole and had wandered through the Warren, that maze of buildings and docks he had seen earlier sprawling out onto the surface of the harbor. As late as it was and despite such terrible weather, several cityfolk had passed him by, hunched over, making their way to and from taverns and inns and other, darker establishments. The storm had raged around him, and there was little light. It had taken him more than an hour to work his way down a multitude of narrow docks, over bridges, across winding wooden stairs, and around tilting shops and warehouses, trying to head east as best he could, where at some point he knew he would eventually come to shore. Once he had gotten to shore, it had taken him yet another hour to search the cobbled back roads of Oldtowne to find Madame Maara's, the inn where his beloved captain was waiting.

Chibb stepped into the room. It was a low-ceilinged, cramped space in the attic. On a table against one wall, a candle burned in a pewter dish. It cast a yellow light over a small bed in the corner. On the floor beside the bed, a bottle of wine sat between two wooden goblets.

"I hope you like Alaran red," Saera said,

shutting the door.

Chibb grinned. "Sure." He shook off his wet cloak and hung it on a hook by the door.

Saera padded barefoot across the floor and filled the goblets. Chibb felt the sweat break out on his palms, and his hands shook slightly. She sat down on the edge of the bed and patted a spot next to her. "Come here," she told him.

Chibb's mouth went dry. He moved to her, took the goblet she held out to him, and drained half the contents.

"Easy, Chibb." She laughed. "Dawn's still far off."

Chibb shrugged. "Sorry." He sat on the bed, unsure of what to do next. He'd only been with a few girls in Ithicar, and they had been his own age. Saera was older by at least a half-dozen summers, maybe more. She had to know things. Things he didn't. Suddenly, he felt sick to his stomach.

She put her hand under a pillow and pulled out a small pouch. "I saved this for you," she told him. It clinked as she tossed it onto his lap.

Chibb opened it. Inside were gold troyals. Several of them. Immediately he thought of the first rule of the *Destiny*. If the others found out, his life wouldn't be worth a copper chip.

"I don't think—" he began.

Saera leaned in and kissed him. She smelled of the sea and her lips tasted like honey. She ran a hand through his hair and gazed at him with those intense blue eyes. "The others won't find out," she said. "How could they? Besides, I'm the captain. I'll do as I please. Take it."

Chibb thought of Yngot. The rumormonger seemed to know everything that happened on the *Destiny*. He would find out. And then Ossillard would know. Chibb could already see the disappointment on Ossillard's wrinkled face. But what if he shared the coin with them? Surely, that would make things right. Chibb dropped the pouch in his pocket. "Thanks," he said.

Saera smiled.

Chibb gulped down the rest of his wine. A warm sensation spread through his belly, easing his nerves a bit. Maybe if they talked awhile, he would feel more comfortable. He needed to relax. He wanted Saera to think of him as a man, not as an overanxious boy. The thought made him scoff. Why was he so anxious? She wasn't his first woman, after all.

"What?" Saera asked.

"Nothing." Chibb took her hand. It was callused from working the wheel, yet surprisingly soft. He kissed her fingertips, one by one. "Tell me something about yourself," he asked her.

"Like what?"

Chibb worked his way down to her wrist. "Like how you became a captain."

"Ah," she said. "Well…"

Chibb kissed the crook of her elbow.

Saera let out a low sigh. "I was in Bosk a few

years ago. Nyland had just entered into a truce with Thalia. After a dozen years of fighting, Felgus thought it better to cut his losses. His coffers were running dry. So, once he made peace, he put half his fleet on the auction blocks. I took one look at the *Destiny* and knew I had to have her. I was still a pirate, but I was sick of living by the sword. I figured it was time to make some honest coin."

Chibb slid up to Saera's neck. "How long were you a pirate?" he whispered.

She moaned and lay back onto the bed, pulling Chibb down with her. "I was five when I was taken aboard the *Reaver*," she told him. Her breath was hot and sweet. "Bloody Bardikk and his men sacked my village. He took me prisoner. Bardikk ended up raising me as his own."

Chibb ran a hand along her cheek. Saera's hair flowed over the pillow like a river of gold. "What of your parents?" he asked. "Surely you must have hated Bardikk for taking you away from them."

Saera shook her head. "I was an orphan. I was glad to be aboard the *Reaver*. Bardikk became the father I never had."

"Where is he now?" Chibb asked.

"Dead," she answered. "But that's enough about me." She rolled off the bed and padded over to the desk. She shook her shoulders once, and her tunic fell in a pool around her feet. Candlelight flickered up the length of her naked body, and Chibb nearly gasped. She was the most beautiful woman he'd ever laid eyes on. This was going to be a night he'd never forget.

Saera bent over and blew out the candle.

*

Chibb trembled as he thought of his captain. She was tough, smart, beautiful, passionate. Extremely passionate. And now she was his. Or he was hers. Either way, it didn't matter. He would visit her again tomorrow night, and the next night, and every night after, until the *Destiny* set out for another month of fishnetting.

He turned his attention to the task before him. Dawn was an hour away, and he was back in the Warren. It was dark and deserted, and the storm raged on around him. He spied a sliver of dock that ran into a shadowed area between two hulking buildings. It was an alley of sorts, and it headed west, toward the Run, the main dock in the Warren where the Hole was located. Once he hit the Run, he could slip over to the Stonewharf and onto the *Destiny*. With luck, Ossillard and Yngot would have been too drunk when they got back to have noticed his absence. Chibb could slip into his bunk, and in the morning the two would be none the wiser. But he'd have to tell them something if he was to share the extra coin Saera had given him.

Doubt settled over Chibb. He was no longer sure taking the coin was such a good idea. But he pushed the thought aside. He would worry about that later. He took a step into the alley, and then stopped. A short distance ahead a cloaked figure was standing in the middle of the dock.

A ripple of alarm passed through Chibb. He had no weapon, no dagger, not even the small sailor's knife he'd left back on his bunk. He spun around, looking for something, anything, he might use to defend himself. A small object lay near the edge of the dock a few feet away. It was about the length of his arm, jagged, with a sharp point. He darted over and snatched it up. It was a broken piece of plank. Better than nothing, Chibb thought, heart racing.

He stared back into the alley, the shard of wood clenched in his fist, but the man was gone. Where'd he go? Chibb wondered as he searched the shadows. Was he seeing things?

He tried to calm himself. He'd grown up on the streets of Ithicar, for Ryke's sake. What could possibly frighten him here? He gritted his teeth and moved further into the alley, his boots clomping loudly as he went.

Chibb walked on for a few moments and then paused, listening. He heard nothing save the pounding of the rain and the wailing of the wind. He took another step, and the black-cloaked figure appeared in front of him. It happened so fast, it was like he materialized straight out of the mist. Then a stench hit Chibb like a fist in the gut. The man reeked of blood and rancid meat. Chibb froze. Panic seized him with icy fingers, and he nearly retched.

The man whipped open his cloak, and Chibb realized it wasn't a cloak at all. It wasn't a man at all. It was a thing, a thing with bat-like wings and skin the color of the moon.

There was a sudden flash of white and a searing pain exploded in Chibb's face, as if a dagger had been driven deep into his cheek. He dropped the shard of wood, and his eyes flew wide. A half-dozen tentacle-like appendages hung from the thing's chest like a nest of snakes. They were long and twitching, like sea worms that had been stretched to the breaking point. One of the tentacles led up to Chibb's face, where it dug its way deeper into his flesh.

The tentacle pulsed as it sucked something from him. Blood. The thing was feeding on him!

Frantically, Chibb tried to pry his fingers beneath the tentacle, but it wouldn't budge. He pounded his fists at it, again and again, but the tentacle held fast. Then a sudden numbness swept through his body. He felt his strength dissolve, and he sunk to his knees.

He was dying.

His thoughts turned to Saera, to her golden hair and blazing blue eyes, to the sweet softness of her skin. Would she wonder what had become of him? Would she mourn when they found his bloodless body? Would Ossillard? Would Yngot?

Sorrow washed over Chibb. A sudden gust of

wind whistled through the alley, and he recalled something Yngot had said.

They say death comes on the wind.

He should have paid more heed to the rumormonger. He shuddered once, and then collapsed onto the dock. He no longer had the strength to move. The thing bent over him, its face hidden in shadow. It said nothing as it fed.

Chibb closed his eyes and sank into the cold, dark depths of nothingness.

SELLSWORDS

"To one a cap, to one a crown,
To one a smile, to one a frown,
To one a madman, one a monk,
To one a jewel, the other junk."
The Illusionist, *9-12*
—*Starroch Phemorel*

RAINDROPS SPLATTERED onto the Run out of a fog-filled morning sky. They landed on dock planks, bounced off the tops of pilings, and fell into catch barrels. They formed little rivers that ran down the rooftops of taverns, inns, whorehouses, warehouses, and other businesses built upon the Warren's oldest, busiest dock.

The wind had died down at dawn after the

passing of the storm. A steady rain remained, though it did little to deter the crowd that had gathered, even at this early hour, to walk along the Run's waterlogged planks.

Shopowners everywhere were unlocking doors, throwing back shutters, and waving cordially to each other as the cityfolk ambled by, heading for their favorite shops or drinking establishments. Beneath a section of awning that jutted out from Kessler's Fine Blades, Ander Ellystun watched the droplets trickle and plop around him. He pulled his black, oilcloth cloak tighter and turned to his twin sister.

"Ryke's beard, Emma, how can you read at a time like this?" he asked.

His sister brushed aside a lock of tawny hair and gave him an exasperated look. Her gray-flecked eyes were filled with a steady intelligence that Ander had never possessed. Though they were twins, they were vastly different. But it was their differences, his unbridled recklessness and her calm, calculating demeanor, that combined to make them two of the most sought-after sellswords in the city.

Emma placed a goosefeather between the yellowed pages of her book. "What would you have me do?" she said. "What's done is done. Besides, it will be days before the Watch finds out. Until then, why worry about it?"

"We do nothing?" Ander pressed. "We could try to figure a way out of this mess."

Emma sighed. "I don't know why you're so concerned—"

"Concerned?" Ander blurted. "I *killed* Ballard. It was self-defense, sure, but what if someone tells the Watch otherwise?"

"Then we'll deal with that when the time comes. Can I read my book in peace? When Kessler opens, we'll get our swords edged, then head to the Savage Poet and go over our options."

His sister turned the hand-bound book over and ran a finger down its plum-red leather spine, caressing it as if it were the cheek of her favorite lover. "Do you know what this is?" she asked him.

Ander didn't know, and he didn't care. He had no time for books, especially now that he might be a wanted man.

"I bought it yesterday at the Sorsagorium," she went on, gesturing to the small curiosity shop across the dock. "It's the complete works of Espare dae Kesh, printed in Cabyll across the Great Waste. It's in great condition. And it's rare. Quite valuable, in fact."

Ander scoffed. "So?"

"So Nach doesn't know what this book's worth. He gave it to me for three silver rounds. For another two he threw in a Thalian blowgun, three poison-tipped darts, and four vials of Molish ink. The good stuff. Black as the Abyss."

"Books and blowguns," Ander snapped.

"Trinkets and junk. What if the Watch decides to come after you as well as me? You're barely capable of drawing your own sword without tripping over it."

His sister's brow rose. "I didn't drive a handspan of steel into Ballard's gut," she said. "I doubt the Watch will come looking for me. But I'm touched by your concern. Perhaps—Oh, my."

Ander followed his sister's stare. A handful of men had just exited Frollard's Fishery. They wore the red and black tabards of the Watch, the gargoyle of Fell's Hollow embroidered on their chests. It was an entire patrol. Ander slid his hand down to the hilt of his sword.

Two of the watchmen broke away from the group and headed toward them. They were tall men and their chainmail clinked as they walked. One wore a gold cord at his shoulder. He was the Commander of the Watch, Rhandellar Larron. Dark, gray-streaked hair fell to his shoulders. His face was hard and haggard and he wore the expression of a man expecting trouble.

Ander cursed under his breath. The Watch had heard of Ballard's death far sooner than even he would have expected, and now Larron and his lackey were too close for him to make a run for it. A cold feeling settled into Ander's stomach. He'd had a few run-ins with Larron in the past. The Commander was not a man to trifle with.

The two watchmen stopped a few feet away.

"There, you see Deven," Larron said to the watchman beside him. "I was right."

Deven, like the Commander, appeared to be in his forties. He wore a haunted look about him. His amber-colored eyes reflected too much suffering, and his lips were turned down in a frown that seemed to have become permanent.

When Deven didn't reply, Larron smirked and went on. "I told you we'd find them lurking around the Run."

Ander stiffened. "Lurking?"

His sister put a hand on his shoulder. "Take it easy, Ander. Surely he meant no insult. Isn't that right, Commander?"

"Be off, Larron. I'm busy," Ander said.

Deven took a step forward and Larron barred him with an arm. "Let's not make this any more unpleasant than it has to be," the Commander said. He pulled off his gloves and stuck them behind his belt. Then he peered up into the rain and gloom. "A fine summer morning, don't you think?"

"What do you want?" Ander asked, though he knew the answer. Tiny sparks of fire raced up his spine as his nerves prepared for the inevitable rush that always came with a fight.

Larron looked at him. "It isn't what I want, Ellystun. It's what the Lord Mayor wants."

Ander squeezed the hilt of his sword. "And what's that?" he asked.

Larron smirked again. "He wants you to pay

for your crime. Murder is not something the Lord Mayor takes lightly, even when it happens in Rogueswarde."

"Murder!" Ander cried. "Ballard drew on me, Commander. Ask anyone who was there. I merely defended myself."

"That is the truth of it," Emma put in. "Had Ander not skewered the stupid bastard—"

Larron turned to Emma. "This doesn't concern you," he said calmly.

"Should I deal with the woman, Commander?" Deven asked.

Ander itched to draw steel. "You'd be dead before you took a step," he warned the second watchman.

Larron held up a hand. "Hold your tongue, Deven. Sellswords can be an excitable lot. We don't want to spill blood this morning." He gave Ander a stern look. "You will come with me to the gaol and stay there until the Lord Mayor decides your fate, or—" The Commander hesitated. He appeared to be mulling something over.

"Or?" Ander prodded.

"Or," Larron said, finally. "You can do the Lord Mayor a service."

Deven pointed a finger at Ander. "We should arrest him. Now. We have other duties to attend to."

Larron gave his lackey a sidelong glance, and the watchman fell silent.

"Why should I do anything for the Lord Mayor?" Ander asked. "I'm guilty of no crime."

"Ander, perhaps you should," Emma began, but Larron cut her off with a laugh.

"Do you actually believe guilt or innocence has anything to do with this?" the Commander asked. "You, Ellystun, are a sellsword with a hot temper. You killed a man in a tavern brawl. The perception is clear enough. You will hang or you will do the Lord Mayor a service."

Ander's anger flared. He hated to be forced into anything. He looked past Larron to the group of watchmen standing in front of Frollard's. It seemed he had no choice.

"Fine," he grunted. "What must I do?"

"You agree, then?" Larron asked.

"I just said that."

Larron gave him a smug smile. "Very well, then." The Commander went quiet for a moment, seeming to choose his words carefully. "There is an assassin in the city," he said after the pause. "He's already made one attempt on the Lord Mayor's life. We've kept it quiet to this point. The people have enough to worry about at the moment. The Lord Mayor, as you can imagine, wants him captured. Alive. Bring him in, Ellystun, and the charges against you will be dropped."

"That sounds like a job for the Watch," Ander told him. "So why me?"

"Because the Watch has other things to deal

with," Larron answered. "More important things."

"More important than catching an assassin?" Emma asked.

Deven's eyebrows shot up. "You haven't heard? I thought you sellswords were better informed."

"We've been rather busy," Ander growled. "Perhaps you could enlighten us?"

Larron pulled his gloves from his belt. "Three ships of war have been spotted in Bosk. They've been fitted for battle. The Triad believes Nyland is preparing for war."

"Against who?" Ander asked.

"Against us," Deven said.

Emma scoffed. "And risk war with Alar and Kern? Surely you're mistaken."

Larron turned to Emma. "We believe the assassin was sent by Nyland. And we've had reports from other sources as well. Apparently King Felgus is no longer concerned with Alar. Or with Kern. He feels he's lived with this uncertain truce long enough. He wants Fell's Hollow, and he's willing to risk a war to get it."

Ander considered the news. Alar, Kern, and Nyland had left Fell's Hollow unmolested for centuries. If one kingdom gained the port city, it would hold a distinct advantage over the other two, for Fell's Hollow could be used as a base of operations to block all traffic in and out of Farstun Bay. As all three kingdoms relied on the bay for trade, they had allowed Fell's Hollow to rule its own destiny. Were one kingdom to attack Fell's Hollow, it was understood they'd be at war with the other two, a war any one of them singly couldn't hope to win.

"Commander," Deven said, "we are due at the Watchtowers. The cannon need to be ranged if we're to protect the entrance to the cove."

Larron nodded. "Look, Ellystun," he said. "My men are busy with more pressing matters. As am I. They have no time to tear the city apart looking for an assassin, not with war on our doorstep. You will bring him to me. Alive."

"And how will I find him?" Ander asked. Fell's Hollow was full of cutthroats, thugs, thieves, and worse. Finding one assassin amongst the crowd would be no easy task.

Larron's brow furrowed as if he were trying to dredge up more details from his memory. "The assassin's a lithe fellow," he told Ander. "Dark hair and eyes. And he's a foreigner. Speaks with an accent I'm not familiar with, so I guess he traveled a great distance to get here. Perhaps from the Midlands. He could be a Cabyllian or a Belani. I don't think he hails from the Nine Kingdoms."

"That's all you can tell me?" Ander said. "I'll need more than that."

Larron shrugged. "That's all I've got." He took a step away, then stopped. "Oh, yes. I almost forgot. The assassin bore a unique weapon, a sword with a small crossguard and a slightly curved blade. I've never seen its like before. He used it to cut through three of my most seasoned men as if they were recruits. Fair warning, Ellystun. The foreigner is a master swordsman."

With that Larron turned on his heel, and the two watchmen headed back to rejoin their patrol.

Emma clapped Ander on the shoulder. "Come, brother, think of it this way. We haven't had a real job in months. We need some steady work."

Ander gave his sister a hard look. "We've made a bit of coin over the last few days."

"For escorting a few frightened merchants around the city?" she said. "That's hardly sellswords' work."

Ander grunted. "I don't like it."

"Nor do I," his twin agreed. "But we have no choice. I would prefer, though, to wrap this up before tomorrow night. We have a show to attend."

"A show?" Ander didn't like the sound of that.

Emma smiled. "Yes. The Cove Theater is putting on a production of Espare dae Kesh's *Har and Iva*. They say it will be Ordin Awl's finest performance."

Ander groaned and looked out into the rain. It was going to be a miserable day.

*

Emma dropped onto a stool beside Ander.

"Wine. Make it red," she said.

The barkeep, a short, older man with a muddy complexion, frowned. He probably didn't get many requests for wine. The Dregs was a cramped tavern in the south end of Rogueswarde. Wedged in a small square where only the poorest lived, its clientele consisted of peasants, servants, thieves, fetches, beggars, and the occasional watchman seeking shelter from the rain or the cold. The drinking room was in the half-cellar of a two-story building. Above were rooms that could be had for a few copper chips a night. Ander knew Emma hated the place, for she had a sour look smeared across her face.

The barkeep gave Ander a bored glance. "And you?" he asked.

"Ale. Make it drinkable," Ander muttered.

"A joke!" Emma clapped him on the back. "I'm rubbing off on you."

"Let's hope not," Ander said.

The barkeep stalked off, mumbling under his breath. Ander shook his head. "Emma, do you really think the assassin will come here?"

She looked around the bar and wrinkled her nose. "No. But," she gestured toward the grime-streaked window by the entrance, "we have a view of the entire square. He's probably hiding somewhere in Rogueswarde. There are fewer watchmen here than anywhere in the city, except perhaps for the Crags."

"What are we going to do if we can't find

him?" Ander didn't deal well with uncertainty. He much preferred when Emma planned things out for him. He could rely on his sister to keep them out of trouble. Most of the time.

"We'll worry about that when it happens," his sister told him.

"Maybe we could find a ship heading to Ukria," Ander suggested. "They say Mennach is a rich city. We could do well there."

Emma shot him a surprised look. "Have you forgotten?" she asked. "We are about to go to war with Nyland. No ships will be heading anywhere, at least not for a while. We're stuck here. Might as well make the best of it."

The barkeep returned, set down their drinks, and stalked back off to the other end of the bar.

Emma took a sip of wine and grimaced. "Let's hope the bloke shows his face before I have to drink another one of these."

Ander stared out the window. A steady drizzle continued to fall. At the back end of the square a handful of carts were gathered in a line, and behind each a grocer or a traveling merchant was hawking his wares. People milled about in every direction. Most were peasants, servants, and other lowborn cityfolk. Only a few wore swords at their sides, though most would have a dirk or a dagger stashed away somewhere. Of those that did have swords, none matched the description Larron had provided.

Ander slipped off his cloak, hung it on a peg

under the bar, and took a swallow of ale. Bits of barley scraped his throat.

Yes, he thought. It was going to be a long, miserable day indeed.

*

Emma elbowed Ander, and he lifted his chin from his chest. Around him, the Dregs hummed with late afternoon activity. He yawned and stretched.

"There," Emma said, pointing out the grimy window.

Ander searched the crowd swarming about the square. Things looked the same as they had an hour ago, before he'd dozed off. People were hunched over in the rain going about their daily business, beggars pulling at sleeves, hawkers shouting and waving, trying to attract a buyer. Then Ander spotted him. A man in a tattered black cloak was skirting his way through the crowd. He carried himself with a grace that only a fellow swordsman would recognize. As the man moved, Ander caught sight of the blade hanging at his side. It had a slight curve to it, with a small, thin crossguard.

They had found their man.

Ander leaped from his stool and, without waiting for his sister, sped out the tavern door. He barreled his way into the crowd, and all around him people howled in anger. He knocked into an old woman, who went sprawling, her newly bought loaf of bread bouncing onto the cobblestones. She let out a curse, but Ander ignored her. He pushed deeper into the square, and then stopped short.

Several paces ahead, the assassin had already turned, his curved blade bared and gleaming. He was a young man, lean, with a swarthy tone to his skin. Ink-black hair framed his thin face and a small, crescent-shaped scar underscored one of his fierce, brown eyes.

The crowd drew back, murmuring in excitement. Daggers in the dark were commonplace in Rogueswarde, but a duel in daylight for anyone to see was a rare event. The Triad had outlawed dueling, and to be caught by the Watch meant a trip to the gallows. But Ander had orders from Rhandellar Larron himself. For the first time in ages, his swordplay would be legal.

"Drop your blade," Ander ordered as he slipped his sword from its scabbard.

The assassin laughed. "I think not," he said. "Drop your own, my friend." The foreigner's voice was thick with a strange accent, an accent that had a somewhat musical quality to it. "Run," he added, "or you will die."

Emma reached Ander's side, puffing. "I would do as my brother asks," she told the assassin. "He's been in a foul mood all day and is aching for a fight."

The foreigner glanced at Emma and grinned,

and Ander knew he would never surrender.

"So be it," Ander said, and rushed at the man.

The foreigner flung himself to the side and backhanded his blade around in a high arc meant for Ander's neck. Ander ducked as he passed and felt the foreigner's sword whistle over his head.

The crowd gasped. The assassin was quick, Ander realized. Too quick. There came another gasp from the crowd, and then a cry of pain.

Ander spun. The assassin stood over Emma, his curved sword raised over his head. How did he get there so fast? His sister lay sprawled on the cobblestones. Her hands were clenched to her thigh. Blood seeped between her fingers.

"Bastard!" Ander cried, and charged at the foreigner.

The man turned to face him.

In three long strides, Ander closed the distance between them and lunged. The assassin dropped to his knee and thrust his blade straight at Ander's stomach. Ander's own sword passed harmlessly over the foreigner, and he tried to halt his momentum. But there was no time. He twisted his body and felt the assassin's cold steel dig into his hip. Pain lanced up the side of his ribs. He gritted his teeth at the fiery agony.

Ander regripped his sword in both hands and hacked downward.

The assassin laughed as he yanked his blade free and brought it up to parry the blow. Pain exploded in Ander's side. His sight blurred and he fought to stay focused.

The foreigner bounded back a step and assumed a relaxed stance, his blade hanging casually from his hand, blood dripping from its tip.

"I told you to run, did I not?" he taunted. The man gave a little bow, like an actor on a stage. "It is better to live with shame than to die with honor," he said.

"The Watch!" warned someone in the crowd. There was a commotion to one side, and Ander risked a glance over his shoulder. Four watchmen had entered the south end of the square and were trying to push their way through the mass of onlookers. They would reach Ander in moments.

"Ander!" Emma shouted.

Idiot! Why had he taken his eyes off the man? Ander whipped his blade around, knowing he was already dead. But the assassin was gone.

He spotted the foreigner racing north through the rain, his tattered cloak billowing behind him. The crowd parted, not wanting anything to do with the dangerous man. In an instant, the assassin shot between two buildings and dashed out of sight.

*

Overnight the rain had stopped and a thick, wet mist had settled over Fell's Hollow. An occasional gust of wind whipped across the waters of the harbor. Somewhere in the gloom a gull cried.

Ander glanced at Emma, who was sitting on the pier next to him, reading. At daybreak they had arrived at an abandoned shipbuilder's warehouse in the Yards, the rough-and-tumble warde at the southwest end of the cove. His sister's wound hadn't been bad, nothing a good needle and thread couldn't handle. Ander had sewn his own wound shut the best he could, and it ached. Sewing wounds was part of a sellsword's job. But one day a wound would run too deep, and there would be no sewing. Until then, or unless he found another career, he would just have to deal with the pain.

"Again with that book?" he grumbled. "Don't you ever get sick of reading?"

Emma looked up. "Do you ever get sick of drinking a good ale? Or swinging a well-balanced blade?"

Ander turned away. He was being foolish. He wanted to forget about Ballard. He wanted to forget about Larron. Life in Fell's Hollow was tough enough without having to deal with this situation. Peace and quiet. That's all he wanted. But to get it, he had to catch this damned assassin before he struck again. Or before he fled the city. Otherwise, Larron would hang Ander for sure.

His sister sighed and closed her book. "What's on your mind?" she asked.

Ander stared out across the mist-covered harbor. "How can we possibly expect to catch him now?" he asked her. "The man is the deadliest swordsman we've encountered. You barely had time to pull your blade before the bastard stuck you in the leg. I've never seen anyone move so fast. Or so gracefully."

Emma shrugged. "Be that as it may, it's still his neck or yours. If we don't bring him in," she gestured across the harbor, "they'll hang you from one of those cranes on the Stonewharf."

Ander scoffed. "We'll never find him. Especially now that he knows we're after him. If he hasn't fled, he's holed up somewhere, and he won't come out until we've given up the hunt."

"We'll find him," Emma assured him.

Ander looked at his twin. "And then what? We're both wounded. You can hardly stand, and I'm stiffening up like a dock plank. We should leave. Stow away on a ship. Let it take us wherever it will."

"Look out there, Ander." She pointed across the harbor. "Do you see anyone leaving?"

Several dozen ships were tied to the Stonewharf. Twice that number were moored out in the deeper waters. None were moving. A few sailors roamed about the docks and decks, but no one was preparing to make way.

"Blasted Nylanders," Ander cursed. "Of all the times to start a war. Every captain in the city is afraid to set sail."

His sister yawned and leaned her back against a piling. "Just keep your eyes open for Gillum." She reached into a pocket and pulled out a pipe.

In a moment, the rich aroma of tabac wafted over Ander.

"Will he show?" Ander asked. He didn't have the connections in the city that Emma had. When it came to finding things out, Emma always knew where to go, and who to talk to.

She nodded. "I left word at Madame Maara's. He likes to go there for the fishermens' stew. I offered him a gold troyal. He'll be here."

"I am here," a voice said behind them.

Ander jumped to his feet, and he felt his stitches stretch. Pain scorched up his side and hammered into his head. Beside him, Emma dropped her pipe, which smacked onto the pier, bounced over the edge, and hit the water with a splunk.

Ander pulled his sword half out of its scabbard as Gillum stepped from behind a thick piling a few strides down the dock. How had he snuck up on them? He must have gotten to the pier before they had. The bastard was nothing if not cautious.

Ander took in the thief's appearance. He was short, thin, perhaps twenty summers old, if Ander guessed right. And everything about him looked ragged. His clothes were old and torn, his brown hair short and mussed, his face dirt-smeared and grimy. He looked like a hapless beggar, but Ander knew better. Gillum was a thief. And a good one. He probably had more coin stashed away than most of the merchants on the Run. Certainly far more coin than Ander would ever earn with his blade. How he hated thieves.

Emma stood slowly, a scowl of irritation plain on her face. "You shite. You owe me a pipe," she told the thief.

Ander slapped his sword back into its scabbard.

Gillum grinned. "You owe me a troyal," he told her. "Hand it over."

Emma fished a coin from her pocket and flipped it to Gillum. The thief caught it and continued to grin.

"Well?" Emma asked.

Gillum leaned against a piling and began to pick at his thumbnail. "No luck," he said.

"You couldn't find him?" Emma sounded shocked.

The thief shrugged. "I heard a rumor or two. But the man you're looking for doesn't want to be found. It's going to take some time."

Ander spat. "Ryke's balls! We don't have time!"

"Then get yourself a fetch," Gillum remarked. "Finding things is what they do. My job is taking things."

"We can't use a fetch," Emma said. "The man we're looking for is an assassin. And he's well trained. He'd spot a fetch a league off. And then there'd be one less fetch in the city."

"An assassin?" Gillum's eyes narrowed ever so slightly. "What do you want with an assassin?"

"That's none of your concern," Ander barked.

Gillum raised a questioning eyebrow at Emma.

"Keep looking," she told him.

Gillum shook his head. "Sorry. Got another job."

"So?" Emma said.

Gillum grinned. "So I'm busy today. And tonight. I could try again tomorrow."

"Tomorrow is too late," Ander stated.

"Then I guess we're done here." The thief turned and started down the pier.

Emma let out a sigh. "Wait."

Gillum paused.

"You mentioned some rumors," his sister said. "At least tell us where you *think* we might find the bloke."

Gillum grinned and held out his hand.

"Don't give him a single copper chip," Ander told his twin. "We can't trust him."

Emma tossed another troyal at the thief. Gillum snatched the gold coin from the air and pocketed it.

"I just told you," Ander began, but his sister held up a hand.

"Try the cellar below Pynn's Inn," Gillum told them.

"Thank you," Emma said.

After Gillum had gone, Ander let out an exasperated breath. "What was that about?"

She put a hand on his shoulder. "He was bluffing. He knew where the assassin was all along. Gillum always finds a way to make an extra

49

troyal or two out of a deal."

Ander scowled. "I hate thieves."

*

Pynn's Inn was a run down, three story building near the center of Stockwarde. It sat facing the corner of River Street and Ankka's Lane, with a warehouse on one side and a tannery on the other. The inn had been abandoned years ago. Half its clapboards were gone, and not a single window was left unshattered. A massive, crumbling brick chimney thrust out of the center of the roof like a russet fist. Slate rooftiles were missing in large patches, and in a few places the roof had rotted away completely, leaving holes the size of a seaman's cart.

Ander rubbed his eyes and yawned. No one had entered or exited the inn all day. From across the street, he and Emma had an unobstructed view and could see most of the inn's back courtyard, including a small stone stair that descended a few steps to a cellar door. The rain had begun again after midday, and now it fell steadily from a darkening sky.

The wind stirred and Ander wrinkled his nose. Around them, two warehouses came together to form an alley of sorts. Empty pallets crammed the space, and it smelled of urine and rot and worse. "He's not coming," he said, shifting himself into a more comfortable position against the wall.

Emma gave him an exasperated look. "Gillum knows every speck of this city, and everything that goes on within it. If he heard the assassin might be hiding here, then this is our best chance."

"It's been hours, Emma. Let's go check out the cellar. I can't wait any longer." Something inside Ander told him this might not be a good idea, but what choice did he have? He had to catch the assassin, soon, or... He didn't want to think about the *or*.

His sister stood up and brushed the dirt from her breeches. "Fine. Let's go."

They made their way across the muddy street. Ander scanned the area for any sign of the foreigner. In one direction an old man led a mule-drawn cart heading toward Oldtowne. The mule looked as old as the man. Its wiry hair was gray and unruly and rain dripped down its sides as it plodded through the mud. In the other direction a pair of men, dockworkers by the looks of them, hunched under a small awning that stuck out over the entrance to another warehouse. A haze of pipesmoke hovered over their heads as they chatted quietly. When Ander reached the corner of the inn, he loosened his blade in its scabbard. Emma pulled a dagger from her boot.

The inn's courtyard was in shambles. Its flagstones were weed-choked, cracked, and heaved up from years of frost and ice. A rotted chair sat next to an iron table red with rust. The rest of the courtyard had become a mass of brush, deathvine, and rubbish. The shards of an old ale barrel lay beneath a twisted black poplar whose bark was scarred from years of knifework.

They inched along the backside of the inn. A rumble of thunder sounded far off in the distance, and the rain turned to a downpour. When they reached the cellar door, Ander eased himself closer, careful not to scuff a boot on the steps. They needed every advantage they could get. After their encounter outside the Dregs, he knew they couldn't capture the assassin on the skill of their blades alone. Surprise was their only hope.

He looked back over his shoulder and Emma nodded.

Ander grasped the door handle and gave it a pull. The door opened a crack, slowly, silently. Darkness filled the cellar. If the assassin was inside, Ander had to move quickly. He drew his blade, yanked the door open, and darted into the darkness. Pain flared in his hip and he tried to stifle a groan.

The open door let in just enough light to make out several rough shapes in the gloom. A wooden pallet covered in scraps of wool lay next to a stone foundation. A chest sat next to the pallet, upon which two candles had burned down to nubs. A heavy odor of mud and mold and something slightly foul filled the cellar.

"Ander!" Emma whispered. "Look." She

pointed to a set of warped, wooden shelves that ran along one wall. The shelves were stacked with forgotten junk: broken tankards, chipped plates, pots, an old frying pan. In a small space between the shelves and the corner of the foundation, a man sat with his back against the wall. He was staring at them.

Ander took two strides and lunged. The tip of his sword landed on the man's chest. "Move and I'll run you through," he said.

The man was silent. Ander squinted in the dim light. He could barely make out the man's pale skin and the shocked expression frozen on his face. It was not the foreigner. Whoever he was, he was dead.

"Ryke's balls," Ander swore. "The assassin's not here, but he's left some of his handiwork."

Emma came closer. "Poor fellow," she said, leaning over the corpse. "He looks familiar. I wonder who he—"

"You'll never know," came an accented voice.

Ander whirled. The assassin stood silhouetted outside the doorway. Before Ander could move, the foreigner slammed the door shut. Complete darkness swallowed the cellar. There came a rasping noise, like wood scraping against wood.

Ander dashed to the door.

"I would kill you now," the assassin taunted from the other side of the door, "but I am already late for an engagement. Fear not, though. I will return." He laughed. "Until then, my heart lives for love and light, whilst yours drowns in the dark!"

Ander reached down, fumbling for the door handle. He found it and pushed. Nothing. He slammed his shoulder against the door. Pain erupted in his hip. The door didn't budge. The assassin had wedged something into the jam.

They were trapped.

"Shite," Emma muttered. "I know where he's going. And I know who the dead man is."

*

Ander shook the rain from his cloak and scanned the crowd. "Are you sure he's here?" he asked.

It had taken them the better part of an hour to hack their way through the cellar door, after which they'd raced out of Stockwarde and down the slick, narrow streets of Oldtowne, all the way to the Cove Theater.

"Yes," Emma said. "Do you remember what he said back in the square?"

Ander scoffed at the thought. He had been fighting for their lives. He could barely remember the man's face, let alone what taunts and jibes he may have spouted. "No," he told her.

Emma pulled back her cloak and gripped the hilt of her sword. "He said *it's better to live with shame than to die with honor.* That's a quote from *Catch a King,* one of Espare dae Kesh's lesser-known plays. I didn't pick up on it before."

"So?" Ander said.

Emma sighed. "So, he quoted dae Kesh again when he trapped us in the cellar. *My heart lives for love and light, whilst yours drowns in the dark.* That's from *Har and Iva*. Which is playing here. Tonight. The show we were coming to see, remember?"

"I don't—"

"And the dead man?" Emma went on. "I've seen him before. Many times. It was Ordin Awl. The actor who was to play the lead role in tonight's performance."

Ander returned his attention to the crowd. If Emma thought the assassin was here, then he was here. Somewhere.

Cityfolk of all sorts, peasants, harlots, merchants, seamen, dockworkers, and more filled the area in front of the stage, shoving, shouting, laughing, talking, arguing. Small bowls of lime burned at the edge of the stage. Shadows danced on crimson curtains that hung from the rafters far above.

"Do you see him?" Ander asked.

Emma shook her head. "Not yet."

The crowd gave a sudden cheer. Ander watched as a man sauntered out from behind the curtains. His breeches were bright white. His tunic was a patchwork of reds and yellows, blues and greens. He wore a floppy orange hat, the tip of which hung down over one shoulder, a bright pink ball bobbing at the end. The crowd quieted.

The man gave an overdramatic bow and spoke. "Though I have brought you scenes of tragic deeds, of Har and Iva and their wicked aunt, believe not all the woeful things you've seen, for oft good comes from what's expected not." He turned and swiftly exited behind the curtain.

Emma whispered in Ander's ear. "Last act of the play. We need to find the assassin. Soon."

The curtains parted, revealing a bare stage. A young woman appeared. Her hair was long, sunlight yellow, and fell halfway down her back. She wore a flowing crimson gown and had a look of terrible sadness in her eyes. Limelight splashed over her, painting her in shades of gray and white. The crowd erupted in applause as she moved to the front of the stage and fell to her knees. She looked out over the audience.

"O Har, my Har, why hast thou 'bandoned me?" she cried. The young actress raised a shaking hand high in the air. There was a slender dagger clutched in her fist. The edge of the blade glinted in the limelight. Someone in the crowd gasped.

"Shall I rend this rended heart of mine?" the actress asked.

"No!" a voice rang out. "Never!" cried another.

Ander tore his eyes from the young woman and elbowed Emma. "Do you see him?"

"No," she hissed. "Let's split up. I'll head toward the stage. You go up to the balcony. Once we're sure he's not in the crowd, we'll search backstage."

Ander shuffled up a set of stairs at the side of the theater. At the top, rows of crowd-packed benches ran from one side of a wide balcony to the other. They were filled with a calmer, wealthier set of patrons. He searched the faces before him, looking for those dark, fierce eyes. At least he remembered the eyes.

Men and women stared with rapture down at the young actress as her voice floated up to them.

"My life without thee, husband, is no life."

Ander checked each person in turn. The assassin wasn't among them.

"And so I'll end it on this widow's knife."

The murmur of the crowd suddenly rose in excitement, and Ander peered out over the balcony.

An old hag had appeared at the back of the stage. She was foul, with a boil-laden face. Rags hung from her boney frame. The hag studied the younger woman for a moment, and then stalked further out to address the crowd.

"What wond'rous joy my wicked plots have hatched," the hag cackled. "Fair Iva dies and so they're both dispatched!"

Ander turned and clomped down the stairs. He was getting tired of this cat-and-mouse game. When he reached the bottom, he stopped. What was he going to do if he found the assassin? Emma hadn't had time to come up with a plan, and he didn't have the strength for a fight. Even if he did, the assassin would surely cut him down. But he supposed he'd prefer to die on the end of a sword than on the end of a rope.

The crowd cheered as a third actor made an entrance. A lean, dark-haired man stalked up behind the hag. He wore beggar's clothes, and a dirty strip of cloth was wound around his face.

The hag turned to the man, and her features hardened. "Begone thou beggar of the night, begone!" she snarled. "You'll not disrupt this deed before it's done."

The man laughed and removed the cloth from his face.

It was the assassin.

He took a step toward the hag, his hands reaching for her neck. "Thy beggar is thy prince beneath this gore!" he cried. "Die, foul witch, and cast thy spells no more."

The hag screamed.

"You!" Ander yelled.

The assassin shot a surprised glare toward the back of the theater. His eyes found Ander and his face contorted in rage. Somewhere near the stage, Emma shouted.

Ander dashed into the crowd.

Cursing, the assassin turned and fled. In a handful of strides he made it to a narrow door hidden near the back of the stage. He threw it open and bolted out of the theater.

The audience erupted in anger. They cursed, bellowing obscenities, furious at the interruption.

Emma pulled herself onto the stage, drew her sword, and half-limped, half-ran toward the door. Somehow she was managing to move at a good pace, even with an injured leg. She would get to the assassin long before Ander would.

"Emma!" Ander shouted, but his cry was swallowed by the roar of the crowd.

His sister reached the door and stumbled through it. Ander shoved his way down to the edge of the stage. The crowd was in a frenzy, howling in outrage. People pointed and cursed at him. A seaman tried to grab his cloak. Ander pushed him away and pulled himself up between two bowls of burning lime. His stitches tore and pain scorched through his hip as he pushed himself to his feet.

The young actress stared at him. The hag had shuffled back, her mouth hanging open. Ander staggered across the stage, out the back door, and into the night.

A cool breeze hit him in the face. Rain spattered down on him. A short distance off, the waters of the harbor lapped against the shore. He was at the back of the theater. Several docks ran out into the mist and disappeared into a maze of buildings set upon thick, pitch-covered pilings. One-, two-, three-story structures teetered in every direction. They looked like enormous blocks of wood bobbing on the surface of the water. There was no sign of Emma. Or the assassin.

"Emma!" Ander yelled. They must have gone down one of the docks, he guessed. He chose one at random and ran, his boots clomping over the planks. The waters of the harbor lapped in the darkness around him. His hip smoldered with pain.

"Emma!" Ander yelled again.

An answering cry came from somewhere in the darkness. He searched for a side dock or walkway, anything that would take him in the direction of the sound. Twenty paces ahead, a narrow dock split off and edged between two buildings. Ander drew his sword and raced toward it.

He reached the dock, took a few running strides down it, and then stopped short. There was Emma, lying on her back. Blood was pooling slowly around her, like wine leaking from a punctured winesack. The assassin loomed over her, Emma's own sword clutched in both his hands.

Horror shot through Ander. "No!" he cried, and launched himself at the foreigner.

The assassin brought Emma's blade around just in time to parry Ander's attack, then he jumped to the side and swept the sword at Ander's head. The stroke was awkward. Emma's blade was heavier than the man was used to. He appeared to struggle with the heft of it.

Ander dropped to his knee and dodged the blow.

The assassin took a step back. "I am going to enjoy killing you," he said, "as I enjoyed killing your friend here."

White hot rage surged through Ander. He leaped from his knee, driving his blade at the foreigner like a quarrel shot from a crossbow. The assassin batted it aside at the last moment.

Ander knew it was only a matter of time. The heavier blade was slowing the man. He'd make a mistake soon enough, and then Ander would kill him.

"She was your sister, yes?" the assassin mocked. His accent rang heavier as he panted from the exertion. "Imagine, slain by her own sword. How pathetic."

For a heartbeat Ander's rage bubbled into fury, but he caught himself and pushed aside the taunt. The assassin was goading him, trying to lure him into making a mistake. Ander lunged forward, raising his blade over his head. He brought it down in an arc, slashing at one side of his foe. Then he aimed a backstroke at the other side. Again and again, Ander pressed the attack, and the clang of steel echoed into the night.

The assassin backpedaled under the assault, parrying blow after blow, and then, finally, he stumbled and fell to the dock.

Ander grinned. He reversed his blade, and with both hands plunged it down at the assassin.

The assassin rolled to one side, slicing his sword upward. The blade bit into the underside of Ander's arm, and a flash of pain shot down to his hand. His fingers went numb, and he dropped his sword.

The assassin smiled. "You are quite the fool," he said as he got to his feet.

Ander grasped his arm. Hot blood flowed past his elbow and dripped onto the dock. It was over. Strangely, he felt no regret. He'd lived a good life. He only wished Emma had lived. The ways of the sellsword had never suited her. She had the heart of a poet, not a swordsman.

Ander dropped to his knees and stared into the dark eyes of the foreigner. "Make it quick," he told him.

The assassin nodded. "Death is my specialty."

Ander closed his eyes. He heard the assassin's feet shuffle on the dock. Ander tightened in expectation of the blow, but it didn't come. Instead, there was a short *pssst*, like the sound of a quick breath, and the assassin grunted.

Ander opened his eyes. The foreigner stood before him, a look of shock on his face. A small, feathered dart was stuck in his shoulder. He brought his hand up and tried to knock it loose, but something was wrong. His hands were quivering and his body was beginning to convulse. He staggered toward Ander. Emma's sword slipped from his trembling fingers. He shot an angry, confused glare over Ander's shoulder, stumbled sideways, and fell into the harbor.

Ander scuffled to the edge of dock, just in

time to catch a glimpse of the assassin as he sunk into the murky water.

There came a grunt, and Ander spun around. Emma was on her knees, clutching a bloody hand to her side. In her other hand was a long, thin wooden tube. "Thalian blowgun," she gasped. "Poison dart."

She coughed, then gave Ander a smirk. "Trinkets and junk, huh?" His twin sister's eyes rolled back into her head, and she crumbled onto the dock.

*

Shouts and laughter echoed through the Hole as Ander studied the white and black pegs that dotted the taffyl board. Emma had taken half his knobs and now his king was in danger.

"Another round, Morg!" Emma shouted, holding up an empty tankard.

Ander pegged a knob over a square. "How're your ribs?" he asked her.

Emma shrugged. "I'll survive. How's your arm?"

Ander grunted. "I'll survive."

As his sister looked over the board, Ander glanced around the tavern. It was a busy night. Morg was drawing drafts for a dozen men lined up on the barstools. The barkeep brushed at the swatch of spiked hair sticking up from his scalp like the bristles of a bloody porcupine, grinned at one of the men's jokes, and then turned to carry a couple of tankards to the other end of the bar. Kretch, the muscle-bound Ukrian Morg had recently hired to keep the peace at the Hole, wandered among the patrons who stood about, drinking and gabbing. He gave each a challenging glare down the end of his crumpled nose, as if daring them to start trouble. Past the big man was an enormous porthole set into the front wall of the tavern. During the day it offered a green-glazed view of the Run. Now it looked like a black pit.

"It's your move," Emma said.

Ander was about to turn his attention back to their game, when the tavern door abruptly banged open.

"Is that who I think it is?" his twin asked.

Ander nodded. "Yep. And three guesses who he's looking for."

Watch Commander Rhandellar Larron stalked into the Hole. He appeared even more haggard than the last time Ander had seen him. Dark bags hung below his eyes. His tabard was stained and wrinkled, the gargoyle of Fell's Hollow barely discernible beneath the grime. The man looked as if he hadn't slept in days. It seemed Nyland and the threat of war was not agreeing with the Commander. He spotted Ander almost at once, and then made his way straight for him, his head brushing against the low ceiling. Patrons parted, giving him a wide berth.

"Ellystun," Larron said, adding a curt nod.

"One of my men told me you were in here." He took an empty seat between Ander and Emma and glanced at the taffyl board. "Looks like white's in trouble."

Ander grunted. "Someone's always in trouble. Speaking of trouble, you can tell the Lord Mayor *his* trouble's been dealt with."

Larron's brow rose. "Really?" he said, sarcasm dripping from his voice. "You haven't brought me the assassin, as I ordered."

"We ran into a bit of difficulty," Emma said.

Larron looked the sellswords up and down, his eyes pausing on the patches of blood that still stained their clothes. "I heard," he said. "There are some very angry people at the theater. Seems our assassin murdered Ordin Awl. We found his body in the cellar of Pynn's Inn."

"We know," Ander told him.

Larron shook his head. "I guess the foreigner fancied himself an actor as well as an assassin. He turned up at the theater the morning of the show. Awl hadn't been seen in days. They said the foreigner knew all the lines."

"He doesn't anymore," Ander commented.

Larron's eyes narrowed. "He's dead? Are you sure, Ellystun?"

Emma pegged a black knob over a square. "Someone will fish him out of the harbor before the week's done," she told the Commander. "You'll have your body then."

"I wanted him alive," Larron complained,

displeasure clear in his voice. "That was the deal."

"There was never a deal," Ander spat. "You blackmailed us into doing your dirty work."

"Blackmail?" Larron laughed. "That's such a nasty word. I like to think of it as a favor for a favor."

"Goodbye, Commander," Ander said. "We've done what you've asked, and now we'd like to get back to our game, if you don't mind."

Larron smirked. "Oh, but I do mind. You see, I have another job for you."

Ander stood. Pain flared in his arm and his hip throbbed angrily. "We are done with you," he said.

Larron reached beneath his wrinkled tabard and pulled out a small pouch. He tossed it on the table and it landed with a clink.

Ander stared at the pouch, and a bad feeling settled over him. "What's that for?" he asked.

The Commander shrugged. "Despite what you think, I pay for the services I receive."

"What about Ballard?" Emma asked.

Larron slapped his knee and snorted. "What about him? He had a worse temper than your brother here. The man was bound to get skewered at some point."

Ander felt a twinge of suspicion. "I don't understand."

"It's simple." Larron got to his feet and tried to smooth the wrinkles from his tabard. Then he stared down at Ander. "You work for me now."

"I will not!" Ander's hand dropped to the hilt of his sword.

Larron grabbed a handful of Ander's tunic. The Watch Commander's face looked even worse up close. His eyes were bloodshot and his breath reeked of sour ale. "You work for me, else I'll find another way to hang you." He glanced at Emma. "That goes for you, too."

Larron let go of Ander. "Meet me at the Garrison in a few days. In the meantime, get some rest and heal up." With that, he turned and left the Hole.

When the tavern door slammed shut, Emma burst into laughter.

Ander glared at her. "What's so funny?"

"Look at it this way," Emma said, picking up the pouch from the table and hefting it in her hand. "At least we've found some steady work."

DAEMONS AND RINGS

"They haunt our dreams, astound, confound,
With twisted reason, madness sound,
Daemons dark and shadow bound."
Rhailiffaeben, *Act III, Sc. 1*
—*Flenter dae Chode*

RATS INFESTED THE DAVACRE. They had been there since the beginning, centuries ago, when the citizens of Fell's Hollow had cleared a small plot of land near the north end of Oldtowne. The plot had become the city's first burial ground, a sanctuary where the bones of loved ones could slumber in eternal peace. Year after year the citizens added tombs, crypts, and mausoleums, and year after year they would

69

return to visit the dead. Until one day the Davacre's last tomb was filled. Then, over the slow, lonely passage of time, the visits eventually stopped, and the Davacre fell into ruin.

Still the rats scurried through the Davacre's twisted, weed-choked paths. They scrabbled across the peaks of its tombs and scampered down the sides of its moss-covered mausoleums. They skittered about aimlessly in the dark, darting between thigh-thick poplar roots, up scarred and ragged cypress trunks, and through the skeletal branches of alder trees that hung heavy with deathvine.

Jessa Luness studied three blotched and boney rats as they huddled at the foot of one crypt, a rough-cut, spired edifice set with a rusted iron door. The reek of dead leaves filled the damp, midnight air. One rat jerked its head up. It stared about, red eyes burning in the mist. The other two followed, their ears pricking forward as they swiveled their heads this way and that. Then, abruptly, the rats turned and scattered into the night.

Jessa raised a sprig of lilac to her nose. She never left her home in Southside without stopping in her garden to break off a piece to carry with her. Its sweet smell eased her nerves and gave her comfort. She inhaled deeply and savored its soothing aroma.

"He'll have it," she said in a hushed voice. "You'll see, Mother. I know he will."

She scanned the Davacre for any sign of the young man. It was dark and misty, the only light coming from a few distant oil lamps that hung on iron posts near the entrance to the graveyard. She felt alone. Almost alone. She had Mother with her, as always. Mother had been inside her for years, since the night Father had strangled her in a drunken rage. "Isn't that right, Mother?" Jessa whispered. "You've been with me ever since."

Oh, yes, Dear. Ever since.

"And we don't need anyone else, do we?" she asked.

No. No one else.

Jessa moved to a stone bench beside the path. "He'll be here any moment, Mother. Then we'll have only one task left to perform."

One task. Yes, Dear, only one more task.

The thought of revenge sparked a flare of anger in Jessa's breast. Rorham Nach had told her that he would always love her. He had promised to leave his wife. He had promised... He had promised her everything. But that was over, and she was back to being alone. Her life was ruined.

Ruined, oh, yes. He ruined everything.

And it was all because of the thing growing inside her. His thing. When she had told him about it, Nach had tossed her to the street like a bucket of slop. She'd tried to change his mind, tried to convince him.

Convince him, yes, Dear. You tried to convince him.

But the man would hear none of it. The

Sorsagorium was his only priority. The curiosity shop needed his complete attention. And Nach didn't want children. It had all been a mistake. Jessa had been a mistake. Right before he slammed the door to the Sorsagorium, he had told her he never wanted to see her again.

Jessa tossed the sprig of lilac to the ground. Her eyes welled and she wiped them on the sleeve of her dress. She could feel her fury building, and was tempted to touch the Gift, to caress the energy she felt pulsing around her, shimmering in every tree, every stone, every blade of grass. She wanted to pull it in, all of it, and then unleash it upon Nach. She wanted to watch him burn, watch him wither before her eyes. She wanted him to die. Painfully. But even a painful death was too good for Nach. Oh, yes, much too good.

Yes, yes. That would be much too good, Dear. Much too good.

Jessa had a better plan.

She heard footfalls, soft, barely a wisp in the night. They came closer, and she tensed. Rumors were running through the city of late, talk of a madman loose in the streets, murdering anyone foolish enough to cross his path. Bodies had been found, bloodless and broken. She had to be careful.

Careful. We must be careful, Dear.

"Shush, Mother. He's coming."

The footfalls padded closer, and then a man

72

stepped out of the shadows of an ancient alder. It was Gillum, the young thief she'd hired at that pigsty of a bar in Rogueswarde. He was thin and as dirt-smeared as the first time she'd seen him, wrapped in a ripped and ragged cloak that had more holes than cloth. An arrogant look hung about his dark eyes. Jessa didn't like him. He was far too young to be so full of himself.

Gillum stopped a few feet from her. "Were you talking to someone?" he asked.

Jessa pursed her lips. "Of course not," she huffed. She never told anyone about Mother. At least, not anymore. She'd told a man once, her first lover several years back, and he had abandoned her the next day. After she'd killed him, she had made up her mind. Mother must remain her little secret.

"Well?" the thief said. "Do you have the coin?"

"Do you have the ring?" she countered.

The ring! Does he have the ring?

Jessa ignored Mother and studied the young thief's face. She knew men like him. Had known them all her life. And she knew what was running through his mind. He was trying to decide if he could kill her and take her money as well as the ring. His eyes narrowed slightly, almost imperceptibly.

Jessa pointed a finger at him. "Before you do anything rash, let me warn you. I can touch the Gift."

Gillum's brow lifted. "A sorceress, eh?" He grinned. "There'll be no need of that. I've got the ring. If you have the coin, we can both walk out of here—"

Jessa produced a leather pouch from the folds of her dress and tossed it in the dirt at his feet. Gillum clamped his mouth shut. Irritation spread across his face. The young thief bent slowly and picked up the pouch, never taking his eyes from her. She knew he didn't trust her. And she didn't trust him. But he was the best, or so she'd been told.

The best, oh, yes, Dear. Everyone said he was the best.

Gillum opened the pouch and poked a finger among the troyals. When he was satisfied, he slipped it beneath his cloak and took from under his belt a small pouch of his own.

"Show me," she said.

The thief upended the pouch, and a ring dropped into his hand. Even in the mist-filled darkness, it shimmered like a hunk of gold in the sun. Jessa recognized it at once. It was Nach's signet ring. His most valued possession.

"If you don't mind me asking," Gillum said with a smirk, "why did you want his ring?"

Jessa looked at him, but said nothing. Her heart was thudding with excitement.

"I mean," the thief went on, holding the ring up and giving it a close inspection, "there were a lot of things more valuable in Nach's manorhouse than this."

Jessa smiled. "That ring has been in Nach's family for more generations than anyone can remember. It was a gift from a Cabyllian king. Losing it will cause him to suffer greatly."

"Ah, I see," the thief said. "So it's a matter of revenge." He grinned and bowed mockingly. "Remind me never to cross you."

Jessa did not like this man. Not one bit. She gave him a sneer. "See that you don't. Now give me the ring and leave."

Gillum slipped the ring back into the pouch and handed it to Jessa. He nodded, and without another word turned and left, his footfalls fading back into the darkness from where he'd come.

"We'll do more than cause Nach a little suffering, won't we Mother?"

Oh, yes. Much more.

"Do you remember the plan, Mother?"

Oh, yes, Dear. The plan. I remember the plan.

"Now that we have the ring, there is only one item left to acquire."

One more. Just one more.

"And then," Jessa said with a smile, "we'll have everything we need."

*

The morning sun was nowhere to be seen. Gray clouds cloaked the sky. A light rain was falling, and a cool breeze blew between the buildings of the Warren. It had been raining on and off for days. Though the tempest had passed, the remnants of it clung to the city like deathvine, refusing to let go, soaking the city to the bone.

She'd come to the Warren at dawn, edging her way past buildings, over bridges, and down narrow, crooked docks, all of it constructed upon the waters of the harbor and supported by countless pitch-coated pilings. In places the docks were barely wide enough for two to pass, the clapboarded sides of some buildings shoved right up to and often right on top of the docks. The closeness of it all made Jessa feel as if she were weaving her way through a labyrinth.

She passed an old seaman heading in the opposite direction. He had a pole slung over his shoulder. A bucket slopped in one hand. She caught the sharp odor of sweat and fish and jerked her sprig of lilac to her nose. The old seaman grunted a greeting and continued on, and Jessa hurried deeper into the Warren.

Teetering around her, the buildings housed businesses of all kinds. Most sold goods of the cheapest sort, where even the poor could find what they needed for a few copper chips. But there were some shops in the Warren that offered rarer, more expensive items. Items that were either not of interest to most of the citizenry, or were illegal in nature, or both. Items like the one Jessa sought.

At last she came to a single story structure with an iron-studded front door. Above the door, a thin wooden placard was nailed to the clapboards.

Whitewashed and faded, it had a broken black pot painted at its center. The apothecary, known as the Cracked Crucible to those who could touch the Gift, specialized in peculiar and exotic materials. Jessa had explained to the shopkeeper exactly what she wanted. Wauker had said obtaining it would be difficult, but to check back in a few weeks.

Her hand shook with anticipation as she pushed open the door and stepped inside. All about the shop, cabinets, counters, and shelves overflowed with a wild array of objects: bottles of viscous fluids and powders of every color imaginable, small animal skulls and bits of bone, dried flesh and feathers of geese and gulls and birds she didn't recognize. Resting on a long bench against one wall were stacks of stones, shells, bundles of herbs and twigs, and even the head of some unfortunate fellow bobbing in an oversized jar.

At the back of the shop, Allomandius Wauker sat behind a small table. His forehead was beaded with sweat and his tiny black eyes widened as they shot past the tall man that stood before him and landed upon Jessa.

"L-Lady Luness," the shopkeeper stammered. "I-I'll be right with you as soon as I finish with this g-g-gentleman."

Something was wrong.

Wrong! Something is wrong!

She approached the table, and the tall man

77

turned to her. Recognition dawned on Jessa, and a ripple of fear slid down her back.

Urik Ungar ran his gaze from Jessa's face to her feet and back again. She felt as if he was tearing off her skin with his eyes in order to study her bones. The man was one of the few sorcerers in Fell's Hollow who was unafraid to let people know he could touch the Gift. Powerful and deadly, he had a reputation for using the Gift in the cruelest of fashions. There were those who insisted that Ungar, tormented by the loss of his wife, consorted with daemons and shadowspawn, concocting the most intricate tortures for those who crossed him. Lean and middle-aged, he wore his silver-gray hair tied back by a golden cord. His keen, bright eyes glittered with a sharp intensity, and his teeth were like chips of polished ivory.

The sorcerer returned his attention to the shopkeeper. "I will take an ounce of ambergris as well," he told him.

"Of c-c-course," Wauker said with a stutter, taking a flask of grayish-black powder from a shelf. With shaking hands he placed a lead weight onto one side of a balance that sat at the center of the table, then he poured some of the powder into the pan on the other side. He added a touch more powder until the balance was level and then transferred the contents to a small glass vial.

Wauker handed the vial to Ungar. "Will there b-b-be anything else?" His eyes darted to Jessa. A trickle of sweat ran down the shopkeeper's temple.

Wrong! Wrong!

Ungar handed Wauker a fistful of troyals. There must have been fifteen or twenty of them. That was a lot of coin for an ounce of ambergris.

"I will return in a few days for some scorpion blood," the sorcerer informed the trembling shopkeeper. "See that you have it." With that, Ungar stalked out of the shop.

Wauker muttered something under his breath. He turned to Jessa. His face bore a half-fearful, half-sorrowful expression. "I'm t-t-terribly sorry," he moaned.

A bad feeling settled into Jessa's stomach. "Sorry about what?" she demanded.

"I found a d-d-daemon's fang for you, but—"

Her bad feeling burst into rage. "You didn't!" she cried.

He did! Oh, Dear, he did. He sold it!

Another bead of sweat coursed down the side of the shopkeeper's face. "I had no ch-ch-choice!" he wailed.

Jessa opened herself to the Gift. Instantly she sensed it pulsing in the room. It vibrated in every object, throbbed in every bottle, book, vial, and herb in the shop. It shimmered in Wauker. It flowed through every feather, every bit of bone, and every stone and shell. She reached out with her mind and touched it. It soaked into her like water into a sponge. She drank it in, savored it as every nerve in her body began to tingle.

"*Quirum.*" She spoke the word of power, wrapping it with the Gift as the word left her lips. A ball of fire appeared in her hand, white hot, though it felt cool to her flesh. It wouldn't be so cool to Wauker. It would consume him like a moth in a flame.

Wauker's eyes shot wide. "P-Please d-d-don't!"

"Who did you sell it to?" She wanted to kill him. She'd been waiting too long. Everything was ready. All she needed was this last item, a single daemon's fang, and then she could perform the ritual. She'd dreamt about it for months. She would summon a daemon to drag Rorham Nach straight into the Abyss, where his black spirit would suffer an eternity of torment. But now...

"I asked you a question," Jessa snarled through clenched teeth.

Wauker's wide eyes grew wider. Then they shifted over her shoulder to the shop door.

Realization struck Jessa. "You didn't," she whispered.

Wauker began to weep. "I t-told him the fang was one-of-a-k-k-kind. I told him it was spoken for. But he w-w-wouldn't listen."

Jessa spun around, raced to the door, and flung it wide. Outside, the dock was empty.

Urik Ungar was gone.

*

She stormed up the High Road. The midday sun had once again failed to cut through the mist and fog. The buildings of Oldtowne remained shuttered, and the lamplighters had left many of the streetlamps burning from the night before. The roads in this part of the city were cobbled and narrow and smeared with a layer of reddish-yellow mud that had recently washed down from the Heights. There were no carriages to be seen. A few cityfolk meandered through the gloom, and the occasional horseman clopped sloppily along, splattering anyone too slow to step aside.

Mud sucked at Jessa's feet as she walked. She thought of Ungar's infamous manorhouse tucked away at the top of the Street of Ten Steps. It was said that Ungar lived alone in one of the most lavish residences in the Heights. She'd never been near the place, but had heard it was a towering structure of stone and stained glass, with a front gate that made the entrance to the Tershium look like the back door of a brothel. She had no idea what she was going to do when she got there. She knew only that she had to retrieve the daemon's fang. Her revenge depended upon it.

Frustration gnawed at her belly, and she rubbed at the bulge that held Nach's spawn. Life had finally been worth living when she'd met Rorham. They'd spent so much time together, walking the city, dining in the finest taverns and inns, taking in plays at the Cove Theater, or a night of beast-baiting at Fuller's and Fangs. She had not enjoyed the company of another living person in years. Rorham had been so nice, treated her like a lady from the day she'd first met him in his curiosity shop. But then she had come down with his child, and he had scraped her from his life as if she were a foul blotch on his boot.

Something foul we were. Oh, yes. Foul indeed.

Jessa ignored Mother and trudged up a side street that led north into the Heights. The buildings here were spaced further apart, dotting the tree-lined slope that eventually led all the way to the base of the cliffs that surrounded the cove. High stone walls encircled most of the properties, preventing Jessa from seeing much more than red-tiled roofs and chimney tops. Nach lived in the Heights as well, near the border of Faettewarde. The thought made her stomach burn.

Suffer! We will make him suffer!

"Yes, Mother. Nach will suffer."

An elderly woman walking nearby shot her a questioning stare and then picked up her pace. Abruptly, Jessa laughed. How ironic things can be, she thought. She had bought the scroll from Nach himself. The dumb fool didn't know what it was. He rarely knew what sat upon the shelves of his shop. He just collected the strangest objects he could gather from the sailors that came into port. More often than not he'd sell them for a staggering profit. Sometimes, however, he would let a treasure go for a copper chip. He had no idea the scroll contained the very spell that would send him screaming into the Abyss.

Jessa clenched her fists. She had to get the daemon's fang. She had the iron brazier, tempered in grakkyn blood, and the camphor, and Nach's ring. The ring would connect Nach to the ritual. She wasn't sure exactly how that would happen, but without the daemon's fang, it wouldn't happen at all.

We will banish him to the Abyss!

Jessa sighed. "Yes, Mother, we will."

After a while, Jessa turned onto another road, this one far steeper than the rest. The Street of Ten Steps led straight up into a stand of thick yew and cypress trees. Beyond the stand on the crest of a small hill stood a dark, castle-like structure. It had to be the home of Urik Ungar. She slogged up the street. Around her, the foliage was thick and green, and the smell of wet soil and mold hung beneath the trees. Moss clung to trunks twice as thick as Jessa. Her legs were tired from the climb into the Heights, so she moved off the road to a cluster of rhododendron that had grown particularly close together. A log, half rotted, lay on the ground beside an outcropping of rock. She smoothed her dress and sat. Through the tangle of leaves she had a perfect view of Ungar's manorhouse.

We must get the daemon's fang! We must!

"Patience, Mother," she said. "All in good time."

*

Night had fallen and the darkness was near complete. Jessa stood and groaned. Her back had stiffened, but the pain was worth it. A while ago, Ungar's carriage had left the manorhouse, carrying him down into the city. She had waited to be sure he wasn't simply taking a short ride, but he hadn't returned. Knowing his reputation, he would most likely spend the entire evening at one of the theaters, or at Edden's gambling house. She would have hours.

Jessa stumbled back to the road. Brushing off her dress, she worked her way up to the manorhouse. As she neared the entrance, she strained to take in the details of the place. It was constructed entirely of black carterock. Four fat towers jutted up at the corners. In the center of the manorhouse, a larger tower rose like a thick spike into the low-hanging mist. Slits of stained glass, red, blue, and green, were set into the stone at intervals. At the front of the manorhouse, a pair of enormous silver-studded doors sat within an archway twice the height of a man. On either side of the doors, a torch burned in an iron sconce.

She gave the place a long look. How was she to get inside? She wasn't a thief, like Gillum. She couldn't scale the walls and slip in through a window. And she couldn't use the Gift. Ungar would have put protections in place. But she did know one word. An old and obscure word that she'd learned from a Thalian witch as a child. There was a chance Ungar knew it as well, and if he did, he would have cast the counterspell upon those massive front doors of his. But maybe, just maybe, the witch's word would work.

Jessa crept up the steps. This is madness, she thought. She was about to sneak into the home of the most dangerous sorcerer in Fell's Hollow. To steal a daemon's fang. Her hands started to tremble. What if she were caught? Or what if Ungar came looking for her afterwards? He might know of ways to locate anyone daring enough, or stupid enough, to steal from him. But if he did, she supposed, she would simply have to deal with that later. Her revenge was worth any risk. She would face a thousand Ungars to make Nach suffer.

Make him suffer. Yes, oh, yes, we will.

"Shush, Mother," she whispered.

Jessa opened herself to the Gift and spoke, cloaking the word with power. *"Esiduvum."*

The doors swung silently open, and she felt a flash of pleasure. She squinted her eyes as a blaze of firelight spilled out onto the front steps. Slipping inside, she shut the doors. Her heart thumped wildly in her chest and her mouth went dry as she examined the inside of Ungar's home.

She was in an antechamber. Along one wall an ornately carved bench sat beneath a black tapestry. A small, marble-topped table hugged the other wall. On it, three candles burned in silver holders. At the far end of the antechamber, an archway led into a brightly lit room where she could hear a fire crackling within.

Jessa slipped up to the archway. Spanning nearly forty paces in all directions, the room beyond was vast and elegant. It was filled with furniture of every sort: velvet-lined chairs, divans, sofas. An intricately carved cabinet stood open on one side of the room, its shelves lined with strange objects not unlike those in Wauker's shop. A handful of human skulls stared down at her from the top shelf. At the back of the room, a fire roared within a monstrous fireplace. There were several doors along the other walls and next to the fireplace a wide staircase ran up into darkness.

She could hear her own breath coming in quick, shallow gasps. She skirted around the furniture, shot over to the cabinet, and searched the shelves. No daemon's fang.

We need the fang, Dear. Find the fang!

Ignoring Mother, Jessa tried to think. Where would Ungar keep it? Where would she keep it, if she had just acquired a daemon's fang? She'd keep it close, she realized. Certainly not here. Somewhere more private, perhaps.

Yes, Dear. Somewhere more private.

She studied the doors. They could lead anywhere. To a kitchen, a storage area, a servant's room. Fear flooded into Jessa's belly. She hadn't thought of that! What if Ungar didn't live alone?

What if he had servants? And one found her sneaking through the manorhouse?

What if? What if? Hurry! Find the daemon's fang!

She'd have to trust to her luck. She scurried across the room and bounded up the stairs. Ungar's private rooms would certainly be on an upper level of the manorhouse.

The darkness grew deeper, and Jessa had to slow her pace to let her eyes adjust. She stopped at the top of the stairs. A long hall stretched out in front of her. A narrow carpet ran the length of it and ended at a door of dark, glossy wood. She crept down the hall. Along one side were several windows of colored glass.

She reached the door and pushed it open. The room beyond was nearly black, save for a splash of red that spilled in through the leaded panes of a single window. Shadowy shapes filled the room. One, rectangular and larger than the rest, dominated the center. A bed. Next to it, a long dresser was pushed against the wall. She could just make out the drawer handles on the front. A handful of small objects were scattered across its top.

She crossed the room and picked up one of the objects. It was an ivory comb as thick as her thumb. She set the comb down, and her stomach climbed into her throat. Next to the dresser, something had moved. Jessa turned her head slowly and stared straight into the face of a nightmare. There, staring back at her, was a woman. She was gaunt. Her face was drawn and washed in a pale red glow. Her eyes were wide, exactly like her own. Her hair fell in a tangle of dark curls to her shaking—It was a mirror!

"Shite," Jessa hissed. Her hands shook as she returned her attention to the dresser. She had never been so frightened in her life. She shuffled through the rest of Ungar's personal items until, near the edge of the dresser, she saw it. The daemon's fang. It was about a handswidth in length, black and curved and tapered to a sharp point. Snatching it up, she turned to leave. And there, standing before her, was the dark figure of a man.

The man spoke. There was a blinding flash of light, and then nothing.

*

Jessa awoke, groggy, disoriented, and shivering. She was naked, lying on a stone slab in a small, dank cellar. Above her a dim yellow light danced across a low, wooden ceiling. She had to be below the manorhouse. She tried to move. There came a clank of metal and the bite of iron on her flesh. Shackles encircled her wrists and ankles. Lengths of chain ran to iron ringlets set into the corners of the slab.

A torrent of terror crashed over her, and she opened herself to the Gift. Instantly, pain exploded behind her eyes, a sudden, fiery, overwhelming agony unlike anything she'd ever endured. She screamed as she cut off the flow of power. It felt as if someone had poured molten iron through a hole in her forehead.

"She stirs, master," said a rough voice. A figure moved at the foot of the slab. A servant, by the looks of him. His clothes were rumpled and stained. He was short and stocky, with strands of grimy black hair that hung down in front of his round, pockmarked face.

"I have given you a draught of galbanum," said another voice, deep and resonant. From behind her, Urik Ungar stepped into view. He grasped a handful of her hair and held her head firmly. He leaned in closer, studying something in her eyes. "Using the Gift will be quite painful for some time yet," he informed her.

Jessa's fear swelled. She struggled to clear her head. How long had she been unconscious?

Ungar wore a long, flowing black robe. Strange glyphs were inked onto his face and hands. His silver-gray hair was pulled back, and he stared at her with eyes filled with a blazing intensity.

"Is there anything I can do, master?" the servant asked.

Ungar glanced at him. "No, Zaul. Not until we begin the ritual."

Ritual? What was he planning!

Escape! We must escape!

Jessa ignored Mother and screamed. She yanked at the shackles. "Let me go!" she howled.

Ungar laughed. "After you were so kind to pay

us a visit? I think not. You've saved me a lot of trouble. I had wondered where I would find so lovely a host."

The sorcerer dragged a small, wooden workbench up to the slab. Jessa could see he had sketched more of the glyphs onto its surface. She stared down at her own naked form. Black symbols covered her as well, from head to toe.

Ungar set a stone mortar onto the workbench. Gingerly, he placed into it what appeared to be the tip of a cleanly severed finger. Then he added a drop of red liquid from a glass vial and, with a pestle gripped in one hand, crushed the contents into a thick crimson paste. From somewhere beneath the workbench he pulled out more bottles. They clinked together as he mumbled to himself, continuing his preparations.

Once more, Jessa opened herself to the Gift. And once more, liquid fire flooded into her head. She cried out in pain.

Ungar chuckled. "I warned you."

Do something! Anything!

Panic threatened to overwhelm her. What was she going to do!

Ungar gestured to Zaul, who took an oil lamp from an iron stand in the corner and carried it closer to the slab. A sickly yellow light fell over Ungar's face as he moved to Jessa's side. He raised a long, curved knife in one hand.

Jessa yanked herself away. Chains clanked and the shackles bit into her ankles. "Let me go or I swear I'll kill you!" she shrieked.

Zaul snorted, and Ungar shook his head. "You are a strong-willed woman, aren't you?" the sorcerer noted. "And smart, too. I don't know how you managed to get past my front doors. Thankfully, I had other wards in place." He turned to Zaul. "Hold her down."

Jessa brushed aside her pain and tried to wrench free from the shackles, but they were too tight. Hard metal cut into her wrists.

Zaul set the lamp on the slab and shuffled closer. A terrible stench followed him like a cloud. He took from a pocket a swatch of cloth and wrapped it around her face. Everything went black. Then he snatched her shoulders and pinned them to the table. She felt him lean over her, and the pressure on her shoulders increased. Tendons stretched and nearly tore. She groaned as she struggled under the servant's weight. Zaul laughed as his reek washed over her.

Fight! You must fight them!

She felt the tip of Ungar's knife nick her breast, and she jerked. A warm trickle ran down to the center of her chest. There came a clink, then a cold, wet tendril touched her skin. A brush. Ungar was painting more symbols on her flesh. Jessa howled and tried to pull her body away as best she could, but Zaul was too strong. She barely moved.

Ungar slid the brush over her breast. There was another clink, more cold. Then came a long hiss. It was a burning sound. Ungar had tossed something into the fire of the lamp. A pungent aroma suddenly filled the cellar.

"*I sudurit equos purivuset!*" the sorcerer chanted. "O powers of the Abyss, come forth. Return to me my wife. Return to me my Bel."

"No!" Jessa cried.

"*Bevur vut tideum us evicesurum,*" he went on. "Take this spirit in exchange."

Jessa twisted with all her might, but Zaul clamped down even harder. Pain shot through her shoulders. She screamed again as she fought against the servant. Suddenly, the temperature in the cellar dropped. The servant gasped, and she felt his dirty fingers grip even tighter. Then a voice spoke. It was not human. Deep and guttural, the words were in a language unknown to her. They sounded as if they'd been dredged up from the cold, dark depths of a well.

"What?" the sorcerer snapped. He sounded shocked, upset. A cold hand pressed against Jessa's naked belly. It felt like bones.

Ungar let out a low growl. "She is with child. *I pitubut a, Daemon*. Begone, until I summon thee again."

There came another string of words, inhuman, cold, wet. Foul. Then the air in the cellar warmed and Zaul released her. She exhaled in relief as the pressure on her shoulders vanished and with it most of the pain. She whipped her head from side to side and the blindfold fell away, restoring her sight. "Release me!" she demanded.

Both men ignored her.

"You sent the daemon back," Zaul said. "Why, master? How did I fail this time?" A look of terror was on the servant's face.

Ungar remained silent, considering the question. He had the daemon's fang in one hand. He studied it for a moment, testing its point on the pad of a finger. "There are two spirits in her body, Zaul," the sorcerer said. "The spirit-switch would not work. There must be an equal exchange."

Zaul stared at Jessa, and his eyes filled with lust. "I can have her, then?"

A wave of nausea washed over Jessa.

He wants us! Don't let him befoul us!

Ungar tossed the daemon's fang onto the workbench. "I think not," he told the servant. "We will try this again. Tomorrow, perhaps."

"How?" Zaul asked.

Ungar frowned. "First I will need to replenish the materials we've wasted." He moved to the foot of a small wooden stair that led up to a door. "Which might not be easy with the threat of war keeping the tradeships out of port. It may take a while."

"I could get them for you, master," Zaul offered.

"No," the sorcerer told him. "I will visit Wauker myself. He may have what we need." Ungar glanced at Jessa. "I'll need a few strands of

93

stargrass, as well. To expel the child. Then our sweet host will be ready to accept my wife."

A strong sensation, warm, protective, and unfamiliar, swelled within Jessa and mingled with her fear.

"As you wish, master," the servant said. He turned to Jessa and raked his eyes over her naked flesh. "Shall I wash off the ink?" he asked Ungar.

The sorcerer nodded. "Yes. Then lock her in the cage."

*

A creak echoed in the darkness and Jessa opened her eyes. She was still naked. And cold. The bastards hadn't even given her a blanket.

A yellow light fluttered at the top of the stairs. Zaul appeared and took a few steps down. He held out a lamp in one hand and peered in her direction.

Jessa shut her eyes and lay still. For what had seemed an eternity, the vile servant had scrubbed the ink from her flesh. Then he had locked her in an iron cage at the back of the cellar. She'd spent hours trying to escape. The cage and the lock were new. There was nothing within arm's reach outside the cage, nothing she could use to pry apart the thumb-thick bars, nothing to snap the lock. She'd tried to open herself to the Gift, but that had only resulted in more pain. Eventually she had realized the truth. She would have to fight her way out. Pushing aside her fear, she tried to keep her breathing shallow and even. If Zaul thought she was asleep, perhaps she could surprise him.

The servant ventured to the bottom of the stairs and gave a grunt. Jessa could hear his feet scuffling through the dirt as he came closer. "Oh, so beautiful," he muttered. "Ungar will beat me for days, but it will be worth it."

Disgust and terror double-punched Jessa in the belly. Ungar must have left the manorhouse, and now the little man's lust had won over his fear.

Don't let him take us!

Mother was awake. That was all Jessa needed.

There came the scratch of metal on metal, and the cage door squeaked open. This was her chance. She would take it, or die trying. The servant's foul stench enveloped her, and she held her breath.

"Mmm," he whispered.

Do something! What are you waiting for?

There was a clank as Zaul set down the lamp. Her chest burned as she tried to keep still, not daring to breathe, lest she gag on his reek. The servant shuffled closer and a rough hand touched her leg.

No!

Jessa opened her eyes and kicked.

Zaul lurched backwards. "Wha—?"

Her foot slammed into his thigh, and he grunted. She leaped toward him and her hands found his neck. The two fell out of the cage in a tangle of limbs.

"Bitch!" Zaul cursed. He snatched Jessa's wrists as she drove her thumbs into his throat. Across the floor, their shadows fluttered and flailed.

Kill him!

The servant made a gurgling sound, and his eyes widened. He pulled at her wrists, trying to break free. He was strong, but Jessa tightened her hold. She squeezed with all her strength, burying her thumbs deeper and deeper into his windpipe.

Zaul let go of her wrists and punched her in the side of the head. His fist landed like a miner's maul. Sparks flew across her vision. He hit her again, and she lost her grip.

The servant bucked, and Jessa tumbled off him. He coughed and gasped for air. Jessa stumbled to her feet, blood trickling down her cheek.

Run! Flee!

She took two strides toward the stair, and Zaul slammed into her back. They crashed against Ungar's workbench. The mortar thunked off the side and onto the dirt floor. Bottles shattered. Jessa felt the edge of the bench dig into her belly, and she howled in pain.

The servant snatched Jessa by the hair and hammered her face into the broken glass. Once. Twice. Three times. Her skin split and a sharp pain sliced through her forehead. She pushed herself away from the bench. Blood sprayed across her hands.

"You're going to pay for this," Zaul grunted between heavy breaths.

Find a weapon! Anything!

Jessa spun. Blood ran into her eyes. Blindly, she raked out a hand and caught the servant across the face. Her nails dug gouges through his pockmarked skin. Zaul howled and she launched a kick at his groin. He turned at the last moment and caught her foot in both hands. He gave it a vicious twist. Pain tore through her ankle, and she wailed.

Zaul spun her around, grabbed her by the shoulders, and forced her face-down onto the workbench. Glass bit into her naked breasts. He held her in place with one rough hand. With his other hand he fumbled at his breeches.

Do something!

Desperate, Jessa opened herself to the Gift. Fire flared behind her eyes. It was molten agony. It dwarfed the pain of the cut in her forehead, the ache of her twisted ankle. She knew this would kill her, but she didn't stop. She relished it. If she was to die, it would be her way, not his.

She pulled in the power that vibrated in every object in the cellar. She soaked in every scrap from every stone, from every shard of glass, from every speck of dirt upon the floor. Unbearable fire coursed through her body. But she didn't care. She took it all in, and then, in one instant, let it go.

"*Quirum,*" she spat. The word and the power left her in a flood, and she focused it on the wretch behind her. There was a horrifying shriek, and Zaul's hand left her back.

The servant staggered backwards, screeching in agony. White flames danced over his body. His clothes shriveled into black ash. He bellowed as his flesh bubbled and hissed. Black smoke escaped from his mouth, and he crumbled to the floor. Within moments, there was nothing left but a pile of burnt bones.

*

It had taken Jessa till dawn to make it back to Southside. She was exhausted, but sleep could wait. Her forehead stung and her ankle throbbed as she studied her work.

Hot ashes burned in the iron brazier. Tendrils of smoke and the sharp scent of camphor hung in the air. Around the brazier, freshly-painted glyphs spidered across the floor. She had sketched the symbols precisely as the scroll described, exact in every detail. She was taking no chances.

No chances, Dear. Take no chances.

"I won't, Mother," she said.

Jessa shifted her position on her knees and tossed another waxy chunk of camphor onto the coals. It hissed and spat, and more of the pungent fumes wafted up, stinging her eyes. Her hands shook. She had waited months for this moment.

It's time, Dear. Yes, it's finally time!

Jessa opened herself to the Gift. Shimmering power soaked into her. She took it in, relished it, and then released it in a steady stream, wrapping it carefully around each word as she read from the scroll.

"*Isus.* Open, ye gates of the Abyss."

The ashes flared in the brazier.

"*Isus.* Open. I command you."

The ashes flared again, and then, as if a cover to a well had been suddenly flung open, a black hole appeared in the center of the brazier. A wave of cold blasted from the hole, frosting Jessa's breath. She felt her skin turn to gooseflesh. Then she took the daemon's fang in one hand and read once more from the scroll.

"*Vebem, Daemon.* Come to me." She wove the scintillating power around the words as they left her lips and focused them on the brazier.

"*Vebem, Daemon.* I call to you."

The daemon slithered out of the hole, an icy, incorporeal force that threatened to freeze Jessa where she knelt. It surrounded her, snaking around her body, and her stomach roiled. Frost gathered at the edges of the brazier.

Jessa trembled. There was one last step, and then revenge would be hers. She set down the fang and took up the small pouch Gillum had given her. She felt the weight of Nach's ring inside, his most prized possession, and smiled.

"*I quireius ra, Daemon,*" she said. "I free you to claim the spirit of one man. The man connected to this ring." She upended the pouch—and screamed. Instead of Nach's golden ring, a small chunk of dark gray metal dropped into her hand.

No! Betrayed! We've been betrayed!

Fear engulfed her. She had been tricked! Somehow Gillum had switched Nach's ring, replacing it with a shard of lead. She slung it into the brazier, knowing the act was pointless. The ritual would only work if the person had a strong connection to the item.

Flee!

Jessa pushed herself to her feet. Pain raced up her ankle and she stumbled. Then she felt the daemon enter her. Its cold, greasy presence stabbed into the center of her mind. The blood in her veins froze. Darkness consumed her, and she tumbled into another world.

*

She found herself on the battlements of a great fortress, surrounded by darkness. The daemon was out there, somewhere beyond the walls. It was searching. Searching for her. And when he found her, he would devour her.

The daemon moved closer. It knew where she was. She could not hide from it. It was drawn to her. She could feel its malice pulsating in the dark, its hate throbbing like a wound. And then, far below the battlements, it arrived at the fortress gate. It slammed against it, and the fortress shook. It pounded at the gate again and again until Jessa felt the gate crack. Then the daemon hesitated, and Jessa could somehow sense its confusion.

There was another fortress! A smaller one further out in the darkness. Newly formed. Delicate. The daemon abandoned the gate and moved toward it. Who was in that other fortress? Instantly, she knew.

It was Nach's child.

Let it take the wretch!

Something snapped within Jessa. A flood of unfamiliar, raw feeling broke over her, igniting every speck of her being. What was it? she wondered. Protectiveness? Nurturing? Love? Yes, that was it. Love. Suddenly she understood the impact of what Nach had done. He had not abandoned her to a life of loneliness. He had blessed her with a gift. Somehow, someway, Jessa reached out over the battlements and pulled the child into the confines of her own fortress.

It was a girl.

Out in the darkness, the daemon roared in rage. Jessa held the unborn girl close, protecting it with arms that were not arms, shielding it from the daemon. The daemon returned and began battering once again at the fortress gate. It shook and splintered. It would not hold for long.

Give the daemon the child! Give it to him!

No, Jessa thought. She would not give up her baby.

You must!

No*!*

Listen to me! It will never leave without a spirit!

Below the walls, the daemon howled in anger as it hammered at the gate.

Suddenly, without thought, Jessa reached down into the bowels of her fortress. She felt around, blindly, until her hands came upon a thing that was dry and withered, like a pile of old skin and dead leaves.

What are you doing?

Jessa grasped Mother and dragged her up to the battlements. The daemon's hatred washed over the walls, a torrent of ice and frozen fury. The beast beat against the gate, and she felt it crack once more.

Stop! You mustn't! You won't survive without me!

She gave Mother a shove, and Mother toppled into the darkness. Abruptly, the daemon stopped. There came a long wail of satisfaction, and Mother screamed.

NOOoooooooo!

She screamed and screamed until, finally, her screams faded into a cold, empty silence.

Jessa opened her eyes.

She was lying on the floor. The brazier had returned to normal, its red embers glowing warmly. The black hole was gone. Gillum's chunk of lead shimmered in the ashes.

Shaking, she got to her feet. She was done with Nach. She no longer cared if he lived or died. There were other things to care about now.

"I will call you Falla," she said, clasping her hands to her belly. "It means *little sister* in the Old Tongue, isn't that right, Mother?"

There came only silence, and Jessa smiled. It was a silence she could live with.

THE SOLDIER AND THE SON

"Deny not the whetstone of fate
When edging the sword of purpose."
The Weaponsmith of Mol, *77-78*
—*Doman Skythe*

T HE SOUND OF SWORDPLAY rang over the grounds of the Tershium. Built three hundred years ago by the wealthy poet and playwright Starroch Phemorel, the Tershium was once a private residence near the center of Oldtowne. It covered nearly six square blocks and had been famous for its high, thick walls of carterock, its lush, tree-lined gardens, and, most of all, for its quiet tranquility. In its time, the serene atmosphere of the Tershium had rivaled

105

even that of the hilltop parks of Faettewarde. But no more. Its peaceful mystique vanished upon Phemorel's death when the Triad, the ruling council of Fell's Hollow, along with the soldiers of the Watch, claimed the property for their own.

The clang of steel on steel rattled against the Guildhall, a renovated two-story carriage house in the southern end of the Tershium, where merchants, craftsmen, and oft-swindled citizens came before the Guildmaster to have their grievances settled. It clanked about the House of Justice, a former mansion set in the heart of the grounds, where the Lord Mayor liked to read the Triad's latest proclamations from its giant steps of black stone. And it echoed thunderously through the courtyard of the Garrison, a hulking complex on the north side, once home to Phemorel's servants and staff, where watchmen honed their skills from dawn to dusk.

From an open second story window of the Garrison, Watch Commander Rhandellar Larron gazed down at a dozen, rain-soaked recruits garbed in padded practice gear. They launched blows at each other with blunted weapons, snarling and cursing. A few grizzled veterans stood nearby, wrapped in oilcloth cloaks, shouting scraps of encouragement and instruction as the recruits went about their morning routine.

Larron closed the window, dulling the sharp edge of the din. As he crossed the room and took a seat behind his parchment-littered desk, Horm

Norgarde, the Lord Mayor of Fell's Hollow, slapped another parchment on top of the clutter. Norgarde had seen well over sixty summers, had lost most of his white hair, and sported a substantial paunch around his middle. He had small, black eyes, a wide nose, and his normally red face burned even redder than usual.

"Have you read this morning's *Gargoyle*?" he asked. "I swear, that bastard Zoltin Maark is pushing his luck."

Larron rubbed his temples. It seemed every waking moment brought a new problem, a new catastrophe he was expected to resolve. The Watch Commander was only one-third of the Triad, yet Norgarde and Archen Indellisar, the I'm-far-too-busy-for-that Guildmaster, preferred to drop any issue that wasn't specifically related to their domains into Larron's overloaded lap.

Norgarde didn't wait for an answer. He snatched the *Gargoyle* back from the desk and shook it at Larron. "I think Maark is trying to start a panic," he complained. A blue vein pulsed at his temple. "Listen to this: *Until our Lord Mayor summons a shadowhunter from the mainland, people will continue to die.* A shadowhunter! Can you believe that? Protecting the city isn't even my job, it's yours." Norgarde crumpled the parchment in his fist. "Every man, woman, and child from the Heights to Southside will be frightened out of their wits once they read this!"

Larron let out a sigh. He had seen this coming

and had already begun preparations. "The night after the tempest hit, I sent a ship to Alar," he said as he began straightening the mess of paperwork in front of him. "There should be a shadowhunter in Fell's Hollow within a week. Two at the most."

Norgarde's eyes widened. "Without telling me?"

"You were busy," Larron said. "I figured I'd deal with it."

The Lord Mayor gave him a look of consternation. "Next time I would prefer to be kept informed."

Larron shrugged.

"So," Norgarde went on. "You really believe there's a valkar loose in the city?"

Larron scoffed. "No. Those bloodsucking fiends have been extinct for hundreds of years. But why take the chance?"

"You still believe the murders are the result of a madman?"

"I do."

Norgarde studied Larron. "And yet old Pand says no one has escaped the Asylum."

Larron raised an eyebrow.

Norgarde laughed. "Right. Like every madman in Fell's Hollow is locked in the Asylum. But you'll catch the bastard? Soon?"

"I've put a half-dozen men on it," Larron said. "That's all I can afford right now."

Norgarde nodded. "I see. Well, maybe we'll get

lucky. Shall I put out a proclamation?"

"That's up to you," Larron told him.

Norgarde moved to the window. Larron could still hear the muffled sounds of fighting as the young soldiers went about their training.

"And what about that other problem?" Norgarde asked. "Have we confirmed those sellswords of yours actually *killed* that assassin? That foreign bastard nearly skewered me. If you and your men hadn't shown up—"

"But we did show up," Larron interrupted. "And no, the body hasn't washed up yet. It's probably snagged on a piling somewhere. I wouldn't worry about it."

Norgarde let out a snort. "Easy for you to say."

Larron grunted. "Granted."

Norgarde sauntered back to Larron and crossed his arms over his belly. "What of our defenses? Have you fortified the Watchtowers? Are you ready in case Felgus decides to sail his warships into the harbor? Sinking them in the gorge is our only hope. If those Nyland bastards get through—"

"They won't get through," Larron assured him. "I've tripled the men on the towers. The cannon are ranged. We're prepared."

The Lord Mayor took a satisfied breath, and a small smile appeared on his face. "Seems like you've got everything under control."

"As much as can be, I suppose."

"That's wonderful." Norgarde pulled up a chair and settled his bulk into it. He crossed his legs, then smacked his knee with an open palm. "How is everything else, then? How's that boy of yours?"

Blast! Larron had completely forgotten. Today was his son's birthday. How could he forget? Even after Tyna had died of fever and was no longer around to remind him, he never forgot Ghaid's birthday.

Larron was struck with guilt. His own birthday was in two days, and he knew Ghaid wouldn't forget. His son would always give him something special, made from his own hands, something he'd spent weeks carving, or sketching, or constructing from scraps of wood and resin. Last year the boy had built him a shield from the planks of an old crate. Ghaid had painted it red and had painstakingly inked the gargoyle of Fell's Hollow at its center. It was hanging now, on the wall behind his desk. He glanced at it, and a fresh torrent of guilt swept over him.

Larron stood and grabbed his cloak from the back of his chair. "Ghaid's fine. Now, if there's nothing else, I need to make my rounds."

And stop at Arryn's before he closed shop, Larron thought. If he arrived home without a gift for his son… The gift. Ghaid was not going be happy with his gift. Not at all. He pushed the thought from his mind as he headed for the door. He had enough to worry about already.

*

Lamplighters wandered about Welkyn Street, touching flame to wick as the sun set somewhere behind the fog. The air was cool and damp, the rain having let up a few hours ago, and the cobblestone road was cluttered with people hustling home from work or heading out for an early drink before dinner. There were fewer than usual, and most wore expressions of worry on their careworn faces.

Larron settled the small package under his arm as he walked along the shadowy street. He had arrived at Arryn's just as the bookdealer was locking up. The old man hadn't been too happy, but he could hardly turn away the Watch Commander of Fell's Hollow. Arryn had browsed through an old manuscript, muttering to himself, while Larron took nearly an hour to find a present for his son. He wanted to find something the boy might really enjoy, something that might make up for the disappointment Larron knew was coming. In the end he had settled on Bonnost's *The Whippoorwill*. Ren Bonnost, a proponent of heavy drinking, marriageless love, and dueling, was said to be fiendishly addicted to opit. Larron didn't approve of Bonnost, but the playwright was a favorite among the younger crowd in the city. Larron hoped the gift would be enough. Ghaid, he knew, was expecting something entirely different.

As Larron slogged past the Tavern of the Red

Glove, its windows already glowing with firelight, he felt the familiar pang of guilt. He had made a promise to his son, and now he was breaking it. How could he not? Ghaid was only fourteen, still just a boy. How could he give him a sword and let him join the Watch? Yet he had promised Ghaid exactly that, right after Tyna had died. The boy wanted nothing more than to follow in the footsteps of the father he worshiped. With his mother freshly buried, Larron couldn't bring himself to say no. He should have, but he lacked the courage. He couldn't break the boy's heart. It had been broken enough.

A short way up the street, he arrived at his home, a small, modest, red-tiled cottage set back from Welkyn among a handful of oaks and glossy-leaved rhododendrons. He stepped up the walk, went inside, and tossed Ghaid's gift on a small table by the window.

The sitting room, even at this time of summer, was chilly. Larron moved to the fireplace and grabbed a handful of kindling from an old wine barrel sitting next to his favorite armchair. He placed the kindling on the grate, stuffed in some straw, and after a few strokes of flint, had a fire started.

Larron sighed. He could remember a time when he didn't have to worry about coming home to a cold house, or forgetting birthday presents, or dealing with impending invasions, or assassins, or madmen. He could remember a time when all he had to worry about was his little area of Fell's Hollow, a mostly peaceful section of Stockwarde where he, as a young watchman, would patrol the streets, lending a hand here and there, helping anyone who needed help. At worst, he'd have to break up a brawl at Pynn's Inn, or chase down some urchin as the little tyke sprinted by with a loaf of bread stolen from Corolan, the old baker at the end of Ankka's Lane. And after, he would return home to Tyna, a warm meal, and an even warmer embrace.

But no more. Now he had the whole city to worry about. Now he had a son who would soon be facing the dangerous choices of manhood. And he had to deal with it all. Alone. Larron shook off his self-pity. There were things that needed doing, like getting some food on the table.

"Ghaid?" he called out. There came only the crackle and spit of the fire.

"Ghaid!" he called again. He peered up the staircase that led to the bedrooms in the attic. Nothing. That was strange. The boy was usually home by this time, with dinner already simmering in a pot over the hearth. He must be out with his friends, Larron thought, and a tinge of worry settled over him. The boy had been getting into trouble lately. He hoped Ghaid was being careful.

Larron frowned. His son was too much like him, too hot-headed, too quick to action, too willing to stick his neck out to help someone else. It had taken Larron years to learn the wisdom of patience. But he saw his younger, rasher self in Ghaid every time he looked at the boy. Larron often told him they were two coins struck from the same mold. Ghaid loved the expression, but Larron meant it as a warning.

He blew out a tired breath and settled himself into the armchair. He would wait until the boy got home, and then maybe take him to the Red Glove for an ale and a bite of Betta's potato stew. That would cheer the boy up. At least, he hoped it would.

*

The front door creaked open, and Larron woke. The tall, slim form of his son slipped into the house. Outside, a streetlamp fluttered weakly as it burned away its oil. Thick tendrils of fog, the same fog that had plagued the city for over a week now, hung like deathvine in the night air.

Ghaid eased the door shut, and the room sunk back into shadow, save for a red ember glow that spilled out from the hearth. It must be nearly midnight, Larron realized. He felt a stab of annoyance and sat up in his chair.

"Where have you been?" he asked the boy.

Halfway to the staircase, Ghaid froze. "Out with some friends, Pa." he said. "G'night."

"Out where?"

"Just out. G'night."

"Come over here," Larron told him.

Ghaid hesitated, then shuffled closer. As he

neared the hearth, Larron took in his son's appearance. His hair, normally well-kept, was matted and disheveled. One shoulder was slumped more than usual, and the side of his face, the side that Larron could see, was streaked with dirt and grime. He was keeping the other side turned purposefully away.

"Look at me," Larron said.

Ghaid didn't budge. He just stared off into the shadows and stuffed his hands into his pockets.

"I said look at me."

Ghaid faced Larron, and Larron bit back a curse. An ugly, blue-black welt ringed the boy's eye, swelling it nearly shut. His son said nothing as he lowered his head and scuffed the toe of his boot across the floor. But Larron didn't need him to speak. He knew exactly what had happened. The boy had gotten into another fight.

Lately Ghaid had been brawling on a regular basis. A few months ago he'd defended a kid he hadn't even known from a gang of back alley bullies. His son had come home so bloodied and bruised, his lips so torn apart, that two weeks had passed before he could take a solid meal. And the time before that had been even worse. He'd tackled a pickpocket racing down the Run with Rorham Nach's coinpurse. The two had crashed through the dock rails and tumbled into the harbor. The boy had nearly drowned.

Larron shook his head. His son was too much like him. Far too much. It was going to get him killed.

"What happened this time?" Larron asked the boy.

"Nothing," Ghaid muttered. "I fell and—"

Larron cursed. "Ryke's beard! Don't lie to me, boy. You've been sticking your nose into other people's business again. How many times—?"

"Pa," Ghaid broke in. "Can I come with you to the Garrison tomorrow? You promised I could start training with the men when I turned fourteen."

Guilt swelled in Larron's belly. He glanced over at Ghaid's present resting on the table by the window. The boy was too young for a sword, promises or no promises. Bonnost's play would have to do. Reading wouldn't get the boy killed. "Next year, Ghaid," he promised. "Now, tell me what happened."

Ghaid followed Larron's gaze to the package. The boy studied it for a moment, and Larron could see the disappointment spread across his face.

His son bit his lower lip. "It was nothing. A couple of kids were harassing Madame Maara in front of Frollard's Fishery." The boy frowned. "I'm tired, Pa. G'night." He trudged across the room, up the staircase, and disappeared into his bedroom.

Larron opened his mouth to speak, to yell, to apologize, to say anything at all, but no words came to mind, at least, no words that wouldn't make matters worse. He sighed and pinched the bridge of his nose. Suddenly it felt like someone was taking a pickaxe to the back of his eyes. Like it or not, Ghaid was going to have a better life than he had. A safer life. Even if Larron had to die from guilt to give it to him. He looked back at the package, unopened on the table.

"Happy birthday, son," he muttered.

*

The morning air was thick with rain and fog. A cool, brisk breeze slipped through the Warren, the labyrinth of docks, bridges, and buildings that spread out onto the surface of the harbor. The wind brought with it the squawk of gulls and the briny smell of the sea. Larron shivered. It seemed the dismal weather was infecting the city like a disease, refusing to let go, and he didn't need a bonereader to tell him that was a bad omen.

Beside him, Deven Dye, his second in command, walked silently in the gloom. His friend was still a well-muscled man, despite his years, and moved with as much cat-like grace as he had when Larron had first met him. Larron could remember the day the two had joined the Watch back when they were no more than boys. Life had been so much simpler when he was young. And so much safer.

"How did yesterday's ranging go?" Larron asked, but he knew the answer. It had been the same each day for the last week or more. But the question broke the silence, which was beginning to settle over Larron as uncomfortably as the weather.

"Fine," Deven answered. "The cannon are targeted on the center of the gorge. If Felgus dares to bring in his fleet, they'll be blown to bits."

Larron nodded as they clomped their way over a small bridge. The black waters of the harbor lapped beneath, as dark as his mood. "And their sunken ships will plug up the gorge," he said, restating the plan. "That will block passage to the rest of his fleet. It's the only way, Deven. If we can't keep Felgus out of the harbor, we're doomed. I only hope we have enough cannon."

Deven glanced at Larron. His second in command looked as tired as Larron felt. Dark rings hung under his amber-colored eyes, and a week's worth of stubble covered his cheeks. "What about Alar and Kern?" he asked. "Surely they won't let Felgus seize Fell's Hollow. That would give Nyland far too much power."

Larron shook his head. "We can't rely on anyone's help."

"What if Felgus does manage to break through the gorge?"

Larron shrugged. "Then it might become a matter for the Lord Mayor. The Watch does not have the strength to fight off an army. Norgarde will have to negotiate whatever peace he can."

Deven snorted. "Ryke save us if it comes to

that."

"Ryke save us, indeed," Larron echoed.

The two fell silent again as they came to Planer's Way, a wide stretch of dock that ran east to west through the Warren, from the shore of Oldtowne nearly all the way to the Run. It was still early, only a few hours after dawn, yet the cityfolk were already long about their business: shopowners opening shops; seamen stalking about, probably making their way back to their berths after a long night of drinking and whoring; men and women in search of the day's food, a bolt of cloth, a new lantern or trinket for their homes.

Larron wondered if Ghaid was among them, and again he felt the press of guilt. The boy was gone from the house by the time Larron had made his way downstairs for his morning meal. Ghaid was disappointed, he knew. And none too happy. He was probably avoiding him. But Larron could live with that. Ghaid was simply too young to join the Watch. Other boys came to the Watch at fourteen, as he himself had. Boys who had no other choice in life. But not his son. His son would become a craftsman, or perhaps a scribe or clerk at the House of Justice. Norgarde could make the arrangements, if Larron asked. Ghaid would hate it, but he would thank him when he was older.

"Here we are," Deven said, putting a hand on Larron's shoulder.

Larron set aside his worries. Before him stood a low building fronted by a half-dozen windows and a wide, iron-studded door. A wooden placard hung from the store's eave. A pair of barrels was painted on it, above a line of bold blue letters that read *Torr's Drums and Kegs*. The night before, the shopowners on either side of Torr's had brought their concerns to the Watch. The old proprietor of the barrel shop was missing. Murdered by the creature, they surmised.

Larron thought of Zoltin Maark and that fear-mongering article of his. Frustration churned in his gut. He didn't have time for this nonsense. He had to prepare for war. Maark had everyone jumping at shadows. Shaking his head, he moved to the door. It was locked. He wiped the rain from a window and peered inside. The interior was dark, but he could make out the black shapes of barrels stacked across the floor. "Still not open." Larron observed.

Deven moved up and took a look for himself. "The old man hasn't been seen in a week or more," he said.

"Maybe he's sick," Larron guessed. "Have you checked his house?"

His second in command nodded. "I sent two men up to the Crags last night. The house was locked up, but there was no sign of him. You think Torr's been murdered like the others?"

Larron had been avoiding that conclusion. "I don't know. Perhaps, though more likely the old fool is off drinking his profits."

Deven chuckled. "That sounds like Torr."

Larron smiled. It was the first sign of mirth he had seen in Deven in months. "Check the house again," he told him. "Tonight. Keep checking. The old man's bound to turn up at some—"

"Commander!"

Behind Larron came the sound of ironshod boots hammering over dockplanks. He spun. A young watchman, red-faced and dripping with rain, stopped before him. It was Kol, a new recruit he'd taken on last spring. The boy was as thin as a rake and barely older than Ghaid. His chest heaved as he tried to catch his breath. His tabard was soaked, and the gargoyle embroidered on his chest seemed to grin at Larron as if it knew something he didn't. A worm of fear squirmed into Larron's belly. Only bad news would have brought a watchman racing to him at this hour of the morning.

Kol saluted.

"What is it?" Larron asked.

"It's," Kol said, gasping. "It's—"

"Another body?" Deven cut in. "Has that murdering shite struck again?"

"No, sir," Kol told Deven, then he looked at Larron. "Sir, it's your son."

*

Larron's heart pounded as he peered around the corner of the building. There, not forty paces

121

away, was Jurrick's Jewels. The shop was a single story structure in the north of Oldtowne, not far from the Davacre, where Jurrick's family had sold glittering treasures to the rich and glass trinkets to the poor for the last fifty years, maybe more. It sat in the middle of a small open area surrounded by a handful of taller buildings, at the foot of a low hill near the corner of River Street and Hackney Road. Across the front of the shop ran a wide, white porch that led to a large, paned window and a heavy, archenwood door. A middle-aged, thuggish-looking man in a boiled leather jerkin stood there with his back against the door, a crossbow cocked and held firmly in both hands. He was looking straight at Larron.

Larron stepped back out of sight. It had taken him less than a quarter hour to race out of the Warren and through the muddy streets of Oldtowne to Jurrick's. Deven and Kol had struggled to keep up. When Larron had arrived, he'd found another young watchman, Alvette Dulan, waiting for him. The lad was barely twenty, heavily-muscled, with large gray eyes and a crossbow slung over his back. Larron cursed to himself at he looked at the young watchman. There wasn't a veteran in all the city. Anyone with experience was at the Watchtowers, manning the cannon, waiting for Felgus.

"What in the Abyss is going on?" he asked Alvette.

The watchman shuffled forward and saluted.

"Commander," he said awkwardly. "We were making our rounds when your son came staggering out of Jurrick's. I recognized him from when he's visited you at the Garrison. Two men were chasing after him. He screamed for us, but they—" Alvette paused and Larron's gut tightened.

"They what?" Larron demanded.

Alvette looked down at his feet. "They stabbed your son in the back," he said. "Then they knocked him flat with their swordhilts. One of the men dragged him into the shop. The other told us to leave or they'd slit his throat. And old man Jurrick's, as well. We had no choice but to back off. They posted a man at the door. I think there might be four of 'em in all. Not sure. Your son must have stumbled across a burglary." The young watchman shook his head, then continued. "Front door's the only way in or out. We're caught in a bind, Commander. They can't leave. We can't leave. I feel like a knob on a taffyl board."

Larron's chest constricted in fear. Was his son dead? Alive? If he was alive, how badly was he wounded? Then something else took hold of his emotions. Anger. Anger at the thieves. Anger at Ghaid. Stumbled across a burglary? More likely the boy had spotted the thugs and followed them, looking for more trouble to stick his nose into.

Deven drew his sword. "You know, Rhan, we don't have a choice."

123

Rhan. Deven only used Larron's nickname when things were about to get serious. Very serious. Larron felt the weight of his son's life settle onto his shoulders. It was heavy, heavier than the weight of responsibility he'd been carrying around these past ten years as Watch Commander. Heavier than the loss of Tyna. He felt old. Tired. "I know," he said. Blood was going to be shed. There was no stopping it now.

Larron looked over at Kol, and the boy unsheathed his sword. There was no fear in his eyes. It occurred to Larron that he would make a good soldier. He shifted his attention back to Alvette. "Can you shoot that thing?" he asked, nodding at the crossbow.

"Better'n most, sir."

"Good." Larron slipped his sword from its scabbard. "Take out that man on the porch, son. And for Ryke's sake, don't miss."

∗

The thug's eyes shot wide. He brought up his crossbow and took aim at Larron. Larron ignored the threat as he raced toward the porch. Behind him followed Deven and Kol, cries and curses flying as their ironshod boots splashed through the mud.

The feathered shaft of a quarrel slammed into the thug's chest. The man grunted and his crossbow clunked onto the porch. As the thug slumped against the door, Larron took three strides, leaped onto the porch, and launched himself through a window. Glass shattered, and a glittering spray slashed through the air. Larron hit the floor, rolled once, and came up running, sword at the ready. He felt the sting of a hundred small cuts on his face and hands, but he dismissed it. After two or three strides he stopped and whirled around, raking his eyes over the shop, searching for Ghaid.

He spotted the boy lying face down on the floor near the back wall. He wasn't moving. Ice shot through Larron's veins. Standing over Ghaid were two men, stunned expressions stuck to their grimy faces. One was short and fat, with large ears that stuck out beneath a worn, leather cap. The other was lean, dark, with a nose like a hawk. Both were dressed in rags. Thieves from Rogueswarde, no doubt.

Larron spun and took in the rest of the shop. A third man stood behind a counter that ran along one wall. He had the look of a sellsword: tall, muscled, with a black leather hauberk that fell past his waist. Greasy brown hair hung down over his sunken cheeks. The sellsword was holding the point of his sword against Jurrick's chest. The old jeweler was as white as a pearl, and he was shaking like a fish on a hook.

Larron caught a familiar twitch at the corner of the sellsword's eye. It was a twitch Larron had seen many times before, and it marked the sellsword as a desperate man. A man with nothing to lose. A man about to strike.

Larron raised his sword and threw it with all his strength. It flipped end over end toward the sellsword. The man's mouth dropped open for a heartbeat, then he dove for cover. The sword smashed into the wall behind the counter and clattered out of sight. The old jeweler's eyes rolled into the back of his head, and he crumpled to the floor.

One of the thieves, the fat one, rushed at Larron, a slender shortsword held high over his head. The hawk-nosed thief shouted something, but Larron lost the words in the chaos. Behind Larron came a crash of splintering wood and a roar from Deven, but Larron kept his eyes on the man charging at him. Somewhere nearby, glass crunched under boots.

Weaponless, Larron shot forward and kicked the fat thief in the stomach. There was a woof of air and a groan as the man dropped to his knees. The hawk-nosed thief cursed and came at him next, a dagger in each fist. From behind Larron, Deven lunged past and drove the point of his sword into the charging man's chest. The hawk-nosed thief shrieked, dropped the daggers, and stared at Larron, his eyes filling with shock and disbelief.

The fat one struggled to his feet.

"Commander!" It was Kol. He had climbed through the broken window and the sellsword, who had come out from behind the counter, was now slashing his blade wildly at him. Kol barely had time to block a blow to his head when the sellsword pivoted on his back foot and reversed his stroke. The man's blade bit into Kol's side, and the young recruit howled in pain.

Larron whipped a hand to his belt and yanked out a dagger. Next to him, Deven kicked the hawk-nosed thief off the end of his sword and the man toppled over, blood spraying into the air. Then he took a step forward and struck again. The fat thief's head fell with a splat onto the floor.

"Commander!" There was pain in Kol's voice, but no panic. Larron was eight, maybe nine paces away. It might as well have been fifty. He knew he'd never get there in time.

The sellsword swung his blade at the young recruit and Kol's sword shattered as it hit home. Steel shards flew. The boy staggered backwards, clutching at his side. Blood oozed between his fingers. The sellsword lifted his blade and Larron knew it was the end of Kol. The boy raised his chin and glared at the man.

There came a *thwick*, and before the sellsword could strike, a feathered shaft buried itself into his throat. Blood spurted. The sellsword's blade clanked to the floor and the man clawed at the quarrel. His mouth hung open, and he tried to speak, but all that came forth was more blood. He looked from Kol to Alvette, who stood on the porch in front of the shattered window, crossbow raised to his cheek. The sellsword let out a long gurgle and collapsed.

"Rhan." Deven was kneeling over Ghaid.

Nausea swept through Larron. Was his son—?

"The boy's fine, Rhan," Deven assured him. "The cut on his back's shallow, and his skull seems in one piece. He's only stunned."

Deven gestured at Kol. "Better check on him."

A lightness flooded through Larron. It felt like a block of stone had suddenly been lifted off his chest. Ghaid was fine. His son was alive.

"I'll be okay," Kol grunted. The young recruit shuffled over to Larron. "My mail took most of the blow. Nothing a good needle and thread won't fix."

Alvette climbed through the window and put a supporting arm around his fellow watchman.

"Well done, boy," Larron said as he clapped Kol's shoulder. He gave Alvette a nod of approval. "And you. You're both good soldiers. Good men."

There came a moan from behind the counter as the old jeweler got slowly to his feet. Jurrick must have seen seventy summers at least. He was thin and frail and shook as if he still had last winter's chill in his bones. The old man ran a wrinkled hand over his white hair as he took in the dead men sprawled on the floor. Then his gaze went to Ghaid, who was still lying unconscious next to Deven.

"Is he okay?" the jeweler asked.

"He'll live," Deven said, picking up Ghaid and holding him in his arms. "I'll bring the boy around to your place, Commander. See to his wounds, get him into bed."

Larron nodded.

Jurrick blew out a breath of relief. "Don't know how to thank you, Commander. Them thieves were gonna rob me of everything. And that boy of yours—" The old jeweler smiled. "He's a damn brave lad. You ought to be proud. Wrestled himself free from one of them thugs when he spotted your men through the window. Broke out of the shop and shouted a warning, he did."

Larron's fear subsided and the truth of the situation took hold. He glared at the old jeweler. "Proud? The boy is always sticking his nose into other people's business." Larron pointed a trembling finger at his son. "He'll be dead before he's sixteen. He goes looking for danger, damn him. Or it looks for him, I'm not sure which. But proud? I don't think so. He'll be punished good for this."

Jurrick stared at Larron, his bushy white eyebrows rising. Then the old man's face flushed red. "You lay one hand on that boy," he said, his voice slow and surprisingly steady, "and I swear to Ryke—"

The old man stopped, shook his head, and reached below the counter. After fishing around for a moment, he came out with something dangling from his clenched fist.

"Ghaid came here today on his *own* business, Commander. Like he has every morning for the last two months. He's been working for me, doing odd jobs, to pay for these." He thrust his fist at Larron.

Larron stepped closer. A pair of fine chains hung from the jeweler's hand. Attached to each was a silver round.

"One necklace for you, one for him," the old jeweler said. "Alike in every detail. It took me over a week to find two coins that were identical enough to satisfy the boy."

Sudden realization swept over Larron. Two identical coins. Two coins struck from the same mold. His eyes burned and he felt his throat tighten.

The jeweler was holding his birthday present.

*

Candlelight flickered across the room. Ghaid lay in his bed reading Bonnost's play. The boy had a strip of cloth tied around his head. More strips were wound tightly about his torso. Deven had done a good job cleaning and bandaging the wounds. The boy would be back on his feet in a few days.

Larron stepped through the doorway.

Ghaid glanced up, one eye still black and swollen, and then set the play down next to the candle on the bedside table.

Larron released a ragged breath. After the incident at Jurrick's, the rest of the day had been long and difficult, and he was tired, hungry, and covered in dirt and sweat. He'd been too busy to stop in earlier, but Deven had come by to check on the boy. Several times.

"Pa," Ghaid began, "I—I'm sorry."

"For what?" Larron asked. He eased himself onto the edge of the bed.

Ghaid sat up, wincing. "For risking my life. I know what you said. I shouldn't have—"

"Never mind what I said."

"But—"

Larron reached beneath the bed and pulled out a long, slender bundle wrapped in oilcloth. He had asked Deven to hide it there while Ghaid was sleeping.

A look of slow understanding came over his son's face. "Pa?" he whispered.

Larron pulled away the oilcloth and ran a hand down the length of a newly-forged longsword. The scabbard was sheepskin, boiled and riveted and embossed with decorative tracings. The hilt was fashioned from archenwood wrapped with thin cords of leather. The polished steel of the crossbar glinted in the candlelight. He had picked up the sword at Kessler's that afternoon. The weaponsmith had assured him it was the finest blade in his shop. The finest in all Fell's Hollow.

Ghaid grinned. "For me?"

"For you."

"Why?" his son asked.

Larron shrugged. "Because I can't stop you from being who you are."

"Then I can join the Watch?" Excitement shivered in his son's voice.

Larron nodded. "You'll work with Kol and Alvette. They'll keep you safe. If I can't change you, at least I can see to it that you're properly trained."

Ghaid leaned forward and hugged Larron.

Larron set down the sword and put his arms around the boy. As he held his son his gaze wandered to the bedside table where Ghaid's new necklace lay curled around the bottom of the candle. Beneath his sweat-stained tunic, Larron could feel his own necklace and the press of the silver coin against his chest.

It felt cold and hard and wonderful.

THE LAST VALKAR

"A seed of treach'ry's sown in every heart,
A weed that needs but little chance to root
Character from kings to commoners."
The Death of Rohar, III, *Act V, Sc. 1*
—*Espare dae Kesh*

THE NARROW ROAD SNAKED out of Southside and climbed into the Crags. Ages ago, when silver had bled from a dozen mines carved into the Pass, the Crags had been the liveliest warde in Fell's Hollow. Crammed with hundreds of dwellings wedged between the rocks, the warde had teemed with tough, dirt-smeared miners, wealthy merchants, and the powerful Durekson family, foreigners who had owned the mines and had run their business from a towering stone fortress they called the Kyrg Byair.

For a while the Crags had flourished. The poor and not-so-poor arrived by the wagonload in search of wealth, swelling the warde's population. But eventually the silver bled out. Cityfolk starved. The Dureksons returned to their ancestral estates in far off Aegiss. Many of the rest abandoned their homes and moved down to the lower wardes, where some tried their hands at a life of trade, while others fled to Alar, Nyland, or Kern in search of work. Since then, few claimed the Crags as home.

The road continued upward, and the land rose sharply into the fog-filled night like a giant, rock-strewn stair. The massive chunk of tiered terrain was littered with rubble and boulders the size of warships. The road clawed its way over fragments of bare ledge, squeezed through cracks in the rock, and crept ever higher into the warde. As it ascended, it narrowed even further, passing several clusters of houses, their red-tiled roofs sticking up from the rock like blood-tipped teeth.

Midway up the warde it came to the crumbling foot of the old Durekson fortress, which was now an asylum for the city's insane and infirm. The road edged past its rusty iron gate and wended on, up and up into the fog, until at last it reached the top of the Crags. From there it ran to the base of the cliff that encircled the cove. A handful of miners' shacks squatted there, wet and dripping from the previous day's rain. Beside them, the black mouth of the Pass gaped in the cliff face like a wound. The road, now no more than a ragged cart path in the dirt, slithered off to the east and ended at a small dark house lurking alone in the shadows.

Garret Gillum grinned as he left the road and crept to the door. Kneeling before the lock, he shot a glance over his shoulder. All was dark. Quiet. He hadn't seen anyone since midnight, when two watchmen had come looking for old Torr. They had knocked, waited a while for the barrel merchant to answer the door, and when he hadn't, they'd left without a word. That was more than an hour past. The Watch wouldn't return until morning, if at all. He had the entire night to himself.

He reached into a pocket of his cloak and took out his thief's light. The metal cylinder, a clever invention of his own design, was no bigger than the hilt of a small dagger, and it was warm to the touch. A thin length of chain fell from one end, and he slipped it around his neck. Inside the cylinder, several chunks of coal smoldered on a tiny grate. The coal would provide him with light, undetectable from more than a few feet away. The light was dim enough so it wouldn't ruin his night vision, and it would last long enough to accomplish the task at hand. The bits of coal would burn for an hour, maybe two. He had more coal if the need arose, but he doubted it would. This was an easy job. In and out.

Gillum nudged a sliding plate on the cylinder. A faint, red glow spilled onto the door's brass lockplate, and his grin widened. He produced a pair of picks from another pocket. As he worked at the lock, his thick, golden ring glinted in the glow. The ring was too big for a finger, so he wore it on his thumb, a glittering reminder of his latest larcenous triumph.

There came a soft click. Gillum eased open the door and slipped into the house. The interior was nearly black as the Abyss. As his eyes adjusted to the gloom, the darkness seemed to ease slightly, almost imperceptibly. He could make out several shadowy objects as they took shape. Two chairs. A table. What looked like a doorway, probably to a pantry. Off to the left, something angled up the wall. A staircase.

Torr's desk had to be upstairs. When Gillum had heard the Watch was trying to find the old barrel merchant, and that Torr had been missing for over a week, he knew it was time to act. Several months ago, Rorham Nach, the proprietor of the Sorsagorium, Fell's Hollow's famous curiosity shop, had offered to sell Gillum some information. Information that could lead him to a profitable "encounter," as he'd put it. Information, good information, is what separated professionals like Gillum from the amateurs. He'd paid Nach a dozen gold troyals, and Nach had told him something quite interesting. Old man

Torr had just purchased an antique archenwood desk that Nach had procured from a Molish trader. The desk had a secret compartment cleverly constructed behind the second drawer. It was the perfect place to hide one's wealth, Nach had told Torr. And Torr had agreed.

Gillum had sat on the information, waiting for an opportunity to present itself. And now Torr was missing. No one who disappeared for a day in Fell's Hollow, let alone a week, ever showed up alive. People either got sick of slugging it out on the streets and stowed away on some ship bound for anywhere, or they washed ashore with a fresh set of gills slit into their gullets. Or worse. Especially of late. But they never simply turned up, unharmed, as if nothing had happened. Not in Fell's Hollow.

He eased around the table and crept over to the staircase. He took the stairs one at a time, careful not to make the slightest sound. Torr might be missing, but he also might be sleeping off a pounder. The old man was known to throw back an ale or three at the Hole before taking the long trek from the Warren, where his barrel shop was located, on through Southside, and then up the rocky slope to the top of the Crags. Gillum wondered, and not for the first time, why the old man chose to live so far from where he worked. And in such an inhospitable location at that.

At the top of the staircase he paused at a doorway, straining to pick up the faintest sound, a breath, a cough, the creak of a floorboard.

It was as quiet as a crypt.

He peered into the room and studied the shadowy forms sitting in the dark. A bed. A chair. There was a narrow doorway against the back wall, which most likely led to a privy. A black, rectangular shape lurked beside the bed. That had to be the desk. Gillum returned his attention to the bed. It appeared flat. No lumps. No body. The house was empty.

He relaxed a bit, but forced himself to keep his senses sharp. You never knew what might happen when you're on the job. A complacent thief is a dead thief, he always said. As he listened for signs of danger, he twirled his golden ring around the base of his thumb. When at last he was satisfied, he moved quietly to the desk.

He held out the thief's light, and its red glow reflected dully off the desk's dark, polished wood. Three drawers ran down one side. On top of the desk was the stub of a candle, a thin stack of parchment, and an ink bottle. Next to the bottle, several quills stuck out of an empty tankard.

Gillum dropped to his knees. He eased the second drawer from the desk and set it carefully aside. Then he reached a hand back into the void where the drawer had been. His fingers brushed against something hard. Something rectangular. A small box! A thrill of excitement coursed up Gillum's spine. Nach had been right.

He pulled out the box, placed it on the desk,

and brought the thief's light closer. It was made of a light, knotty wood. Decorative carvings swirled over its surface and around a small silver hasp. He turned the hasp and opened the box. Sparks of color flared red, purple, green, blue, amber. Gemstones. Hundreds of them. They glittered like multi-colored raindrops.

Gillum grinned. The old barrel merchant must have saved every copper chip he'd ever made, converting them to gemstones for safe keeping. But why? And then Gillum understood. Torr was a miser. No wonder he lived so far up in the Crags. It must have been the cheapest place he could find in the city, outside the hovels of Rogueswarde. What a waste, he thought. Torr stashed away every bit of his wealth, never spending any of it, never enjoying a single gemstone's worth. Gillum had quite a bit of wealth hidden away himself. But he was different. One day he would retire, spend it all on a comfortable home in Oldtowne, or perhaps Southside. But with these… He gazed at the sparkling stones. With these he could afford a small manorhouse in Faettewarde, or maybe even a modest home in the Heights. And then he could give up this line of work. It was dangerous. Far too dangerous. How many times had he almost died trying to make off with a merchant's paychest or a soldier's coinpurse? But could he give it up? Give up the thrill? He lived for excitement. The truth was, he didn't know if he could.

He closed the box and was about to turn away when he noticed the top sheet of parchment resting on the desk. Fine, spiderlike handwriting scrawled across its surface. There was something unusual about the handwriting. It was—perfect. That was it. The writing was so neatly scripted, so exacting in its height and stroke and elegance, that it almost looked like one of Zoltin Maark's broadsides. Gillum had never seen such flawless work. Old man Torr must have been a scribe at some point in his life. And he must have practiced for a long time, perhaps a lifetime, to have perfected his skill to this level. Even the best scribes at the House of Justice or on Temple Hill couldn't create handwriting like this. It seemed the old barrel merchant was full of surprises.

Gillum moved the thief's light closer to the parchment. The words were written in Bartertongue, the common trader's language used throughout the realms. He could read a bit, having been taught his letters when he was a young orphan growing up on Temple Hill with the priests of Ryke. He scanned the first few lines.

I know not why after all this time I am overcome with a desire to tell my story. Perhaps the yoke of loneliness weighs too heavily upon my sanity, and I wish to preserve my tale whilst I am able. Perhaps it is because I haven't spoken to anyone in over three hundred years, and I feel I must talk to someone, even if that someone is only these humble sheets of parchment.

Gillum shook his head. Torr was either insane, or he was writing a tale for the booksellers down in Oldtowne. Either way, he admitted, the opening words had caught his interest. He held the thief's light closer to the parchment and began to read.

*

I know not why after all this time I am overcome with a desire to tell my story. Perhaps the yoke of loneliness weighs too heavily upon my sanity, and I wish to preserve my tale whilst I am able. Perhaps it is because I haven't spoken to anyone in over three hundred years, and I feel I must talk to someone, even if that someone is only these humble sheets of parchment. Or perhaps, just perhaps, I feel the end is approaching at last. Whatever the reason, I can only hope that in scratching down these words, I can obtain some semblance of peace.

I am Razeshotan, and I am, I believe, the last of the valkar. I was born over six centuries ago in the deserts of Okobas, where my kind had thrived for a thousand ages feeding off the humans that were once so plentiful in the villages along the Great River. But I will not begin my tale with the days of my youth. My memory of that time has nearly faded into mist, as has my hope of ever finding Tuzsheset.

Ah, my beautiful Tuzsheset. Perhaps it is for

her I am writing this. Perhaps she still lives, and after I am gone she will find these words, and read them, and forgive. But I hold no expectation of that. I am no fool.

What, you may ask, is there to forgive? I will begin my story there.

Late one evening, an hour or so before dawn and with the desert horizon shimmering red in the distance, we had reached the burial ground at the base of Mount Manzarat, where the humans wrapped their dead in strips of honey-soaked linen and entombed them in roughly carved limestone crypts. I clung to the peak of one of the taller crypts and gazed into the valley below. In the dim moonlight I could see them easily, a troop of humans perhaps a mile distant galloping through the sands making straight for us.

"You have broken the Oath," I accused Boghat, who was perched atop another crypt a short ways off. For a moment, hidden in shadow, one might have mistaken him for a human. His face was sharp and pale, his head hairless and smooth, his shoulders strong and broad. His arms and legs were corded with hard muscle. But then he shifted his position, stretched out his large, bat-like wings, and assumed his normal shape: that of a very reckless valkar.

He began picking dirt off one wing as if nothing had happened. His tentares, the six cord-like pseudopods through which we valkar feed, hung from his chest and dangled down over the edge of the crypt.

Tuzsheset, my beloved mate-to-be, stood near him with her back against an outcropping of rock. "Surely that cannot be true," she said. "He would never." My love's red eyes shined brightly as she watched Boghat preen himself. Her skin was milky white, almost iridescent in the pre-dawn light. Her veins throbbed with the blood from our recent feeding. She was so beautiful, my Tuzsheset. The sight of her almost made me forget the approaching humans.

"See for yourself, my love," I told her, gesturing down to the valley. "They come. Now we must slay them all or die in the attempt. Just as Boghat should have done back in the village. Our queen—"

Boghat spat. "Queen? Nefress is no queen. She does nothing but squat on her thrown, growing ever bloated and lazy. When was the last time our queen has hunted for herself?"

I shook my head. "When you came of age, you took the Oath. You swore to die rather than let an enemy follow you back to the hive."

"Bah," Boghat snarled. "How do you know it is I they follow?"

"They follow you, Boghat. Tuzsheset and I slew all we fed upon. We arrived here more than an hour past. None followed us."

I watched Tuzsheset as she gazed up at Boghat with a strange expression on her face, and at that moment I knew she loved him. The realization made me burn with anger and jealousy. Was she betraying me? The thought was shocking, but in some small way it didn't surprise me.

Boghat was easy to love. He had come to the hive when he was very young, after his own hive had been exterminated. Ours was one of the few hives left. Scores of valkar had arrived that night, refugees fleeing sunlight and fire and death. Tuzsheset had been among them. She had been no more than four, a mere child. Nefress took pity on them and gave them shelter, and so Boghat and I had grown up together. He had a way about him. He was impetuous and rash, but he was also cruel. So wondrously cruel. And he made me laugh. He made everyone laugh.

"Come," I said, making a great effort to put aside my suspicions. "We must prepare ourselves. We have little time before the sun rises."

There were nine of them in all, rugged looking humans strapped in boiled leather armor. Each carried a shortsword and a round wooden shield. Boghat, Tuzsheset, and I spread out amongst the crypts and waited for them in the dark. They arrived, dismounted, and dispersed, searching for their quarry. Searching for us.

When one of the humans drew within my reach, I stepped out of the shadows and struck. I lashed out with a tentare and latched onto its unprotected neck. The human cried out as my barb sank into its flesh, and I tore out its throat. Another came at me from my left. I knocked it aside with a swat of my wing. My tentares flashed in the moonlight, and then it was dead as well. I killed two more before the screaming came to an end.

"Are they all slain?" I shouted. I was now somewhere close to the northern edge of the burial ground. I glanced up the rocky slope. Mount Manzarat rose high into the brightening sky. It was a long way to the top, a long flight back to the hive. And there was little time remaining.

When Tuzsheset found me, her tentares bloodstained and twitching, she took my hand and my heart leapt at the touch of her soft skin. She smiled. "I slew two, Razeshotan. They are quite dead."

There came a groan, and Boghat approached. He was dragging one of the humans by its hair. Its face bore the marks of Boghat's tentare, where he had latched on and fed. Boghat preferred to feed through the face. He believed it was the quickest, most painful way to render a human unconscious. "I saved one," he announced. "We could always use another leechet."

A leechet. I remember laughing at the absurdity of it. There we were, the three of us at the base of the mountain, far from the safety of our hive, the sun about to break over the horizon and burn the delicate skin from our bones, and all Boghat could think of was food.

We made it just as the morning's first light

seared across the sands. I landed, tucked in my wings, and stepped quickly through the mouth of the cave and into the cool darkness of the hive. Tuzsheset followed, kissed me, and without a word headed down the main tunnel toward her niche. Then Boghat entered and dropped the human at my feet.

"You carry it a while," he told me. There was something in his voice, something that sounded slightly off, slight discordant. Were he and Tuzsheset lovers? They couldn't be. I refused to believe that the two I cared for most in the world would betray me. They wouldn't dare. They knew the price they would pay for invoking my wrath.

Boghat exited out a side tunnel. I sighed, grabbed the unconscious human, and stalked after my old companion.

For a while we walked in silence down the hive's long, twisting tunnels. The human groaned occasionally. There were few valkar about, most having gone to their niches to sleep. When finally we reached the Great Hall deep in the bowels of the hive, we found a few guards standing near the queen's empty throne, talking in low voices. Behind them, candles burned in sconces set into the walls. Two of the guards looked over at us. They saw the human. One guard nodded. The other yawned and stretched his wings. Boghat returned the nod, and the two of us left the hall through a small tunnel to the east. We said nothing until we arrived at our destination.

The feeding chamber was a small cave not far from the Great Hall. It was a dozen strides wide and several dozen deep. The ceiling was quite low, and from it hung no less than fifteen leechets, humans that had been preserved to feed the hive when fresh blood couldn't be had in the normal fashion.

I let go of my burden. Its head smacked into the dirt, and it let out a long moan of pain. No longer able to contain my patience, I seized Boghat by the shoulders and stared into his red, gleaming eyes. "Is there something you wish to tell me?" I asked him.

For a moment, he returned my stare. Then he pulled away and knelt beside the human. He began stripping off its armor. "This would go faster if we worked together," he grunted as he ripped off a piece of leather and tossed it aside.

I shook my head. Something was not right. With him or with Tuzsheset. Again, I pushed back my worry, and I joined him at his task.

It took only a few minutes to prepare the human. When its armor was removed, we wrapped it in strands of slivus, which we excreted from a large gland near the end of our tentares. The strands formed a cocoon around the human, a cocoon that would sustain it, keeping it alive for decades, perhaps centuries, as it provided blood for the hive.

"I did not break the Oath," Boghat stated as he excreted an especially thick strand and began twisting it into a cord. He attached the cord to the cocoon at the narrow end around the human's ankles. We lifted the new leechet, flipped it upside down, and secured it to the ceiling. Boghat stepped back and examined it as it hung there, swaying slightly. He seemed to be admiring his handiwork. Then the leechet jerked. Once. Twice. The human was regaining consciousness.

Boghat looked at me. "I left none alive."

"Then how did they follow us?" I asked.

He ignored the question. Something was definitely bothering him. Was it something to do with Tuzsheset, or was this about the Oath? Or something else? I was too tired to sort it out.

"I don't know," Boghat answered, finally.

He stretched out a tentare and used his barb to cut away a patch on the cocoon, exposing the brown, sunbaked skin of the human's bare torso. The leechet's twitching slowed. The slivus was doing its work, paralyzing the creature's muscles. It would soon render it incapable of any movement, though the human would retain its other senses. It would feel the pain of each feeding, the sting of each barb cutting into its flesh, the burn of its blood being siphoned from its stomach, over and over again. Hundreds of valkar would feed on it. It would be a long, agonizing death, and the human would suffer greatly. It deserved nothing less.

I turned and walked toward the chamber's entrance. "Come," I said to my friend. "I need to sleep. We can discuss this tomorrow."

Boghat flicked out a tentare and sliced off a small section at the very bottom of the cocoon, revealing the human's face. Its sand-brown eyes were stretched wide, permanently frozen in terror.

"I like it when they can watch," Boghat said. "I think it improves the experience."

I stared at him for a moment, then laughed long and hard as we made our way back up the tunnel toward our niches. It felt nice to laugh. It reminded me of our times together when we were young, racing through the hive, causing as much mayhem as the adults would allow. I didn't want to dwell on Boghat's betrayal. His possible betrayal, I corrected myself. I didn't know what was going on with him, or with Tuzsheset. Tomorrow was another night. I would try to find an opportunity to deal with the unpleasantness then. But the chance never came. The humans attacked just before sundown.

The vile creatures were nothing if not efficient. They murdered the pair of guards stationed in the shadows of the hive entrance, shooting them full of arrows. Then they snuck into the tunnels, dozens of them, carrying bales of oil-soaked straw they must have muscled up the mountain. They lit the bales and a thick, noxious smoke swept through the hive.

I awoke in my niche, gagging, my eyes burning. I was disoriented, yet I knew in an instant what was happening. I had heard the terrible tale of what the humans had done to Boghat and Tuzsheset's hive. It had given me nightmares for a month. Still, I was unsure what to do. I knew it was close to dusk. Had the sun set? Was it safe to flee the hive? And what of Tuzsheset? Was she alive? Was Boghat? A dozen thoughts raced through my mind in the span of a single heartbeat, though it felt like an eternity. Then I heard the screams of my brethren, and at last I broke out of my daze.

I crawled from my niche and staggered up the smoky tunnel, making my way toward the hive's entrance. I could barely see three strides in front of me as the tunnel wound its way upward. I rounded a corner and stumbled upon one of the humans, a tall, thin, cowardly thing with bulging, bug-like eyes. It was breathing through a rag it had wrapped around its face, and it held a blazing torch in one hand. The light was blinding. In its other hand it grasped a sword, which it stabbed into a small hollow carved along the lower side of the tunnel.

There came a sharp cry. The human yanked back its blood-stained blade, and a young valkar tumbled out of the niche. She was no more than six or seven. The girl spasmed in the dirt, her slender tentares flailing helplessly at the human's feet. Her delicate wings shuddered, and then she was still.

I struck, and the human died where it stood.

I killed many more before I finally broke free of the hive. The sun was a thin slice of burning crimson far off in the distance. Instantly I felt its scorching rays upon my flesh. The pain was excruciating. My skin began to blister as surely as if I'd walked into a fire pit. Before me, spread out on the rocky slope, a handful of courageous valkar were holding off a hundred of the foul humans. Tentares flashed in all directions. Wings beat and swords slashed. Arrows filled the air, piercing any valkar who dared to take flight. The mountaintop was awash in blood and screams.

I charged into the fray. I could smell my flesh as it cooked, and the pain was nearly unbearable. Yet I fought on for what seemed like hours. The humans were relentless. I would kill one and two would take its place. I would kill two then find myself facing four. As I dealt death with each slash of my tentares, I waited to die. I wanted to die. By the sword or by the sun, it mattered not to me. In the end, though, it was neither sword nor sun that took my life. In the end, it was a gasp and a glance that ripped out my heart.

I had just sliced open the stomach of a shieldless human, a wild, wailing creature who had come at me with a sword clutched in each hand. The thing's eyes widened as its entrails spilled into the dirt.

I turned to seek another opponent. The sun had finally fallen, blanketing the mountaintop in blessed shadow. Steam misted off my blistered skin, but I ignored it as I ignored the pain. Then a large, bearded human stepped over a pile of corpses and pointed its sword at me. It grunted out a challenge in words that, at the time, I could not understand.

I heard a sudden intake of breath, a sound too low for the large human to hear. I risked a glance toward the sound, back toward the cave's entrance, and saw Tuzsheset. Boghat was with her. They turned and, without so much as a word, launched themselves into the night.

Several humans cried out and a dozen arrows flashed through the darkening sky. But the lack of light hindered the humans' aim. Before they could loose a second volley, Boghat and Tuzsheset were gone.

They had left me there to die.

*

Gillum took the sheet of parchment, one of several he had gone through, and set it aside. Half the stack remained, and yet he couldn't stop himself from considering what he had just read.

Torr's tale was addictive. That was the only word for it. Who would have guessed an old barrel merchant could have created such a story? Torr might have spent his life as one of Fell's Hollow's well-paid, well-pampered playwrights, penning his yarns while sipping wine in the comfort of the Savage Poet. But instead he had chosen to slave away in the Warren, hawking warped and leaking barrels to desperate seamen. The old man had wasted his talents.

Gillum shook his head. Though but a moment had passed, it seemed as if he'd been reading for hours. In just a few sheets of parchment, Torr had taken him to another time, to another place. If he didn't know better, he could almost believe there was such a desert as Okobas, or a mountain called Manzarat, or such creatures as Razeshotan, or Tuzsheset, or Boghat. Yes, he had heard the old stories while growing up on Temple Hill, of how the ancient, blood-thirsty valkar had once infested the realms, feeding on humans in the dead of night. Those had been crude and simple tales, told by priests to strike terror into disobedient orphans.

But this one…

Gillum checked his thief's light. One last bit of coal smoldered on the inner grate. He had maybe a quarter hour left. Plenty of time to finish Torr's tale. After that, he would slip down out of the Crags and start making plans for the future. A future of comfort, thanks to the old barrel merchant.

He twirled the ring on his thumb, grinned, and continued to read.

*

To this day I can't recall what happened next. One moment I was watching my betrayers wing away, and the next I was standing alone, bathed in blood, the bodies of a dozen humans dead at my feet. The head of the large, bearded human bounced away through the dirt. Its body lay sprawled over a nearby rock. I didn't hesitate. While the humans were regrouping after what must have been a blind, fury-driven attack on my part, I took to the air.

There were shouts, and an arrow pierced my side. I felt pain unlike anything I had ever known. But I kept going, banking up and to the west. More arrows hissed around me, but with a few beats of my wings I escaped the range of their bows. Blood, warm and sticky, coursed along my torso and down my leg. I needed to land. Soon. The pain was monumental. A blackness threatened to overtake me, but I forced myself to fly on.

I struggled for hours, making my way slowly northward. My skin burned, my side was throbbing, and my wings ached. By the time I landed, my side had gone numb, and I blacked out. When I awoke, it was close to daybreak.

I found a safe place to rest, a crevice beneath two boulders at the base of a dune. I scraped out a makeshift niche and covered the opening with sand just as the morning sun broke over the desert. Lying there in the dark, I wrenched the arrow from my side. A sudden rush of pain streaked up through my back, and I welcomed the sweet embrace of unconsciousness.

I came to my senses the next night, sore,

blistered, and heartbroken. Then, by the light of that night's bloated moon, I pledged my entire existence to one task: Revenge.

I fled the Southlands in search of those I now hated more than any living creature. I knew there was no place left in the desert where any of my kind could survive. The humans had won. They had exterminated nearly every hive from Okobas to Thellos. Eventually, after ages dwelling amongst them, somehow the Southlanders had discovered the valkar. They had figured out how to find us and how to kill us. Boghat and Tuzsheset had no choice but to travel north. And neither did I. So as my wounds slowly healed, I journeyed out of the desert, all the way to the Midlands, feeding on rodents and wanderers and worse as I went.

I would spend nearly twenty years on the hunt. I came first to Belani, where the humans were lean, swarthy creatures. Compared to the brutish Southlanders, the Belani were a stealthy race. They went without shield or armor, and wielded wicked, slightly curved swords. Their movement in battle was quick and dance-like, and I fed on them with caution. I spent many years wandering their villages, seeking any sign that would indicate the presence of another of my kind. I found none.

So with revenge still burning in my breast, I ventured on to Cabyll, where the only difference came in the variety of humans I encountered.

These were a taller, paler, less graceful sort than the Belani, but equally as dangerous. They girded themselves in steel armor, went about on horseback, and fought with long, iron-tipped lances and heavy, two-handed greatswords. The Cabyllians were not an easy race upon which to feed, and I thought it unlikely that Boghat or Tuzsheset would waste much time around them. Even so, I would not leave until I was sure. For more than a dozen years I traveled from one Cabyllian city to the next, stalking the streets in search of my betrayers. Then, finally satisfied of their absence, I set off for Mesurem, last of the three Midland realms.

It might have been luck, or perhaps some sympathetic god had interfered on my behalf, for I spotted Boghat and Tuzsheset on the very night I arrived at Suris Sudarem, Mesurem's only true city. As I flew high over starlit domes and white stone towers, I caught sight of the two. At first they were nothing more than a pair of shadows flitting through the air below me, yet I knew at once it was them. I swept in closer. The two were descending fast, heading for the roof of a tall, crenulated building near the city's eastern gate. I followed, silent, gliding ever closer, and just as my betrayers landed, I struck. I banked sharply to the right. Then I leveled and lashed out with a single tentare.

Somehow Boghat sensed my approach. He spun, and the expression on his sharp, pale face flashed from surprise, to confusion, to horror, all in an instant. "Razeshotan," he whispered.

My barb sunk into his throat, and as I flew past I ripped him open. Tuzsheset shrieked. Boghat's blood splashed onto the rooftop in a torrent. He must have just fed, for it was like slicing open a wineskin. He fell to his knees and was dead by the time I looped around and landed in front of Tuzsheset.

She had dropped down next to Boghat and was now pulling him into her lap. Bright blood ran in rivers over the iridescent skin of her legs. Her wings were half open and they trembled as she wept. Then she stared up at me. Sorrow swam in her eyes. "Why?" she asked.

My anger flashed and I pointed a finger at her. "You betrayed me," I snarled. I was so consumed with rage, I could barely spit out the words. My hand shook as I pointed at Boghat. "He betrayed me."

Tuzsheset wiped a splash of blood from Boghat's cheek, and her voice cracked as she spoke. "We never betrayed you."

"Liar!" I shouted. "You left me to die."

She shook her head. "We thought you were doomed. We mourned for years. No one could have survived against so many humans."

I laughed bitterly. "But survive I did. And every day since, I have dreamed of this moment. Your lover is dead, and now you, too, will die."

"Lover?" Tuzsheset glared at me. "Boghat was

157

not my lover. He was—" She reached down and closed Boghat's dead eyes. "He was my brother."

Brother? I felt the cold steel of truth bury itself into my breast. I did not need to hear the rest of her tear-wracked explanation. I knew, as soon as that one word left her lips, all that needed to be known.

She and Boghat had come to the hive as refugees, parentless, as so many others had. When they were separated, sent to be reared by different families, they had been too young to remember much of anything. But each remembered they had had a sibling. And somehow the two had discovered their kinship. They knew I would not take well to the news. The depth of my love for Tuzsheset was well known throughout the hive, as was my penchant for violent, irrational jealousy. The two had guessed, rightly so, that I would not appreciate a bond between them. Tuzsheset was mine. I would not share her with anyone, not even her own brother.

This is what the two had been hiding. And their supposed betrayal on the mountaintop? That had been nothing more than Boghat's love for his newly found sister, and his need to get her to safety, even if it meant abandoning me to my fate. I didn't know what to say. I had just slain her brother and the closest companion I had ever known. The rage that I had carried within me for nearly twenty years suddenly melted into self-loathing. "Tuzsheset, forgive me," I begged. "I didn't know. If I could change what I've done…" The weight of my mistake was crushing. My eyes burned, and I knew for the first time in my life what it felt like to weep. I gazed into the night sky, tears scorching down my cheeks. To the east, the stars had begun to disappear into the growing haze of dawn. "Daybreak comes," I told her. "We must find a place to rest."

Tuzsheset stood and fixed me with eyes that had narrowed to slits. Gone was the sorrow I had seen in them only moments before. Now they blazed with an angry, red fire.

"I will never forgive you, Razeshotan," she hissed. "Never. You have murdered my brother, and now you are once more dead to me. And this time I will not mourn. At least, not for you."

I reached out and tried to place a comforting hand on her shoulder. "Tuzsheset, please."

She knocked it away. "You are dead to me," she repeated. Then she turned, stretched out her wings, and launched herself from the rooftop.

And there is little more to tell. Tuzsheset fled Mesurem. I remained, hating myself for longer than I care to admit. The Mesurites were no challenge to feed upon, for they carried no weapons and knew little of warfare. Most were poor, starving creatures that milled about the city in dirty white robes blindly obeying the edicts of their rulers, a council of tattooed priests who dominated the masses from their mighty towers.

Over the long years my self-loathing refused to

lessen, and I became lonely. Terribly lonely. So much so that I knew I would soon go mad. Then, as strange as it may seem, I took a human as a companion. I had been about to feast upon a young, dark-eyed priest when, from his knees and through the use of desperate gestures and crude hand signals, he offered to teach me the ways of his kind, their languages, their manners, their customs, in exchange for sparing his life. I hesitated, and then quickly realized that a more intimate knowledge of humans might be useful. So I retracted my barb and acquiesced.

I spent a decade with the tattooed man. He taught me Mesurish, Bartertongue, and other forms of human speech. I learned their letters and how to scratch them onto parchment. And I learned all there is to know about the cruelty of humankind. That last lesson reminded me that there was something out there worth living for, some future cruelty of which I was meant to play a part. Perhaps with Tuzsheset at my side. When the priest had no more to teach, I fed upon him, tossed aside his dead, dry husk, and left Mesurem in search of my beloved. I was tired of being alone.

That was three hundred years ago. Since, I have scoured Cabyll and Belani. I have returned to the Southlands, the place of my birth. I have crossed the Great Waste and have searched for Tuzsheset in more realms than I can recall: Mol, Puret, Sindella, Ukria. I have even traveled to the distant kingdom of Aegiss. But I have found nothing. No sign, no rumor, no glimpse of her winged form flitting through the shadows of the night.

And now I have arrived here at this rain-soaked, dismal place they call Fell's Hollow. I am more tired and more lonely than you could ever imagine. If I do not find my beloved here, then truly she must have perished, and if that is so, then I no longer wish to exist in this world. If I do not find her here, I will walk into the light of day. I will burn the skin from my bones and, with luck, be united with Tuzsheset in death.

And the valkar will be no more.

*

Gillum turned over the last sheet of parchment and frowned. Torr's tale was fascinating, yet it left him somehow unfulfilled. He wished the old man had survived to finish his story. He yearned to discover the fate of Razeshotan and Tuzsheset. Would Torr reunite them? Or would he send Razeshotan bravely into the sunlight? He supposed he would never know.

The thief's light's red glow had diminished to a feeble glimmer in the dark. Gillum slipped the box of gemstones into a pocket of his cloak. He looked down at the shadowy form of the desk, hesitated, and then scooped up the parchments. Perhaps he could finish the tale himself and sell it to one of the booksellers. The Ink and Blot might be interested, or, if not, surely Arryn Saldonic would offer him a coin or two. He grinned. He could always find a way to make a few extra troyals.

He tucked the parchments under an arm and moved carefully to the staircase. He stopped and listened. Outside, the rain had returned. He could hear it pattering softly against the roof. Rain and fog had been plaguing the city ever since the tempest had ripped through more than a week ago. But beyond the rain, all was quiet.

As he slowly descended the stairs, his thoughts returned to Torr's tale. Now that he was going to finish it, he could determine the ending himself. Should it be a triumph? Or a tragedy? He considered the two possibilities, yet he knew there was really only one choice. Few tales and fewer lives ever ended happily.

Gillum reached the bottom of the staircase and headed for the door. As he skirted around a chair, his face suddenly exploded in pain. It felt as if someone had driven an ice pick into his cheek. Agony and shock streaked through him. He tried to scream, but all that came forth was a harsh gurgle. Something had latched onto his face. He tried to rip it away, but failed. It felt like a thick cord of rope, cold and slimy. It felt like a giant eel. He couldn't see. He couldn't breathe. Panic took over.

Frantically, he again tried to yank the rope free, but whatever it was, it had a hard, sharp barb buried deep into his flesh. Another jolt of pain scorched through his face. What was this thing! Terror threatened to consume his wits. He beat at the slimy rope with his fists, but it was strong. Too strong. Then he noticed something else, something beyond any horror he could have imagined.

A strange coldness had begun to creep through him. He thrashed and twisted. He tried one last attempt at a scream, and failed. Then everything went black.

*

He awoke to pain. It was quiet. There was darkness everywhere, save for a low, flickering light in the distance. A candle?

Gillum tried to move, but for some reason his body wouldn't respond. A spark of panic mixed with his pain. His face was sore. His stomach felt like it was on fire. He tried to remember what had happened, but failed. He couldn't think, not with the intense pressure that was pushing at the back of his eyes, as if all the blood in his body had suddenly rushed to his head.

Where in the Abyss was he? What had happened? Why couldn't he move? He tried to lift an arm. Nothing. Something was preventing him from bending even a single finger. But what? He thought he should know, but he couldn't remember. If he could remain calm, concentrate, maybe it would come to him. Maybe if he could figure out where he was, it might jar his memory.

Gillum beat back his panic and tried to take in his surroundings. He stared at the flickering light, and his head throbbed maddeningly. His vision was blurry, but he definitely thought it was a candle, about five, maybe six paces away. He tried to look around, but like the rest of him, his eyes were locked in place. He settled for studying the edges of his sight.

Was he in a small room? Maybe. It was hard to tell for sure. It was far too dark and everything was out of focus. He thought he could make out a doorway in front of him, between him and the candle. There was something strange about the doorway. And about the candle. Panic threatened to overtake Gillum, and he had to force it back.

A sharp pain ignited in his stomach. It flared for a long moment and then faded to a smoldering burn. Then he heard something. Something had moved. Someone was standing next to him!

Gillum hadn't noticed whoever it was, for the figure had only been partially in view. Terror washed over him, and any attempt at damming up his fear crumbled to dust.

The figure shuffled through the doorway. Its footfalls sounded heavy and tired. Gillum watched as it took form against the fluttering light. And then he understood what had seemed so strange about the doorway and the candle. They were upside down. As was the figure.

Everything was upside down.

The figure turned, and a pair of bat-like wings stretched from its back. A handful of wrist-thick, white appendages dangled from its chest. A dark liquid dripped off the end of one.

The figure, the *thing*, moved toward the candle. There was a long scrape as it dragged something across the floor. A chair. Then the thing sat down, and there came a shuffling, papery sound. After a moment, the room was filled with a steady, purposeful scratching.

Gillum's memory returned in a single blow. It struck his mind with the force of a blacksmith's hammer, and something deep within him, something glass-like and precious, shattered into a thousand tiny pieces.

ONE MAN'S JUSTICE

"All that's fair falls in the end,
For power rots the good in men."
The Magister, *20-21*
—Ren Bonnost

A THICK FISHERMENS' STEW simmered in the kitchen of Madame Maara's. Crammed with potatoes, onions, and hefty chunks of croll and korshark, it was the same fishermens' stew that had been served at the inn for over four dozen years, ever since the day Madame Maara had first opened her doors on Crab Street in the south end of Oldtowne. So near the harbor, the inn had easy access to the freshest catch, and easy access to the fishermen themselves, many of whom took rooms at the inn between their month-long excursions into the Sellum Sea.

The stew bubbled and spat in an enormous copper kettle. Its aroma billowed around a bleary-eyed cook as he stirred in a few lazy pinches of pepper. Before long the smell of the stew filled the kitchen, flowing over two wide work tables, through a dozen iron skillets hanging from a rough beam overhead, and along pantry shelves laden with jars of flour, casks of whokur oil, and crates of fruits and nuts. When it arrived at the far side of the kitchen it gathered for a moment, coiling and coalescing, before spilling out into the inn's candlelit common room.

A dozen cityfolk sat about small tables, talking in low voices. Two young dockworkers were playing taffyl near a many-paned, blue-glass window. Several off-duty watchmen stood huddled together in a group, drinking from wooden tankards. Madame Maara, an aged woman with a kind, weather-lined face, was smoking a pipe near the hearth as she chatted with a barrel-chested man in a bearskin cloak.

The aroma slipped silently through the common room, swirling slowly around the inn's patrons, until it reached a swarthy, haggard-looking man sitting alone by the front door.

The man crinkled his nose. He would never be able to stomach the smell of fish again. And it was because of her, that sellsword bitch who had nearly killed him. Him! Indaro Dapiza Rell! He was a trained assassin, by Tugo's breath! And he'd nearly drowned because of a woman.

The sellsword had shot him with some kind of poison dart, and he'd fallen head first into the harbor. In moments he'd been swept beneath the twisting maze of docks and buildings that stretched out over the water, weaponless and disoriented, and it was all he could do to catch his cloak on a splintered piling before he fell unconscious. The poison must have been old or weak. He had survived, but had been forced to suffer six days and six nights hanging there in a state of semi-conscious torment. He had endured the cold of the water, the heat of a blistering fever, and the perpetual stink of rotting fish. As luck would have it, he had hooked himself directly below a fishgutter's dock. All in all, it had not been a pleasant experience. But he had survived.

Indaro took a last spoonful of gruel and forced it down. He needed to regain his strength. Not for her. He didn't have time for her. The sellsword meant nothing. Less than nothing. Now that he'd returned to Maara's, burned his clothes, and scrubbed the stench from his skin, he could refocus his attention on what had brought him to Fell's Hollow in the first place.

The foul odor hit him again. Grimacing, he pushed aside his empty bowl, reached for a goblet, and took a long swallow of wine.

"I will wait no longer!"

Indaro glanced at a nearby table. A golden-haired woman was glaring at two grizzled men seated across from her. Indaro had seen the woman before. She kept a room in the attic. She was beautiful, with blazing blue eyes and a body most men would not likely forget.

"We can't leave the boy behind," one of the old men told her. He rubbed a gnarled hand across his bald, leathery pate. "Give us another day to find him."

"Ossillard has the right of it," said the other man. "They say bad things happen to those who'd leave a shipmate behind. They say—"

The woman shook her head. "The *Destiny* sails at first light. That storm ripped away our last fishnet, or have you forgotten? And I don't mean to get a new one here. We are sailing for Nyland."

The bald man snorted. "Nyland? With them about to attack this very city?"

Indaro had heard those rumors as well, but they meant little to him. He had his own troubles to worry about.

The woman pushed back her chair and stood. "Nyland weavers make the best nets, so we sail for Nyland. Get the crew ready. Chibb's been missing for nearly a fortnight. He's either set off on another ship, or he's found work elsewhere."

"Ain't no ships coming or going," the bald man pointed out. "Everyone's too afraid they'll sail right into Felgus's war fleet."

"Could be the lad's dead," the other man

suggested.

A sad expression crossed the woman's face. "Could be. This place is full of cutthroats. But it doesn't matter what happened to the boy, he's no longer our concern. I will see you both on the ship at dawn."

The bald man grunted. "We can't sail at dawn," he complained. "Fog'll be too thick."

The woman shrugged. "Then we sail as soon as it burns off." She nodded to the men, slipped up the stairs at the back of the common room, and disappeared into the attic.

The bald man sighed. "Saera's a stubborn lass, no doubt. And she's going to get us killed."

The other man scratched at his stubbled chin. "Most likely," he agreed, and then snatched up a tankard. "Look at it this way," he went on. "We get to leave. Everyone else is stuck here. I for one am sick of this blasted fog. I long for the fresh air of the sea."

Stuck here? That possibility hadn't occurred to Indaro. He took a sip of wine. He had botched his first attempt at justice, and now the Watch was sending sellswords after him. If he—*when* he finally did get his justice, they would come after him with everything they had, war or no war. He needed a way out of the city. And thanks to this golden-haired captain and her stubbornness, he might just have one. But that meant he would have to act fast. Tonight.

"More gruel?" Madame Maara had come

across the room. She stood before Indaro, pipe dangling from her lips. "Or perhaps some stew? Everyone loves my stew."

Indaro's stomach roiled. "Gruel," he told her.

The old innkeep nodded and took the empty bowl.

"And more wine," he added.

Madame Maara gave him a wrinkled smile and shuffled off toward the kitchen.

A dull pain began to throb behind Indaro's eyes. Would he have the strength? He hoped so. Grimacing, he held up a hand and it shook slightly. Strength or no strength, tonight one more tyrant was going to die.

*

Indaro pulled up the cowl of his cloak. He stood in a small alley between two buildings, watching the foggy street beyond. It was closing in on midnight, and it was cold, wet, and dark. The only light came from a line of torches across the street which glowed in sconces along the walls of the Tershium. The stone walls towered twenty feet into the darkness, and they encircled several acres of central Oldtowne. By day one could find the Triad within, the three men who governed Fell's Hollow. Two, Indaro had discovered over the past couple of weeks, went back to their own homes at night. It seemed the Guildmaster and the Watch Commander were nothing more than advisors. The Lord Mayor, however, lived at the

Tershium. He was the real power, and therefore the real corruption, in Fell's Hollow. And so it would be the Lord Mayor who would die.

There came a sudden creak and a flare of torchlight. A short distance off a small door set into the wall opened, and three armored men in red and black tabards stepped into the fog. Watchmen, coming off duty. Even in the gloom, they looked young, no more than boys. The first was tall and thin and walked with a bit of a limp. He had a longsword at his hip and a shield slung over his back, as did the second watchman. The third was a muscular fellow who carried a crossbow and a quiver thick with quarrels. The door shut behind them and the street fell back into shadow. The first two watchmen turned and headed north, boot heels clomping over the cobblestones. The third muttered something in a low voice and started off in the other direction.

When the last watchman had gone a few hundred paces, Indaro slipped out of the alley. There were no cityfolk about. This added to the difficulty of the task, of course, as there were no other people to blend in with, but he had done this before. Many times. The young watchman would never know he was being followed.

Indaro stalked the soldier down narrow lanes and through alleys black as blood until they came to Shore Street, a wide, cobbled avenue that ran from the base of Temple Hill, along the border of Rogueswarde and Oldtowne, and all the way to the harbor. The first thing Indaro had done when arriving at Fell's Hollow was commit the layout of the city to memory. It took him two days of constant walking to learn the location of the nine wardes and the main roads that ran through them all. An assassin should always know his surroundings.

It was less dark on Shore Street. Oil lamps swung from iron posts every fifty paces or so, and a ruddy light spilled out of several taverns. A handful of people milled about, strolling along the street, heading from one building to another. A few cityfolk clopped by on horseback. He paused to take in the scene. Ahead the watchman had stopped and was gazing through the window of a weaponsmith's shop. Indaro sidestepped into a doorway and waited.

After several moments, the watchman moved on and Indaro followed. At the edge of Rogueswarde, the young soldier came to a crossroad. In one direction, Shore Street veered off toward the harbor. In the other, a narrow, unpaved road led into Southside. The watchman took the smaller road, and Indaro kept after him.

Soon the streetlamps were gone. All around Indaro two- and three-story buildings, mostly modest family homes, squeezed up next to the road. It was dark, the only light coming from an occasional window where someone had left a fire burning into the night. He eased closer to the watchman.

Ahead the young soldier stopped at a street corner. Next to him a dim light glowed from the window of an inn. The inn was old and badly in need of repair. Above the watchman a wooden sign swayed from an iron hanger. Painted on the sign was an old man hunched over a desk, scratching away at a piece of parchment with a long goosefeather quill. The man's hair was white and disheveled and there was a definite madness behind his bloodshot eyes. The watchman crossed the street, then he trudged up a staircase at the side of a two-story building and disappeared through a door.

The young man had been heading home, as Indaro had suspected. And, by the look of things, he probably lived alone. The way the gables and peaks of the roof cut into the second story, there couldn't be much room up there. That was good.

When a light appeared in the watchman's window, Indaro found a niche between two buildings and settled into the shadows. He would wait until the watchman went to sleep, and then he'd act.

A chill breeze slithered by and he shivered. He felt terrible. Weak. But an assassin worked with more than strength. An assassin worked with cunning as well. He would just have to be smart and trust to his luck. As bad as he felt, it was nothing compared to what he'd already endured. He had suffered for years. Endless training in combat, with perana, dagger, crossbow, spear, bare hands, bare feet. Endless practice at stealth, at lockpicking, at climbing, at moving soundlessly across all types of terrain. He had spent months alone in the wilderness, cold, wet, hungry, surviving off nothing but woodgrubs and worms and whatever else he could skewer on the tip of his dagger. He was used to suffering. But that suffering had paid off.

In the last year alone he'd slain two Belani warlords and a Cabyllian king. The encounter with the king, admittedly, had been anything but perfect, and it was only with Tugo's own luck that he'd escaped unscathed over the Great Waste and into the Nine Kingdoms. And as soon as he arrived, he had continued his quest.

Within three days he'd slit the throat of a Thalian prince and then stowed away in the bowels of a single-masted trader, stuffed behind a great iron cage that had held some winged, black-scaled beast. The beast had been ferocious, and he had heard it had taken the traders the better part of a week to muster up the courage to remove it from the hold after they'd arrived at Fell's Hollow.

So now he was here in this miserable, fog-filled city, where he would continue his quest. He would take great joy in ridding the world of yet another fat, greedy, bloodsucking tyrant. Another leech squatting on a throne draining the life out of the innocent. The Lord Mayor of Fell's Hollow would die for his crimes, even if Indaro didn't know exactly what those crimes were. It hardly mattered. The Lord Mayor lorded over men, and that was all Indaro needed to know. He had sworn an oath, had dedicated his life to slaying all such tyrants, all such parasites. All such *murderers*. He'd given up everything for his quest, including his greatest love: acting and the stage. All for the quest. All for justice.

Across the street the watchman's window went dark. Indaro smiled. It wouldn't be long now. He would break in and question the young man. Harshly. But not too harshly. Some men couldn't take that, as he had recently discovered. Shortly after arriving at Fell's Hollow, Indaro had kidnapped an actor from the Cove Theater. He had only meant to hold the man captive for a few days or so, just long enough to usurp his place for one last performance of *Har and Iva*. One last moment of joy. He thought it only fair for the favor he was about to bestow upon the city. But when Indaro had dragged the actor off his horse and into the cellar of an abandoned inn, the man had clutched at his chest, gurgled a few times, and then abruptly died of fright. The guilt of that encounter was still fresh in Indaro's gut.

He shook his head, returning his attention to the watchman's window. His hand moved to where his perana should have been, the single-edged, slightly curved blade that was as much a part of himself as his own arm, but it was gone. Abandoned at the Cove Theater when he had to flee from that sellsword bitch and her brother. Now he had no weapon other than a dagger, but that would be enough. Enough to make a young watchman tell him everything he needed to know. Soon Indaro would discover precisely how to slip into the Tershium unseen, and precisely where to find the Lord Mayor without attracting unwanted attention. Then he'd kill the tyrant. And with a bit more of Tugo's luck, he would make it to the *Destiny* by dawn, stow away, and escape Fell's Hollow before the city erupted into chaos.

He wiped a clammy sheen of sweat from his forehead, stepped out of the niche, and made his way across the street to the foot of the staircase.

The staircase was old. He would have to be careful. He placed a foot on the first step and slowly added his weight. Nothing. No creak. No sound. He raised his other foot, and stopped.

Something was wrong. What was it? All was quiet. Dark. He felt a surge of panic. He had sensed something, something subtle, something right at the edge of perception. He inhaled deeply in an attempt to calm himself, and there it was. A fleeting wisp of a smell, sweet and pleasant. The smell of flowers. The smell of a—Indaro shot a look over his shoulder. A cloaked figure stood a few paces from him. It was a woman. Where had she come from? She raised a hand and spoke.

"Iceos beum."

A sudden numbness swept through Indaro. He tried to launch himself at the woman, but his legs refused to move. He tried to reach for his dagger, but his hand remained at his side. He was paralyzed! Then the world around him flared, blinding and white. There came a roar, like the rush of wind and thunder. He felt as if he were falling, falling into a whirlpool of cold, white mist…

*

His mother reached the front of the makeshift stage, her gown shimmering white in the light of the setting sun. Her face was pale and sad and her hair, black as ink, fell soft and straight to the middle of her back.

Before her, filling the small village square, the folk of Amarto watched, enraptured, though they had seen the play many times before. Kari Dapiza Rell excelled at tragedy. Her talent could inject genius into the poorest of plays. This play, however, was written by the great Espare dae Kesh himself, court bard to the old kings of Cabyll. The people of Belani would walk an hour to see his mother perform, but they'd walk a week to see her perform one of dae Kesh's masterpieces.

His mother stared out into the crowd and raised a delicate hand. The villagers fell silent. Several wiped tears from their eyes.

"Rohar," she said, her voice cracking, "our most blessed and cursed of kings, has fallen to the prince's murd'rous sting."

A low murmur rose from the villagers. An older woman near the stage sobbed openly. His mother let her hand fall. She knew precisely how to work an audience. At that moment she was no longer Kari Dapiza Rell, a lowly baker's wife. She was Queen Pantora in the flesh, reborn in all her beauty and all her tragedy.

His mother drew out a small vial from the folds of her gown, removed the cork, and placed the vial to her lips. After a pause, she dropped to her knees, and the vial skittered over the edge of the stage. She gazed up into the sky. "O joy of joys! My husband's gentle face!" she cried.

Some of the villagers looked upward. Indaro looked as well, and could almost see the ghost of Rohar hovering there above the audience, beckoning his queen to join him in the afterlife.

Kari Dapiza Rell gestured to the villagers gathered before her. "I leave to you this dark and dreadful place." With a sigh, she collapsed. Someone in the crowd moaned.

Around Indaro, the other actors of the play had gathered to watch his mother end the performance. Lorenzi Manell stood next to him. He was the village blacksmith who played the part of Rohar. Tall, gray-haired, as lean as a wolf, he would always return to the side of the stage to witness the death of his queen.

Indaro waited, fingers tightening around the rope that would close the curtains to the makeshift stage. He wanted to give the villagers a moment to take in the vision of the tortured queen. He wanted them to remember that sight forever.

There came a sudden shout from the back of the crowd. Then another. Two men were pushing their way through the villagers. Soldiers. They were tall, swarthy men cloaked in black. Slender peranas hung at their sides. They were the warlord's men, and their appearance sent hushed whispers rippling through the crowd.

When the two soldiers reached the front of the stage, one of them, a round-faced man with a month's growth of beard on his jowls, pointed at Indaro's mother. "Are you Kari, the baker's wife?" he demanded.

His mother glared at the soldier and then, slowly, gracefully, got to her feet. Though the soldiers had ruined the end of her performance, she retained the aura of a queen. "I am," she told him, coolly. "What do you want? Why have you interrupted our play?"

The other soldier climbed onto the stage. "You are the wife of Salo the baker?" the second soldier asked, scratching at an ugly scar at the base of his neck.

Indaro's mother nodded. The scarred soldier struck her with the back of his hand. She cried out and fell to her knees. The crowd erupted in anger. Several threw curses and insults at the soldiers. The actors around Indaro gasped.

A fiery rage shot through Indaro, just as

Lorenzi's hand clutched his shoulder. "Wait," he warned.

His mother shook her head. Blood ran freely from her split lip. "How dare you?" she spat. "You have no—"

The scarred soldier raised a hand again, and his mother broke off her words. A terrible anger swelled in Indaro, boiling his blood. He tried to break free of Lorenzi's grasp, but the blacksmith held him fast.

"Let me go!" Indaro bellowed.

Lorenzi clasped his other hand over Indaro's mouth. "You will only make this worse," he whispered. "Whatever they are here for, let them state their purpose, and then we will deal with what comes."

Indaro struggled against Lorenzi, but it was futile. The man's grip was incredibly strong.

Abruptly the crowd fell silent. The actors around Indaro murmured nervously. Then the crowd parted. A towering beast of a man led a dozen more black-cloaked soldiers up to the stage. The sight of him stunned Indaro. It was Valos Razett, warlord of the northern villages.

Razett mounted the stage in a single leap, and several of his soldiers clambered up after him. "Is this the baker's wife?" the warlord asked.

The scarred soldier smirked and nodded. "It's her."

Razett turned to the crowd. "My people, here is the wife of a traitor!"

Shock bloomed on his mother's bloodstained face. Indaro's fury flared. He heaved against Lorenzi, but the blacksmith held him fast.

Razett turned back to his mother. "Your husband is required to provide my soldiers with fifty loaves of bread a day, yes?" he asked her.

Indaro's mother glared up at Razett. "He is, my lord, but as you know there's been no rainfall for three months. The price of wheat in the market has doubled. We can't afford—" His mother lowered her head. "My husband has done everything possible."

Razett scoffed and signaled to one of the soldiers, who stepped forward. The soldier held up a small wicker basket. A bread basket. Indaro recognized it as one of his father's.

"Your husband had enough wheat to keep his own pantry stocked," the warlord stated. "And to keep you well fed, I see." He reached a hand into the basket. "Your husband placed himself before me. Before my men. He is a traitor and has been put to death."

The warlord pulled a bloody object from the basket. A stunned silence fell over the villagers. Indaro's mother screamed. From the warlord's fist swung his father's severed head.

What little self-control Indaro had left vanished in an instant. He twisted and fought like a wild boar to break out of Lorenzi's grasp. But the blacksmith's arms tightened even more, crushing the wind from his lungs.

Razett dropped his father's head back into the basket and drew his perana. "And as the wife of a traitor I sentence you to—" The warlord whipped around and his perana flashed in the sunlight.

His mother's eyes widened as the front of her gown fell open. Blood and entrails spilled onto her feet. She wobbled on her knees for a moment, and then crumpled to the stage.

"A traitor's death," Razett finished.

A white mist closed like a curtain over Indaro's vision. There came a rushing roar, like wind and thunder. His world went suddenly cold. The screams of the crowd crescendoed and then faded away.

Lorenzi's voice echoed faintly in his ear. "Your father and mother will get their justice, Indaro. You will get it for them. I will show you how…"

*

Indaro opened his eyes, anger raging in his gut. He was sitting on a chair in the middle of a cramped, sparsely furnished room. Several candles flickered on a table in the corner. There was a cloak on the table as well, along with a wooden bowl that held several sprigs of lilac. There was a door on the opposite wall, which, Indaro guessed, most likely opened into a bedroom. On the floor beside the door, an iron brazier sat atop a low, wooden trunk. To his left a wide gable led to a single window. He realized instantly that he must be in the watchman's room.

There was a movement behind him, and a figure stepped from around the chair. It was the woman from the street. She was dark-haired and petite, nearly gaunt, save for a small bulge at her belly. Her gown was ankle-length and had faded to gray, though it once might have been as black as pitch.

Indaro tried to stand, but failed. His arms were shackled to the chair behind his back. Cold metal bit into his wrists. He yanked at the shackles, but the sellsword's poison had left him weak. There was no chance of breaking free.

The woman crossed her arms. "What do you want with Alvette?" she asked. "Why were you following him?"

"Release me," Indaro demanded.

The woman's eyes widened slightly. "A foreigner? I don't recognize your accent. Where are you from?"

Indaro said nothing. How careless he'd been! He'd let this woman, this *witch*, take him by surprise. She must have cast a spell over him, a spell that had gotten him up the stairs, into the room, and shackled to a chair. A spell that had set him to dreaming. To *remembering*.

He felt a twinge of fear. He had never crossed paths with a witch before. Most had been beheaded or burned at the stake by the warlords. But Indaro had heard that some still existed. And that they were dangerous. He had to stall for time, had to keep her talking until he could figure a way out of this mess.

"I am from Belani," he told her. "From the village of Amarto."

"From the Midlands?" the witch said. "And what brought you here? Why were you following Alvette?"

Behind her the door opened and the young watchman shuffled into the room, eyes squinted against the light of the candles. He yawned, stretched, and then froze when he spotted Indaro. "What's going on?" he grumbled.

The witch hurried to the watchman and took his hand. "He was following you, my love," she told him. "I was in the Savage Poet enjoying a goblet of spiced wine, waiting for you to come home. I saw you walk past the inn and then I saw him. He was right behind you. When you came up here, he slipped into the alley across the street. He looked suspicious so I kept my eye on him for a while. After you went to bed, he tried to sneak in."

That woke the watchman. A look of concern came over his face. He pulled his hand from the witch's and shuffled closer to Indaro.

"You've locked him in my shackles," he noted, surprise ringing in his voice. "How did you manage that? You're no stronger than a mouse, Jessa. This man's twice your size."

How? Indaro thought. She had caught him in a spell, that's how! Him! Indaro Dapiza Rell! Abruptly, he realized the young watchman didn't know. The poor fool had no idea who he was dealing with.

Indaro laughed. "I hate to be the one to tell you, but you're bedding a witch, my friend."

The watchman's jaw clenched. That was good, Indaro thought. The man was susceptible to anger. And an angry opponent is a distracted opponent. Indaro had won many a fight simply by insulting his foe.

The watchman raised a fist. "Say that again, and you'll be swallowing your teeth."

Indaro thrust his chin at the witch. "Ask her. How else could she have done this?" He shook the shackles behind his back.

The witch glared at Indaro. Hatred flashed in her eyes. Then her features softened, and she threw her arms around the young watchman. "I was going to tell you, my love," she whispered. "I was waiting for the right moment. Yes, I possess the Gift. But he," she thrust a boney finger at Indaro. "He was going to *murder* you. I know it."

The watchman studied Indaro for a moment, obviously trying to make some sense of the situation. Then he removed himself from the witch's embrace.

"Love?" the young watchman asked the witch. "I've only known you for two days. And now I find out you're a sorceress." He turned his attention at Indaro. "And you. I don't know who you are or what you could possibly want with me. My coinpurse, no doubt."

The watchman stood there for a few heartbeats, saying nothing. Then he shook his head, stalked back through the door, and returned with his crossbow and quiver. His armor and tabard hung in a bundle over his shoulder.

"No!" the witch wailed. "Please, Alvette. I love you. Don't leave me. I was going to tell you. What does it matter if I have the Gift?"

"You lied to me," the watchman told her. He stormed past Indaro, and Indaro heard another door open behind him. "You can keep the shackles," the young soldier said. "Goodbye, Jessa." There came the sound of a door closing softly.

Indaro had gotten it wrong. This wasn't the watchman's room after all. It was the witch's. He should have known better than to act without discovering everything he could about the watchman, and about these quarters. But he'd been in a hurry. He had rushed himself so he could stow away on the *Destiny* by dawn. That had been a mistake. A mistake for which he feared he was about to pay dearly.

The witch wrung her hands and threw her head back. "You can't leave me!" she shouted.

"Let me go," Indaro said.

The witch cut off her cry. She stared at Indaro, and then a strange expression crossed her face. She began to tremble. One of her eyes twitched wildly. "Helloooo, Mother," she said softly. "Yes, Mother, I know. He will suffer. He will suffer greatly, I assure you."

Mother? Who was she talking to? There was no one else in the room, no one she could possibly be—A terrible realization came to Indaro. The witch was insane. He struggled against the shackles, but they held him fast.

The witch smiled, then spoke in a low voice. "*Quirum.*"

A ball of fire blazed into life in the witch's outstretched hand. She stepped in front of Indaro. "I am going to burn you," she said. "Burn you slowly, until the flesh falls from your bones."

Indaro pulled back from the flames. He could feel the blistering heat upon his face. "Why?" he stammered. "What have I done to deserve this?"

The witch's eyes narrowed dangerously. "You cost me my lover," she said.

Indaro reeled. "That was not my intent. I—" What could he tell her? His thoughts raced. What lie would set him free? Could he even chance a lie? He didn't think so. The slightest misstep and he would burn.

"I came to Fell's Hollow to free you," he confessed.

"Free me?" The witch laughed. "Free me from what?"

"From your Lord Mayor. From his tyranny."

The witch let out a snort. "Norgarde is no tyrant."

"All rulers are tyrants," Indaro corrected her. "They are greedy, filthy murderers that prey on the innocent."

The witch scoffed. "You have clearly been misinformed. Norgarde may be an incompetent bungler, but he is no tyrant." She cocked her head slightly to one side, and her eyes drifted away from Indaro. "Yessss, Mother," she said. "He will pay for what he's done."

The witch stepped forward and set the flames against Indaro's cheek. He heard a sizzling sound, and then a knife of pure agony stabbed through his face. He screamed.

"No! There is no justice in this!"

The witch pulled back the flames. "Justice? What do you know of justice?"

Indaro's cheek pulsed with pain. He almost gagged at the smell of his own burnt flesh. He let out a ragged groan. "I came to Fell's Hollow for justice. Justice for my parents. They were murdered by a tyrant, a warlord of Belani. And so I swore I would claim their justice from him and from every other tyrant I could find across the realms."

"How sad," the witch said. She studied him for a moment, and then took a step backward. "You have wasted your time here. Norgarde is no tyrant. There are—" She hesitated for a moment. "There are others in this city that play that role," she finished.

Indaro let out a grunt. "I am not here for the others. I am here to execute the ruler of this city. That is where corruption is always found. Then I will move on. After Norgarde, I will find another tyrant sucking the life out of his people. And I will kill him as well."

The witch sighed. The ball of flame in her hand vanished. She strode over to the wooden trunk by the door and pushed aside the brazier. She opened the trunk and removed a roll of yellowed parchment. She unrolled it gently, and then hissed. "Silence, Mother."

"What are you doing?" Indaro asked. The pain in his cheek was almost more than he could bear. Every word he spoke sent a throbbing agony through his face.

"Mother wants me to kill you," the witch informed him. "You want me to let you go. And I am unsure what to do." She gestured to the parchment. "I will let this decide your fate."

He felt a pang of panic. "What is that?" he asked, but Indaro knew. The mad witch was going to cast another spell on him.

She looked down at the parchment.

"*Relibutum*," she said.

*

He found himself alone in the middle of a great circular chamber. Constructed entirely of black stone, its walls, floor, domed ceiling high overhead, all were polished to a startling luster. There were no doors. There were no windows. It was as if the place had been built around him, stone by stone, like a mausoleum over some long dead Cabyllian king. There was no sign of lamp, lantern, or torch, yet the chamber shimmered with a strange, golden luminescence.

Indaro noticed he was dressed in a black cloak that hung nearly to the floor. A wide cloth belt encircled his waist. There was something cold pressed against his face. He touched it lightly. It was a mask. A metal mask. He tried to pry a thumb beneath it, but it was stuck to his skin. It wouldn't budge. In his right hand he clutched the hilt of a perana, long, slender, and deadly.

Where in the Abyss was he?

There came the scuff of a boot on stone. About ten paces away a man stood watching him. Indaro's heart leaped in his chest. He hadn't been there only a moment ago. The man was tall and garbed as Indaro was, in a black cloak that fell from his broad shoulders to his boots. He wore a golden mask that resembled a man's face, yet it was featureless and betrayed no sign of emotion. In his hand was a perana.

The man crouched slightly, balancing himself on the balls of his feet. He raised his perana before him and pointed the tip straight at Indaro. He had assumed the tunaga, the guarded stance of Ki, the fighting style taught to all men of Belani.

Who was this man? And why did he want to fight Indaro? Indaro tried to ask him, but no sound passed his lips. It was as if the mask swallowed his words.

The man took one slow step forward, and Indaro dropped instinctively into the tunaga. What in Tugo's name was happening? The witch had banished him to some kind of chamber, where it seemed he must fight some unknown opponent. But why? Was this a test? Was this some form of magical justice? He didn't want to fight this man. He had no idea who he was. Was the man also summoned here by the witch? For some crime Indaro knew nothing of? Or was he some random warrior plucked from Belani to champion the witch's cause? If the man were a warlord, Indaro wouldn't hesitate. He would strike him dead where he stood. But what if the man were simply an innocent commoner brought here against his will?

The man lunged forward, his perana lashing out like viper at Indaro's chest. Indaro swirled his blade around in a semicircular motion and clanged the man's thrust to the side. The man quickly shuffled back and resumed his guard.

Indaro tried to scream at the man, tried to get him to stop so they could figure out what was happening. But once more his words were absorbed by his mask. He held up a hand, gesturing for the man to wait.

The man shot toward Indaro, this time feinting toward Indaro's chest, then redirecting his perana in a sweep toward his leg. Indaro backstepped, and the man's blade swished harmlessly by.

Indaro took another step back. What was he

going to do? He couldn't defend himself forever. The man had some skill. Eventually he would get lucky, or Indaro would tire, and then Indaro would die. But he didn't want to kill this man. Not without knowing who he was and why he was here.

The man rushed at Indaro. Holding his perana high, he brought it down with the force of an axe. Indaro knocked the blow aside, but the man continued on. He drove a shoulder into Indaro, sending Indaro stumbling backwards. The man raised his perana again, and this time Indaro dove out of the way. The man's blade bit into the stone floor.

Indaro rolled and sprang to his feet. He assumed the tunaga, blade outstretched before him, and as he did he felt a twinge of panic. What was he going to do? The witch was giving him no choice. He was going to have to kill this man, a man who might not be anything more than a farmer, or a tailor, or a baker. That last thought reminded him of his father. Damn the witch! He would not kill this man. Not this way.

The man launched himself at Indaro, stabbing straight at Indaro's face. Indaro jumped back, his blade working in a semicircle once more, pushing the man's perana out of the way. But the man pressed on. He slashed at Indaro's midsection. Indaro blocked the attack, and then, in a moment of sudden reflex, he slid his blade straight down the length of the man's perana. The point of

Indaro's sword slipped past the man's crossguard and bit into his stomach.

Indaro felt a stab of guilt. He took several steps back and lowered his blade. The man held a hand against his wound. Blood weeped through his fingers.

Indaro roared in frustration, but the mask ate his curse.

The man looked at Indaro, and then charged. His perana rose and fell in a series of desperate blows. Indaro batted the man's blade away again and again, retreating more and more with each attack, until finally his back slammed against the chamber wall. He had run out of room.

The man raised his perana once more. Indaro had nowhere to go, no other choice. He struck out and drove the tip of his blade into the man's throat.

The man froze. His perana slipped from his fingers and rang loudly against the floor. He stared at Indaro for a moment, the featureless, emotionless mask of gold tilted slightly to one side, as if the man could not believe what had just happened. And then the mask dissolved in a puff of glittering smoke.

Indaro stared into the face of Lorenzi Manell. The actor from his mother's troupe, the blacksmith who had trained Indaro as an assassin, the man who had become his best and only friend in the world, smiled for one brief instant and then collapsed to the floor.

The horror of what he had just done crashed over him, and Indaro screamed a silent scream. He had just slain the man to whom he owed everything. The man who made him what he was. The man who had transformed Indaro into the most feared killer in all the realms. The man who had given him the tools to carve his parents' justice into one tyrant after another.

A black shape caught the corner of Indaro's eye. Several paces away stood another cloaked figure, already in the tunaga. He held a perana before him in a two-handed grip. The man's golden mask glowed brightly. He was waiting for him.

No! This couldn't be happening! Who was it this time? Will the witch force him to kill another person he loved? Another innocent man who had nothing to do with the loss of her watchman lover? That was Indaro's fault, not Lorenzi's. Nor this person's. Where was the justice in this?

The man took a careful step closer. Indaro bolted to one side, trying to put as much distance as he could between himself and this new opponent. Pivoting in place, the man followed Indaro as he moved. Indaro stopped, faced the man, and assumed the tunaga. He could not do this. He would not do this.

Like a Belani kopa dancer, the man stepped closer. One step. Two steps. Then he lunged, raising the point of his blade so that it flashed straight at Indaro's face. Indaro backstepped, bringing up his perana in a sweep, trying to catch the attack. At the last second, the man bent his wrist downward. His perana switched trajectory and streaked towards Indaro's midsection. Indaro reversed the direction of his parry, snapping his blade toward the floor, and barely blocked the thrust.

This man was a far better swordsman than Lorenzi, Indaro realized. Perhaps as good a swordsman as himself.

Instead of resuming his guard, the man took a false half-step back and then came at Indaro again. The move caught Indaro by surprise, and he dove to the right. The tip of the man's blade snagged at his cloak, but missed his flesh. Indaro hit the floor, rolled, and came up in the tunaga.

This man was good, he thought. Too good. Who was he? Indaro tried to remember if there was anyone he loved, anyone he cared for deeply, that was as good a swordsman as this man. He could think of no one. He backed away, increasing the distance between him and his opponent. How could he warn the man? How could he get him to stop fighting? How could he explain to him they were here due to some mad witch's warped sense of justice?

The man danced closer, and then attacked. Indaro blocked a blow aimed at his head, then one to his leg. The man pressed on, stabbing, hacking, slashing. Indaro backpedaled, parrying once, then again, and then he leaped to one side.

The man's blade streaked out and caught the back of Indaro's thigh. A flash of pain raced up his leg. It was only a shallow gash, but it stung like the Abyss.

Once more, the man resumed his guard, and again pointed the tip of his blade at Indaro. Indaro looked past the man to where Lorenzi's body lay sprawled on the floor. He did not want to kill another innocent man. Maybe he could end the fight another way. Perhaps with a serious but non-deadly wound? It was his only hope. Indaro dropped into the tunaga, and then charged.

Expecting the man to retreat, Indaro was stunned as the man simply stood there, blade out, ready to engage. His opponent was fearless.

Indaro aimed the first blow at the man's arm, but the man simply flicked his perana around and captured the end of Indaro's blade. Indaro launched a kick at the man's groin. The man spun sideways, avoiding the kick, and regripped his perana with both hands. Then his opponent drove his blade toward Indaro's chest. With a twist of his body, Indaro beat the blade away and disengaged. He took a few extra steps back and returned to the tunaga.

The man began to circle. Indaro sidestepped, keeping pace. Again, Indaro noted the man's proficiency with a blade. It had taken Indaro only a year to equal Lorenzi's skill, and another to surpass it. Lorenzi had said he had taken to the perana as if he'd been born with one hanging on his hip. This man was easily Indaro's equal.

With a sudden leap, the man closed the distance between them and then dropped to his knees. He slashed his blade around in a wide arc meant to take Indaro in the ankle. Indaro, surprised by the boldness of the move, jumped. The man's blade cut through the air beneath his feet, and Indaro landed with a grunt. He thought the man would disengage, leap back and return to the tunaga, but the man stayed on his knees and reversed his stroke. Indaro tried to jump again, but was too late. He felt the man's blade bite deep into his calf, and he screamed as steel hit bone. With no other option, Indaro threw himself backwards to avoid the next attack that he knew was coming. He slammed onto the stone floor, the wind expelling from his lungs in a whoosh.

He tried to stand, but his leg wouldn't take the weight, so he used his perana to force himself quickly upright. The pain was brilliant. Blinding. Balanced on one leg, he faced the man, who had already returned to his guard.

Indaro knew the end had come. He could sacrifice his own defense, he thought. Strike a lethal blow just as the man's perana was entering into his body. Anyone skilled in Ki knew that you could defeat the fiercest opponent if you were willing to die to do so. But did he want to kill this man? Who was he? The man had been summoned here to fight Indaro, to secure justice for the witch. The man was here, like Lorenzi had been, so Indaro would lose someone he loved. Just like the witch had lost someone she'd loved.

Indaro shot a quick glance to his right. A good man lay dead on the floor. A man he had loved dearly. He felt the crush of guilt and suddenly understood what he had to do.

In a rush, the man charged at Indaro. Indaro raised his perana in both hands, trying to keep himself steady on his one good leg. While just out of range, the man made a half-lunge to Indaro's left, a move meant to throw off Indaro's timing.

Indaro waited.

The man landed hard on his front foot and then as he came into range, redirected a full lunge to Indaro's right. Indaro knew the move well. Lorenzi had called it the hima laram, the little right left. The man's blade shot toward Indaro. Indaro squeezed the hilt of his perana and summoned every bit of courage he possessed. His arms strained, muscle memory demanding that he parry the man's thrust. His brain rebelled, shrieking at him to enact some kind of defense, to do something, anything, to save his own life. But Indaro held fast.

The man's blade slid into Indaro's chest. The pain was so fierce, it took Indaro's breath away, and he dropped to his knees. The man yanked his perana free and stood before him, watching as Indaro's blood spurted down the front of his cloak. As he stared at Indaro, the man's golden mask shimmered and disappeared. Disbelief hit

Indaro like a fist in the jaw, and he coughed up a mouthful of blood. The man had Indaro's own face.

He had been fighting himself.

Confusion swept over Indaro. Was this some final joke? Some demented form of justice? Had he sacrificed himself for nothing?

His other self smiled down at him. It was not a mocking or cruel smile, but rather a kind, loving smile a proud father might give to a son.

Abruptly, the black stone of the chamber, the ceiling, the floor, the walls, all of it dissolved into white mist. Within moments, the mist surrounded Indaro. It was numbing and cold. So cold. He heard a rush of wind and a roar of thunder. And then he felt himself die.

*

Indaro opened his eyes. He was at a crossroad, a crossroad he recognized at once. To one side, Shore Street ran along the border of Oldtowne and Rogueswarde in the direction of Temple Hill. To the other, it veered off toward the harbor. And at his back was the narrow, unpaved road he had recently taken into Southside.

He put a hand to his chest. There was no wound, no pain. The chamber, Lorenzi, the fight with himself, it had all been a part of the witch's spell. Indaro felt a rush of relief. If he weren't wounded, then somewhere back in Belani, Lorenzi was alive and well. He touched his cheek, and a fiery pain lanced through his face. That part, at least, had been real.

He took a closer look around him. Two- and three-story buildings huddled up to the road. It was still foggy and dark, but the sky to the east was less black than it had been earlier. A few cityfolk were already throwing back their shutters to let in some morning air.

Indaro realized he had a choice to make. Should he head back to the Tershium and risk finding a way inside? If he took that road, he would never make it to the *Destiny* in time to flee the city. Should he stay and kill the Lord Mayor? Kill the tyrant?

The witch's words came back to him.

Norgarde is no tyrant.

Could he take the word of a witch, a witch who was insane? She'd cast some spell over him, a spell to test him, to judge him. He must have passed her test, for she had let him go. Insane or not, she was willing to accept the verdict of the spell. There was some justice in that, he thought. Maybe she was right.

A gull cried somewhere off in the fog, as a door opened in a building a short ways from Indaro. A man in a baker's apron stepped onto the street. He noticed Indaro, nodded, and started off in the direction of Oldtowne.

Should he follow the man? he wondered. Head to the Tershium and kill Norgarde? The answer came to him, and he cursed.

He would leave Fell's Hollow, at least for now. There was still plenty of time for Norgarde's power to eat away at his conscience, at his honor. Plenty of time for the Lord Mayor to become just like all the other murdering tyrants in the world. And when that happened, Indaro would return to finish the job he started. In the meantime, he had a ship to catch. A ship to Nyland, where he'd start his quest anew.

With his cheek throbbing, Indaro pulled the cowl of his cloak over his head and marched off toward the harbor.

FATE OF THE FETCH

"The chafe of chains, the lash of whip,
The blackened eye, the broken lip,
With all the pain, none's crueler than,
The death of one's self-worth."
A Slave's Lament, *35-36*
—*Grober Trenee*

SINCE THE PASSING OF THE TEMPEST over a
fortnight ago, the fog had come nearly
every evening to smother the beauty of the
Scaradem.

Set atop the highest hilltop of Faettewarde, the
Scaradem had once been a public park, a place
where people of all walks of life could come and
enjoy a wide variety of flora, winding walkways,

and a stunning view of Fell's Hollow. But when the city's coffers had run dry a century or so back, the Lord Mayor at the time, one Arik Durst, had no choice but to sell the property.

For a pittance, eleven wealthy families purchased the Scaradem. They built luxurious villas and mansions amid its lush landscape. They hired a multitude of gardeners who toiled a year or more to install a five-tiered fountain and a hand-dug fishpond near the center of the grounds. When the work was complete, the families brought in a team of masons to construct a twelve-foot-high stone rampart to surround the property, into which they set a massive iron gate that for a hundred years had kept out the public. The gate, however, did little to deter the fog.

The thick mist billowed through its iron bars and rolled past flowerbeds filled with wilted acanthus and nigella. It passed by well-kept homes and flowed along watersoaked walkways. It swept across the Scaradem's puddled, manicured lawns until, at last, it came to the foot of a small stone manorhouse. The manorhouse was in a terrible state. Black gaps ran between its stones where the mortar had long ago crumbled to dust. Deathvine dripped from its tiled roof. Thin tendrils of fog drifted up to a grime-stained attic window that flickered with a yellow light.

Behind the window, Vara Dayne held up a candle. Her anger simmered as she studied her reflection. The scar on her cheek was barely discernible, but she knew it was there. It had been a parting gift from Rorham Nach. How she hated the man! Last winter her father had forced her to become Nach's mistress on a pledge from the wealthy merchant that he would soon be rid of his wife. Vara had begged her father to change his mind, but he had refused. Nach, smitten by her beauty, had promised that when he and Vara were married, he would help restore the Dayne manorhouse to its former splendor. Her father had foolishly lost his fortune on poor investments, and he wanted nothing more than to regain his wealth and power, so he'd given Vara no choice in the matter. Without a second thought, he had sent her away to live in a small room above the Sorsagorium, Nach's place of business on the Run.

Her eyes burned at the memory. Nach had beaten her. Often. On her first night with him he had hit her with an angry backhand after she'd spilled a goblet of Kernish red in his lap. Nach wore a signet ring of heavy gold, a family heirloom that bore the Rorham crest, and it had split her lip in two. That had been the first of many beatings. Nach had a quick and violent temper, and at times she thought he beat her for no other reason than to watch her weep. And though the beatings were terrible, the nights in their bed were worse.

Vara forced the foul thoughts from her mind. Hands shaking, she set down the candle. At least that nightmare was over, she told herself. Nach had moved on to a more willing mistress, though not before giving Vara one last beating. Her fingers touched her cheek where the wound had been. That beating had been the worst of all.

She turned from the window. Beside her, a small canvas rested on a paint-stained easel, and she dabbed at it with a long brush. Her self-portrait was nearly finished. Vara examined it and frowned. Three weeks of work and it looked nothing like her. It was vague, ill-defined, a mass of auburn curls framing a pale, featureless face that could have been anyone's. She added a touch more umber, blending it with a tinge of white around the cheek, but still the woman that looked back at her was not her. It was missing something.

A hard rap sounded on the door. Vara sighed and tossed her brush into a jar of spirits on the windowsill. "Come in," she called.

The door opened, and her father limped into the room. He clutched a cane in a gnarled, age-spotted fist, and he had a tired look about him, as if he'd just woken from a nap. His short gray hair was mussed, his long robe was wrinkled, and there were black rings below his hard brown eyes. Vara's mother stood in the hall behind him, hands folded, head down.

Her father's gaze fell upon the painting and annoyance spread across his face. "Must you bother with that?" he asked.

Vara tensed. They had had this argument more times than she could count, and she knew what he was going to say: Women shouldn't waste their time with foolery when there was cooking and cleaning and men to be cared for. But painting enabled her to escape from life. When she painted, she went into another world where she was in control, free to do whatever she wished, even if it was only to choose her brushes, her subjects, her colors. "It's what I love, Father," Vara told him.

He hesitated, then apparently decided to drop the matter. "There's someone downstairs. He needs your help. See to it."

Vara groaned. As her father was too old and too proud to work, he instead hired her out as a fetch. It was a job she both loved and loathed. Whatever it was she had to do for this man, it would most likely take all night. "I'm tired," she argued. "Can this wait until morning?"

Her father shook his head. "He paid in gold, girl. Enough to keep our bellies full for a month. Besides," he went on, pointing the tip of his cane at her, "you ruined the opportunity to regain our fortune. Nach would have made us rich again. So now you must earn our money the hard way."

Vara was about to refuse when she felt a familiar tug at her neck. Her necklace, a flamite rose on a silver chain, had grown suddenly heavier, as if its weight had tripled in an instant. Her father noticed her reaction, but said nothing.

He didn't have to. He had been the one who had placed the rose around her neck when she had come of age. It was a patristone, and it had been in the Dayne family for generations, handed down from father to son for as long as anyone could remember, to be presented to their wives on their wedding day. As Vara's mother no longer needed it, and as her father had no son to pass it to, he forced her to wear it.

"Father, please," she implored.

"Ogden," her mother said in a low voice from the hall. "Surely—"

Her father shot a glare over his shoulder, and her mother flinched. She lowered her gaze to the floor. He looked back at Vara. "You'll do as I say, girl. Now get going."

Vara's mother gave her a sad look, a look that said she understood, but there was nothing either of them could do. It was simply the way of things.

Vara snatched the patristone and tried to rip it from her neck. She had tried before. Many times. She had tried the day her father had sent her to Nach. She had tried every night as she lay in bed waiting for Nach to come upstairs after closing the Sorsagorium for the night. She had tried until her fingernails were cracked and her neck was raw and bleeding.

The patristone's silver chain held fast, as it always had. The black stone grew heavier, until it felt like a dozen men were standing on her shoulders, forcing her to the ground. She tried to slip the chain over her head, but it constricted, tightening around her throat. It bit against her windpipe, and the black stone grew heavier still. Vara dropped to her knees. She couldn't take much more. Finally, she gasped.

"Yes, Father."

Her father let out a satisfied grunt, then turned and limped down the hall, his cane clacking on the hardwood. The chain loosened, and the black stone returned to its original heft. Vara closed her eyes and wept.

After a few moments, her mother placed a gentle hand on her shoulder. "Come, Vara. You mustn't keep your father waiting."

Vara looked up. Her mother's eyes shone with unshed tears. "Why?" Vara asked. "Why must I wear this evil thing?"

"It is how we learn," her mother told her. "All women must be taught to serve their husbands. Or their fathers. I wore it for years. And it's not evil, Vara. It simply reminds us when we're not acting in the interest of our men."

Vara got to her feet. "Then why do you weep?"

Her mother sighed. "Learning to be obedient is a hard lesson, Vara. It took me a long time. And I can see it is going to take you even longer. The ordeal will not be pleasant. You must accept your fate. The sooner you do, the sooner you can live your life free from pain."

"Is your life free from pain?" Vara knew the answer to that.

"It is free from any pain brought on by disobedience," her mother answered. "That is enough. It has been enough for all Dayne women, ever since the sorcerers of Cabyll created that patristone over five hundred years ago. Back then, all men of noble birth used patristones to keep their women in order."

Vara scoffed. "It's barbaric."

"It is tradition," her mother countered. "We Daynes are the last in Fell's Hollow to use a patristone. Your father is very proud of that."

"How can he be proud of something that strips away a person's dignity?" Her voice rang with her contempt. "Look at what it's done to you."

Her mother took Vara by the arm. "It is the way of things. Accept it, Vara, and life will get easier for you. And for me. I hate to see you suffer. Now, come."

Vara glanced back at the easel. The faceless self-portrait stared back at her, unrecognizable, and she suddenly realized what it was missing. It had no identity, no individuality, no features that marked Vara for who she was. It was what her mother had become, years ago, and what she was becoming now. It revealed nothing but an empty shell of a woman.

*

212

The fog had continued to gather, a swirling mass of mist that infused the Scaradem with an oppressive, salty dampness. The night was dark and quiet. The smell of sea and mold and wet leaves wafted thickly through the air.

The guard at the gate, a stout old man with a wiry beard and a bulbous nose, stood aside. Vara nodded, and she and her new client stepped out onto the road. Vara pulled her cloak about her. Though it was midsummer, it was always cooler in the hills of Faettewarde, especially at night.

She was so full rage that she was surprised she could feel the cold at all. Perhaps she had reached the end of her strength and was losing her will to fight. She realized now that she'd been fighting all these years to keep some part of her identity, some semblance of her true self intact. But each time she rebelled, each time she was forced by the patristone to do something against her will, she lost more of her independence, became more of a slave.

Vara tried to put her anger aside and turned her attention to the man beside her. He was tall, broad-shouldered, and walked with a catlike grace. From beneath his cloak the tip of a scabbard swayed back and forth as he moved, and the lantern he held clanked with a steady, metallic rhythm. His every movement was like water over stone.

The two headed into the dark, the soft glow of

the lantern lighting the way. Ahead the cobbled road ran straight down the hill, hemmed in on both sides by a thick swath of elm, pine, and cedar. Vara studied the man as they descended, their footfalls echoing into the mist. He was perhaps in his forties, though it was difficult to tell. He wore a cloak of heavy oilcloth that fell to his knees, and with the cowl pulled up against the mist, she could only make out the gray at his temples and the hard glint of his sad, amber-colored eyes.

She wanted to hate the man, but couldn't. It wasn't his fault she was bound to the will of her father. It wasn't his fault her father had been hiring her out as a fetch since he'd placed the patristone around her neck, sending her after missing children, lost jewels, errant husbands, mislaid items of all kinds, and, on occasion, after the perpetrator of some crime or other that had left the Watch particularly baffled. The money her father collected for her services supported their family, but just barely. The cost of living in the Scaradem was something few could afford.

No, she couldn't hate this man. He had come to her for help. And his situation was worse than hers. Far worse. His only daughter had been missing for months, and he feared she was dead. Vara was his last hope. The fact was, she wanted to help him. She only wished, for once, she'd been given a choice.

"What's your name?" Vara asked him as she

pulled her cloak even tighter about her shoulders.

The man looked at her for a moment, as if deciding whether or not to speak. She had the feeling he was accustomed to asking questions, not answering them.

"Deven," he said, after a moment.

Vara gestured to the sword beneath his cloak. "Are you a watchman?"

The two walked on for bit before he answered.

"Perhaps. Why?"

Vara shrugged. "I've worked for watchmen before. They make people nervous. And when people get nervous, bad things tend to happen."

He gave her a sad look. "I'm just a father trying to find his daughter." Worry edged his voice.

Vara suddenly felt sorry for the man. It happened often with her clients. Though she tried to remain distant, most times she couldn't help but sympathize with them, share their pain, their suffering. Over the last few years she'd seen more misery than most people saw in a lifetime. "We'll find her," she assured him.

He said nothing, and they walked on in silence. When they reached the bottom of the hill, they came to another road, this one wider and well-paved, its stones better set to accommodate the wheels of wagons, carts, and carriages.

"Crooked Lane," Deven pointed out. "North takes us to Oldtowne. South heads around Temple Hill and into Rogueswarde." Crickets

215

chirruped somewhere in the foggy night. There was no one else on the road. The watchman looked at Vara expectantly. "Well?" he prodded.

She pulled the patristone from beneath her tunic and clenched it in her fist. She faced north. "Where?" she asked it. The stone was smooth and cool to the touch. Nothing. She turned slowly, inch by inch, and when it pulsed with a sudden heat, she knew the way. Though the patristone forced her into obedience, it also provided her with help, a guidance of sorts, to serve the interests of her father, and, by extension, her clients. That guidance had made her one of the highest paid fetchs in Fell's Hollow. Vara slipped the patristone beneath her tunic. "Your daughter's—"

"Her name's Renna," Deven cut in. The sadness seemed to grow deeper in his eyes.

Vara gave him a smile and gestured to the south. "Renna is that way, though I can't tell how far."

Deven let out a slow, sorrowful moan. "I feared as much. She's in Rogueswarde, I'd bet my life on it."

*

Buckler Street sliced through the center of Rogueswarde. It was roughly cobbled, where it was cobbled at all, with tall buildings looming on either side, more than half of them old and dilapidated and in need of repair. Traces of fog swirled through shafts of light cast from half-shuttered windows and tavern doors. Cityfolk milled about in every direction, seeking excitement, trouble, or a place to spend their last copper chip. It was a vast change from the solitude of Temple Hill over which they had just hiked, where the few people they had encountered were either robed priests rushing between the temples, or a handful of humble parishioners who'd come to lay an offering basket at the altar of Ryke or one of the sea gods worshiped in the city.

Deven threw back his cowl and opened the front of his cloak, exposing the leather-wrapped hilt of his sword. He placed a hand on it, calm, casual. He was a watchman all right, Vara thought. As the military, the constabulary, and the only force for order in the city, they said a watchman had to be prepared for anything at any time, whether on duty or off. Deven looked like he was ready for a battle.

He gave Vara a questioning look, and she took out the patristone. "Where?" she asked it. Again, it was cool to the touch. The stone remained unchanged as her gaze swept over an ill-kept alehouse on one side of the road. A placard painted with a bloody fist hung over its open door. Down on a corner where Buckler met the Street of Seven Lamps, several burly men stood arguing in front of Fullers and Fangs, one of three beast-baiting arenas in Rogueswarde. And beyond the men, two women leaned casually against a lamp post. The lamp had nearly burned through its oil, but in its fading light Vara could make out the garish red rouge that marked them as prostitutes.

She turned slightly and let her sight continue on, past more buildings, some empty and run down, others alive with light and people and noise. Abruptly, the stone burned hot in her hand. A dark structure loomed on a bend far down the road. It sat in shadows, the nearest lamp having burned out. The building appeared abandoned. Several windows were boarded up, and the front door was missing. Vara pointed to it.

"She's in there."

*

Someone was in the building. As they approached the front, Vara could hear a low murmur of voices, the shuffle of boots on wood, and what she thought might have been a faint groan leak out of the darkness beyond the doorway. A bad feeling settled over her.

"Let's go," Deven urged. "I may need your help when we find her."

Vara put a hand on his arm. "I'd rather wait here," she said.

The watchman looked at her, his amber-colored eyes pleading, and she felt the pull of the patristone as it took on weight. The flamite rose became an anchor hanging from her neck. Her anger sparked. She might have decided to go with him on her own, but the patristone was making the decision for her. Slowly, her anger faded and she lowered her head. "Fine," she conceded.

Deven nodded. "Stick close," he told her, and then stepped into the building, lantern held out before him. Vara followed.

The lantern's light spilled into a large room. Its floors were of old wood, scratched and scarred. Plaster peeled from the walls. Dark alcoves and arched entryways flanked the room on either side. The ceiling rose high overhead, and a wide staircase ran up the back to a balcony bathed in shadow. The air in the place had a musty, aged odor about it and a subtle trace of something bitter. It smelled like burnt acorns. As the two entered, the occupants of the room, several ragged looking men in threadbare clothes, scurried like rats out of the lantern light.

Deven sniffed. "Ryke save me," he breathed.

"Sandar?" came a voice from the balcony. "Is that you? I need more—"

"Quiet, fool, it ain't Sandar," said another voice, deep and booming. A man stepped from an alcove. He was enormous, at least a head taller than Deven, with a thick neck and a large paunch where his middle had turned to fat. He wore weathered leather breeches and a stained tunic that did little to conceal the corded muscles of his arms. In one fist he gripped a naked sword, and as he moved to the center of the room he raised it slightly, pointing it straight at Deven. "Who in the Abyss are ya?" the big man challenged.

Vara looked at Deven. His chin was resting on his chest, his shoulders slumped. "An opit den," he whispered. "Oh, Renna."

Pity filled Vara's heart. Opit dens had been popping up in Fell's Hollow over the last few years, ever since Thalian tradeships had sailed in from the east, bringing with them a vast array of strange spices, silk, and their infamously addictive drug. The Watch raided the dens often, but the opit peddlers would simply move on to another abandoned building where they could ply their wares.

"I said, who are ya?" repeated the big man. "Whaddaya want?"

Vara knew who the man must be. Every opit peddler placed a guardian over their den, someone to scare away undesirables and keep the customers in line. And to bribe any less-than-honest watchman who happened to wander in.

"I've come for my daughter," Deven said. His voice sounded even sadder than it had before, as the enormity of Renna's plight settled over him. If she was in an opit den, then she was addicted to the drug, a slave to its power and to the whims of the drug peddlers.

"Get lost," spat the guardian as he stepped closer. "Before I split you in two." He raised his sword. Somewhere in the shadows, the ragged men murmured excitedly to each other as they watched.

"Listen," Deven said softly. "I don't care about anything except my little girl. Let me have her, and I'll leave you in peace."

"Scram," the guardian said. "Now."

Deven sighed and set down the lantern. Vara backed into the doorway, a feather of fear fluttering in her chest. She watched as, in one fluid motion, Deven unsheathed his blade and sprang at the big man. He looked like a panther charging his prey, his cloak flapping behind him as he moved.

The guardian's eyes widened. He threw up his sword just in time to block the watchman's attack. Metal clanged on metal. Sparks flew, and the big man stumbled backwards.

"Give me my daughter," Deven rasped, "and I won't kill you."

"It's you who'll be dyin' tonight," the guardian retorted as he launched an attack of his own.

A collective gasp came from the shadows as the big man's sword rose and fell like a miner's maul, directly at Deven's head. Vara caught her breath. Though the guardian was enormous, he was deceivingly quick.

Deven sidestepped, and the big man's sword thunked into the floor. Deven kicked the man in the stomach, and swung his blade around in a backhanded blow. The guardian grunted and ducked, and Deven's blade whistled over his head.

Dropping low, the big man slashed at Deven's midsection. Off balance, Deven tried to bring his blade around to block the blow, but he was too late. The guardian's sword sliced into Deven's side, and Vara knew the stroke would have killed him if he hadn't kept at his parry, for his blade battered against the guardian's sword even as it entered his flesh, sending it bouncing back in a shower of sparks and blood.

Deven leaped back and with one hand tore off his cloak. A crimson splotch already soaked the side of his tunic.

"I'm gonna enjoy killin' ya," the big man taunted as he circled Deven. "And then I'm gonna enjoy killin' yer pretty little friend there." The man shot an evil look at Vara. "But not 'afore I've had some fun with her," he added.

Vara went cold. This wasn't part of the bargain. She'd brought Deven to his daughter. Renna was somewhere in this Ryke forsaken place. Now the rest was up to him. She'd done her part. She wasn't going to risk herself any further. She turned to leave, and the black stone pulled down on her neck like a block of lead. She nearly crumpled under its sudden weight. Deven had asked for her help, and the patristone was binding her to his will.

Her anger flashed, but then faded like a distant dying fire. It had been fading for years and was now nearly gone. Futility had started to take its place. The futility of being in a situation she could never change. She was stuck at the watchman's side, and there was nothing she could do but watch her doom play out before her. Vara reached into her cloak and pulled a thin dagger from a sheath at the small of her back. A vision of Rorham Nach, naked, grunting, sweat-soaked, flashed before her eyes. Never again, she promised herself. She would die first.

She turned back to the room.

Deven's blade hung limp in his hand as he tried to keep the circling man in front of him. The guardian grinned. Then he lunged at Deven, sword point plunging straight at the watchman's chest.

Deven spun sideways, and it was plain to Vara that the wound in his side had slowed him tremendously. The panther had become the prey. The guardian's sword sliced through linen and left a weeping red line across Deven's chest. The watchman staggered away, gritting his teeth in pain.

The big man was well skilled with a sword if he could handle a member of the Watch with such ease, Vara realized. The drug peddler who ran this den had chosen his guardian wisely.

As he continued to circle Deven, the big man held his sword casually in one hand, letting its tip drag across the floor. He knew he had the advantage. It was only a matter of time before he'd kill Deven, and then he'd come for her.

Suddenly, he shot forward, swinging his sword in a wide arc. Deven brought up his blade and the two weapons collided. There was a loud crack, and the watchman's blade shattered into pieces. Deven dropped to his knees. Gasps escaped from the shadows, and the big man laughed.

"Time to die," he said. He lifted his sword over his head.

In a flash of movement, Deven snatched a knife from a boot-sheath and slung it with a flick of his wrist. The guardian's mouth dropped open as the knife turned over once in the air and sank into his chest. His sword fell with a clatter, and he took a step toward Deven, hands clawing at the air. Then he gurgled something unintelligible and crashed to the floor.

Relief surged through Vara. She raced over to Deven and put a hand on his shoulder. "Are you all right?" she asked.

Deven looked up at her, pain clear in his eyes. "Where is she?" he grunted.

*

Vara trudged through the iron gate and back into the Scaradem. The fog was thicker than ever. It smothered the grounds, choking everything in a wet, gray blanket. Were it not for the light of the oil lamps along the path, the place would have been lost in the murk.

Try as she might, she couldn't get that gut-wrenching wail out of her head, and her thoughts flitted back to the opit den. She had led Deven into the building's cellar, where he had found Renna lying in a corner, naked, wrapped in a torn and tattered piece of cloth. She'd been so gaunt and so pale. Deven had swept her out of the mud. "Find someone to help her," he had begged. "Please."

Vara had yanked out the patristone, asked for its guidance, but no guidance had come. The black stone had remained as cold as a shard of ice. "I'm so sorry," she'd told him.

Deven had pulled Renna to his blood-stained breast, realizing only then what Vara had already known, had known from the moment she'd seen the poor girl's face. His daughter was dead. The watchman had let out a cry filled with such hopelessness, Vara thought she would die from the sound of it. It still echoed in her ears.

She wiped a hand across her eyes and tried once more to forget. Ahead of her the path forked, and she chose her way absently, paying little attention to her surroundings. She came to a massive, five-tiered fountain and then to a fishpond, where she picked another path that took her, at last, back home.

Exhausted, wanting only a bite to eat and a long, dreamless sleep, she opened the front door and stepped into the foyer. It was dark, save for an edge of yellow light at the end where the door to her father's sitting room stood ajar.

It was well past midnight, and her father was

still awake. Vara wondered if he was waiting up for her. That was doubtful, she told herself; he'd never done that before. She moved closer to the light and then she heard them. Voices, low in conversation. Perhaps her mother was awake as well, but Vara didn't think so. Something was amiss, and a sense of worry stole over her.

She pushed the door open. Her father was seated in a chair by the fireplace, a goblet in one hand, a pipe stuck between his lips. He was chatting with a middle-aged man who was seated next to him.

It was Rorham Nach. Nausea flooded into her stomach as she took in the sight of the man. He was dressed, as usual, in the finest fashions. He wore a deep blue silk tunic, and his black breeches were run up the legs with silver snaps. His pale gray-blonde hair was cut short. His face still held those hard, ice blue eyes and a mouth that turned down in a permanent scowl. Bushy sideburns ran down the edges of his jaw, accentuating his weak chin. The man was as ugly on the outside as he was on the inside. When he saw Vara, his mouth twisted into a mockery of a smile. "Good evening," he said. "I'm glad to see you're as beautiful as ever. Finest looking woman I've ever laid eyes on, as I've said before."

"What do you want?" Vara snapped.

"Now, now, Vara," her father chided. "That's the attitude that ruined things the first time. But lucky for us, Master Nach has decided to give you another chance."

Vara felt like vomiting. "Never," she said.

Nach snorted. "You have no say in the matter, girl. This is between your father and me. And as you can see," he waggled a pouch that jangled with coins, "the matter's already been settled." He passed the pouch to her father, who took it, nodding his head as he stowed it somewhere in his robes.

Vara's stomach churned. "Father, please. Please don't do this."

"You will go with Master Nach," her father told her. "Tonight. Pack what you need. You can send for the rest of your things on the morrow."

"And this time you can leave your pretty paints behind," Nach added. "You'll have no time for that kind of nonsense."

"I'm not going anywhere," Vara spat. She felt the patristone pull at her neck, and a jolt of panic raced through her. "He doesn't want a wife, Father. He wants a whore!"

Her father gazed into the fire, disinterested.

"That is not entirely true," Nach said. "First, I need your services as a fetch. Do you remember my ring? The one thing I treasure above all my possessions?"

Vara's hand went to her cheek.

"Ah, yes." Nach chuckled. "I see that you do. Well, some bastard of a thief has stolen it, and I want it back. You'll get it for me and then rejoin me as my mistress. Or whore, if you prefer. This time I've paid your father enough to at least be honest about it."

"Father!" Vara pleaded. The patristone pulled harder still, and her legs began to tremble.

Her father turned to her. He watched, waiting, cold detachment clearly written in his face. The patristone, heirloom of the Daynes, grew heavier still.

"No," Vara begged. "Please, no."

Her father sat there, watching, saying nothing. Next to him, Nach smirked. The black stone grew heavier once more, and Vara's knees buckled. She hit the floor and the stone dragged her down, down, until she was prostrated before the two men. Suddenly, the silver chain tightened around her throat. She gasped as the chain cut off her air.

Nach laughed. "When will you learn, girl? You were born to serve men like your father and me. And serve you will."

Tears flooded Vara's eyes. Tiny lights danced across her vision. She clawed at the chain. The weight of the stone grew again, and she was pressed flat to the floor. She had the weight of the world on her back, and she groaned in agony.

"You will go with Master Nach," her father commanded. "I will not tell you again."

Vara fought against the patristone, fought as she had never fought before. She rolled on her side and shoved her fingers beneath the chain. Her nails scraped away skin, sending furrows of pain lancing through her neck. She writhed on the floor, yanking at the chain with all her strength, and it cut into her fingers. Blood trickled down her hands.

The chain constricted further. More worlds climbed upon her back. Darkness crept over her vision. She was dying.

"Well?" her father asked.

She gave one last wrench at the chain, once last attempt at freedom, but the chain held fast. And then she went still. Vara moved her lips, forming the words with the last bit of breath she possessed.

"Yes, Father."

*

Vara stumbled into her room and sprawled to the floor. Tears spilled down her cheeks. She pulled herself to her knees. There was only one thing she could do. She reached to the small of her back and drew out her dagger. It felt heavy in her hand as she set the tip against her stomach. This is the end, she thought. She couldn't live like this any longer. Too many years she'd suffered under the oppression of the patristone. Too much had been taken from her.

She gazed over at her portrait sitting on the easel. Like the painting, she had no face, no identity. Those had been taken from her, bit by bit over the years, and now there was nothing left. She was empty.

She took a deep breath and tried to plunge the dagger into her bowels. But the dagger didn't move. She half expected the patristone to stop her, to keep her from ending her life, from betraying the commands her father and Nach had placed upon her, but the vile black stone rested quietly between her breasts. She tried to stab herself again, and failed. The dagger would come no closer. If only she could end the pain of it all! One quick thrust and she would be done with all the torment. Yet she couldn't do it. She had lost even the will to take her own pathetic life.

With that realization, one final piece of her identity, one last scrap of her self-worth, broke away and dissolved into mist. A cold, numbing feeling swept through her. The anger, the futility, the rage, it all disappeared. There remained only the cold.

Leaving her paints behind, she grabbed a few belongings and left the manorhouse. She walked along quietly in the fog, making her way back toward the gate. When she was standing out on the road under the dim light of a lamppost, she took out the patristone.

The black rose was cold and heavy in her hand. She had a ring to fetch, she told herself. And a new master to serve. It was simply the way of things. It was her lot in life. Vara wiped the tears from her face.

"Where?" she asked.

THE SHADOWHUNTER

"There's oft more nerve in those who fight themselves,
Than those who storm the mightiest of keeps."
At Talmor's Seige, *Act II, Sc. 3*
—*Starroch Phemorel*

T HE GULLS SHRIEKED as they fought. Their cries carried down the length of the Stonewharf, a long crescent of Crag-mined carterock blocks that cut the harbor in half, separating the deeper waters from the labyrinth of docks and tilting structures that staggered out from the shore, along the tops of pilings, and straight up to the Stonewharf's edge.

The wharf was centuries old, built by the men of Fell's Hollow over the course of a single year, a year in which no man was permitted to work at anything that didn't contribute to the massive project. Chandlers had set aside candlemaking in favor of fashioning stacks of torches, which provided light for the night crews. Blacksmiths had given up their usual trade in order to supply workers with thousands of picks, chisels, and other mining and masonry tools. Barrel merchants had turned to crafting great wooden sleds on which the blocks of carterock were eased down from the Crags and hoisted onto specially made barges lashed together by the city's shipwrights. Though man-made, the Stonewharf looked as if it had been placed into the harbor, block by block, by the hands of giants.

Everywhere gulls screamed as they skittered across the stones. They wrestled over fish heads and brawled over bits of crab. They sparred over shards of broken clam shell. One cluster of especially belligerent birds scuffled too close to a handful of dockworkers that were finishing up their work for the day. The men kicked absently at the gulls as they rolled a barrel of whokur oil toward a single-masted trawler. The gulls screeched and shot into the fog. Most settled onto the wooden beams of a crane that towered in the mist at one end of the wharf. A handful of others found refuge in the riggings of various ships docked nearby.

A travel-worn man in a doeskin cloak stood at the prow of one ship, watching disinterestedly as a particularly old and ruffled-looking gull landed on the bowsprit before him. The gull let out a loud squawk and began preening under a wing, a wing that was missing more than a few feathers. Reminded of his own deformity, the man adjusted a triangular patch of leather that covered one eye, an accoutrement which, though it hid the gaping hole where his eye had once been, did little to mask the terrible scar that zagged from his forehead all the way to his stubbled chin.

Tye Brandigar fingered his scar for a moment and then turned his attention to the girl standing beside him. His apprentice was similarly dressed, in roughspun tunic and breeches, doeskin cloak, and heavy boots. And she was similarly armed, with a longsword at her hip, daggers in thigh-sheaths, and a short bow and quiver strapped to her back. She was a fine looking girl, nearly a woman at seventeen. Over the past few years she'd grown as tall as Tye himself. She'd also become quicker of foot and could nearly best him with a blade. Unlike Tye, Onya Oker was born to be a shadowhunter.

"An ugly city, don't you think?" Tye asked the girl.

He watched as his apprentice took in the shite-stained stones of the wharf, the smell of salt and fish, the clutter of poorly constructed buildings both on and beyond the water. The girl peered out at the looming cliffs that encircled the hidden cove. Everything in view was smothered in a thin, dirty fog. It was a depressing sight.

"Ugly," the girl agreed, and then she gave Tye a questioning look. "Do you really believe there's a valkar here?"

That was something Tye had been considering for a while, ever since he'd received his orders. The Watch Commander of Fell's Hollow had sent an urgent message to the Brotherhood. He suspected a valkar, or some other breed of shadowspawn, was loose in the city. Men and women were disappearing. Some were found days later, dead and drained of blood, with strange circular marks on their faces. The Watch Commander had his hands full preparing for Nyland's eventual assault. He could spare no watchmen to track down the creature, whatever it was. He needed a shadowhunter.

Was it truly a valkar that haunted the streets of Fell's Hollow? Tye was doubtful. No valkar had been seen for hundreds of years. But he had a sense something was here. He could feel it in his bones.

Tye put a hand beneath his tunic and pulled out a thick chain from which hung a chunk of black flamite, a shiny stone mined near the northern border of Cabyll. It was carved in the shape of a skull that lacked a lower jaw. From its upper jaw, two overlong fangs thrust down like daggers. It was one of the twelve velistones, a magical amulet given to him by the Brotherhood on the day he'd become a shadowhunter.

He felt the stone grow suddenly warm in his hand. There were shadowspawn nearby. A twinge of anger sparked within him as he absently adjusted his eye patch. When he'd been about Onya's age, a band of ukun had trapped him and his father in a narrow pass that cut through the highlands of Sindella. They were returning home, ponies laden with tradegoods they'd acquired in Craston. The ukun had set upon them at once. The misshapen, man-like beasts murdered his father and quickly turned to torturing Tye. One ukun had just spitted Tye's eye on the tip of its claw, after another had run a rusty dagger down the side of his face, when a shadowhunter appeared. He had been working in the area and had heard Tye's screams. He feathered the ukun with black-fletched arrows, killing most of them. A few escaped into the mountains. The shadowhunter bound Tye's wounds, buried his father, and brought Tye back to Ithicar, where things went from bad to unbearable.

When Tye had arrived home, his betrothed, unable to stomach the sight of his ravaged face, broke off their engagement. Maimed and devastated, Tye had tried to carry on, but his efforts were futile. The life he had dreamed of for so long was destroyed. There would be no love for him. No wife. No children. No family. So he gave up his dream and joined the Brotherhood. He became a shadowhunter, dedicating the remainder of his life to the destruction of shadowspawn in all their guises: ukun, ghaolin, wroths, merks, skols. And now a valkar, the deadliest of all the shadowspawn, might be within his grasp. The possibility, slim as it was, sent an itch of worry down his back.

"Well?" Onya asked. "Are there any close?"

Tye ripped himself from the nightmare of his past and stuffed the amulet back into his tunic. It had been a long time since he'd dwelled on those memories.

"Yes," he told her. "Within the city, I suspect."

Two lanky sailors lumbered over and threw down a long wooden plank at a gap in the rail. It clunked onto the Stonewharf, startling the old gull on the bowsprit. The gull squawked irritably and took to flight. A single scraggly feather floated in the air behind it.

Tye flipped a coinpurse to one of the sailors. "For you and the rest of the men. Not many would have risked running into Felgus's war fleet." The two smiled, and Tye continued. "We won't be long, a few days at most. Be ready to sail when we return."

The sailors nodded and headed off to other tasks. They were part of a small, captainless crew that ran a fast-running schooner half-owned by the Brotherhood, which was the only reason Tye had secured passage. There had been no other ships willing to take him and the girl to Fell's Hollow. Not with war on the wind.

Tye put a hand on Onya's shoulder. "Let's get

this over with," he said, and then made his way down the plank and off the ship. His apprentice followed.

Tye's boot no sooner hit the Stonewharf when he spotted two men standing a short distance off. They were staring at him. The first had the look of a common sellsword. He was tall, lean, muscular. His tawny hair was tied back with a strip of leather, and he wore a black oilcloth cloak. A well-used longsword hung in a battered scabbard at his side. The second man was clearly a city watchman, grim-looking, with gray and black hair that fell freely to his shoulders. The red and black tabard that covered most of his chainmail bore the gargoyle of Fell's Hollow embroidered across the chest. A gold cord was at his shoulder. Tye figured him to be the Watch Commander.

The men approached, and the watchman, after peeling off his gloves, offered his hand. "I'm Rhandellar Larron," he said gruffly. "I presume you're the shadowhunter?"

With no other ships entering or leaving the harbor, Tye mused, it must not have been too hard for the Watch Commander to guess his identity. "I am," Tye said, shaking Larron's hand. "And this is my apprentice," he added.

Larron nodded at Onya and then gestured to the man beside him. "This is Ander Ellystun, a local swordsman I've hired to escort you around the city."

The sellsword said nothing, his expression as stony as the block under Tye's feet.

"I want these killings to stop," Larron said. "Find whatever is responsible. Find it and slay it. And do it quickly. Now if you'll excuse me, I have pressing business." With that, the Commander spun on his heel and marched a short ways down the Stonewharf to where a group of watchmen were gathered. They were positioning what appeared to be several crates of arrows around a black-stained bucket. Tye knew enough about war to know the bucket was full of pitch. The watchmen were preparing for a last stand against Felgus and his warships. There were other groups of watchmen further down the Stonewharf setting up similar stations. A brave idea, but Tye doubted flaming arrows would do them much good.

He turned to the sellsword, who stepped to the side and made a somewhat mocking sweep with his arm. "After you," the man said.

*

Tye studied the road before him. It was narrow and steep and wound sharply up the rocky slope, skirting around massive stone outcroppings, running over chunks of ledge, and weaving through clusters of houses that clung to the slope like barnacles. The road was drenched in fog, fog that had gone from whitish-gray to charcoal to near-black since the sun had set over an hour ago.

The sellsword pointed to a stone marker at the side of the road. "Southside ends here. Up there is the Crags, which runs all the way to the foot of the cliffs. Not a lot of folk live up there. Just a fistful of miners and their families. And those who can't afford to live anywhere else."

Tye took out the velistone. The skull grew warm in his hand, warmer than it had been when they'd entered Southside. And twice as warm as it had been in Rogueswarde. They were getting closer.

"Which way?" Onya asked.

"Up," Tye answered, and the three began the hike, the sellsword leading the way.

They went in silence, trudging up the winding road. The evening grew darker and darker still. There were no streetlamps about, no shards of firelight escaping from open windows. And with the fog, there was no moon and no stars. But Tye was accustomed to the dark. He had spent years strengthening his night vision. And Onya's eyes were young and sharp. Tye half expected the sellsword to baulk, or to suggest they turn back for a lantern, but the tawny-haired man continued on ahead, a tall shadow unhindered by the lack of light. After a while they came to a rusty iron gate set into a low wall of crumbling stone near the side of the road. The wall encircled what appeared to be an old fortress or keep.

"Stop here," Tye told them.

The sellsword grunted and ground to a halt.

Onya drew up beside Tye. The girl opened the front of her cloak and loosened her sword in its scabbard. Tye grinned. That had been one of the first lessons he had taught the girl. At times steel can stick to leather. If it sticks at the wrong time, you're a dead man. Or a dead girl.

"Is it close?" his apprentice asked.

Tye thought he caught an edge to the girl's voice, but her face revealed no hint of fear. He checked the amulet. "Closer. But not here. Further up, I think."

The sellsword glanced back at Tye and scowled. "What sorcery is that?"

"It's not sorcery," Onya informed him in a clearly offended tone.

"Smells like sorcery to me," the sellsword replied. "Makes the hair on my arms stand up."

"It isn't—" Onya began, but Tye interrupted.

"This amulet was crafted ages ago," he told the sellsword. "By Cabyllian sorcerers during the War of Shadows. It's called a velistone, and I can use it to detect the presence of shadowspawn. It grows warm when there's one nearby. The closer the shadowspawn, the warmer it gets. There are twelve velistones known to exist, which is why there are only twelve shadowhunters at any one time. Never more, never less. So yes, in a sense this is sorcery. But then again, it's not. I myself am not a sorcerer. I do not possess the Gift."

The sellsword grumbled something under his breath, turned, and headed up the narrow road.

Tye shook his head. Sellswords were a suspicious lot. As most men were, he had discovered over the years. He tucked away the amulet and followed him, Onya trudging quietly along at his side.

They continued on, picking their way further up into the Crags, until the girl slowed to a halt.

"What is it?" Tye asked her.

Onya hesitated and then said, "Shouldn't we wait until daylight?"

"Why?"

"Because a valkar can't survive in the sun. They burst into flames. Everyone knows that."

Tye sighed. "First, valkar don't burst into flames. That's a myth. Their skin was so sensitive, it would cook in the sun, like a sunburn you or I might get, only a thousand times worse. Second, I seriously doubt we're dealing with a valkar. It's probably an ukun. Or a small band of skols. Or maybe it's a wroth that's slithered out of some cave. There are cliffs nearby. It stands to reason there're a lot of caves around here as well."

Onya's brow furrowed. "But—"

"We aren't going to wait for morning," he told her. "We do, and the shadowspawn could strike again, take another innocent life during the night. As a shadowhunter, you need to learn when to be cautious and when to be bold."

The girl fell silent, and Tye turned to his own thoughts as they hiked up the winding road. In truth, he wasn't sure what was waiting for them.

If it was a valkar, then caution would be the better choice. But there were no valkar left. Shadowhunters had killed them off ages ago. This was most likely some lesser shadowspawn, and he hadn't met one yet that he couldn't send to the Abyss with a stroke of his blade.

Tye adjusted his eyepatch and then loosened his sword in its scabbard. Bold or cautious, he wasn't stupid. He'd be ready when the time came, whatever it turned out to be.

*

The road, which had narrowed to the width of a cart path, snaked up to a group of shacks that huddled together at the foot of the cliff. From there it curved east, slid past a great black crack in the cliff face, and ended at a small house that sat alone in the darker shadows. There was no one about.

"That's the Pass," whispered the sellsword, pointing at the crack. "Where the miners work. It's a steep ravine that twists its way out of the cove to the top of bluffs."

The three were crouched behind a large boulder. Tye pulled out the amulet once again. It was hot to the touch. A shadowspawn was close. Very close. "It's in the house," Tye told them, keeping his voice as low as possible.

"Are you sure?" Onya breathed. "Wouldn't a shadowspawn prefer to nest somewhere in the ravine?"

"You would think so," Tye agreed.

The sellsword unsheathed his sword. "Then let's go."

Tye put a hand on the man's arm. "Wait. We need a plan. We can't just barge in through the front door."

"Why not?" the sellsword asked.

Onya slipped out her sword and held it across her knees.

"Listen, Ansen—" Tye began, but the sellsword cut him off.

"Ryke's balls, the name's Ander," the sellsword spat. "And I'm not going to waste time with talk. I told that bastard Larron this was the last job I'm doing for him. I'm a sellsword, not a watchman. I mean to be done with this, and with him, right now." The man stood and stalked toward the house.

"Shite," Tye muttered. He stripped the bow and quiver from his back, dropped them to the ground, and drew his sword. He looked over at Onya. "Swords only, girl. Seems we're doing this the bold way."

The two caught up with the sellsword just as he reached the house, which now appeared little more than a shack itself. It had a second floor with a single, shuttered window beneath its peak. The first floor boasted more windows and more shutters, many of which hung broken on their hinges. The front door consisted of a series of weathered oak slats bound together by strips of iron. Except for its brass handle and lock plate, it looked poorly constructed.

The sellsword gripped the handle and pushed. The door didn't budge. He tried again. Nothing. He took a few steps back and launched himself at the door. His shoulder slammed into the wood. Brasswork twisted and oak slats snapped. The door broke open and the sellsword stumbled into the house.

Tye charged in after him. The interior was nearly black as pitch, though he could make out several shadowy shapes in the room. There was a table and a couple of chairs in the center. Beyond them, a dark doorway opened to another room. To the left, a staircase led up to what had to be an attic of sorts.

The sellsword hit the stairs at a run. Onya stormed into the house behind Tye, her sword poised for a thrust.

"Stay here," Tye ordered, and then he rushed around the table to the doorway. He peered through it into the darkness beyond, where he found a smaller room. Shelves lined the walls. What might have been a washbasin was sitting in the corner. Was it a privy? A pantry? It didn't matter. The room was empty.

A loud shout erupted from the attic. There came a terrible crash, and then a high-pitched scream that seemed to go on forever, until it ended in a low, bubbly gurgle. Tye bolted toward the stairs where Onya was already halfway to the top.

"Wait!" Tye barked. The girl either didn't hear his command, or she deliberately ignored it. Onya reached the top and disappeared. "Shite!" Tye cursed. The girl was going to get herself killed.

He flew up the stairs taking two at a time and burst into the attic right on Onya's boot heels. They came into a bedroom. There was a window in one wall. A narrow bed was pushed against another wall next to a desk, upon which sat a stack of parchment, quills, and a single fluttering candle. On the floor beside the desk lay the sellsword. Ander's throat had been torn open, and a pool of black blood was forming around his head.

"No!" Onya howled. The girl raised her sword and plunged across the room to where a man-shaped thing stood before another doorway. The thing was naked save for a strip of cloth hanging over its loins. Its skin was white as death, and bat-like wings stuck up over its shoulders. A half-dozen arm-thick tentacles sprouted from its bare chest, squirming and writhing like a batch of seven-foot snakes.

Shock slammed into Tye. It *was* a valkar! Before Tye could move, the thing struck. Tentacles lashed and Onya was suddenly flying through the air. She hit the wall with a crunch. The girl groaned, collapsed to the floor, and was still.

Tye reeled. A valkar! Ryke save him, but he

never thought it possible. And his doubt had just cost the sellsword his life. And Onya's. And, he realized, most likely his own.

His anger burned hotly as he faced the thing. It didn't move. It just stood there, a pale abomination, waiting to see what he would do, as a cat might watch a cornered mouse. He had heard that valkars were faster than humans. And now he'd seen it for himself. It was fast. Too fast. It would strike him dead long before his sword ever hit home. But he had no choice.

Tye lunged toward the valkar and then, in a change of tactic, switched his thrust to a parry in expectation of the thing's attack. As his sword rose, there was a flash of white. He felt something slam into his blade.

The valkar shrieked and staggered back. Hot blood splattered Tye in the face as a piece of pale tentacle hit the floor. It had a ring of serrated discs on its end, which pulsed and quivered. In the center of the discs, a shard of razor-sharp bone shivered and then slipped gruesomely back into a fold of flesh.

Tye looked up just in time to see another flash of white. This time the barrage of tentacles snatched hold of him. They wrapped around him like a sailor's mooring line and lifted him off his feet. Then he too was hurtling across the room.

Wood splintered as he crashed into the desk. Pain exploded in the small of his back. Candle, parchment, ink, quills, it all went scattering across the floor. He heard his sword clang and thunk down the staircase as he came to rest face down on the floor next to the sellsword's body. The room grew darker as the candle sputtered and died.

The agony in Tye's back shot down his legs and straight to his feet, which started to go numb. He heard the valkar slither closer. And then he was seized again. Tentacles roped around his legs and then up his torso, pinning his arms to his side. Fiery pain flared down his back and he screamed. He was flipped over, and there was the valkar's face, inches from his own. The thing's eyes burned red with hate. Its breath stank of rotted meat, and its fangs were as white as stars.

Without thought, Tye summoned every bit of strength he had. He gave a great twist, and nearly passed out from the pain that jetted down his legs. But he held on to consciousness. The sudden move was enough to startle the valkar. Tye felt its tentacles loosen for a brief heartbeat, and he yanked an arm free. He snatched the velistone from beneath his tunic, snapped it from its chain, and drove its fangs into the valkar's eye.

The thing screeched and jerked away, releasing its hold of Tye. It raised a hand to its face and it came away smeared in blood. Even in the gloom, Tye could see its eye was a pulpy ruin. The thing seethed and drew back its lips in a fang-filled snarl.

"Your torment will last for ages," it said in a

sibilant voice. It spoke the words in Bartertongue, the common trading language used across the realms. The dialect was strange, though, and sounded vile on its inhuman tongue.

"I will feed upon you the old way," the valkar promised. "With nothing but by my teeth. And you will watch me do it, each and every time."

The thing took a step toward Tye, when there came a sound of splintering wood from below. Then a deep voice bellowed up the staircase.

"Torr, you old bastard! Your door's broke open!"

"You finally home?" came another voice.

The valkar flinched and shot a one-eyed glance toward the staircase. A flickering yellow light leaked into the attic from below. The thing hissed wildly, then it turned, bolted the length of the room, and crashed through the window.

*

Tye ignored the pain pulsing in his back as he knelt next to Onya. He put the velistone in a pocket of his cloak and pressed a finger to the girl's neck. There was a heartbeat, strong as ever.

Onya groaned and opened her eyes. "What happened?" she asked.

Tye blew out a breath of relief. "You foolish girl! What were you thinking?"

Before she could muster a reply, boots thundered up the staircase and two dirt-stained men in leather smocks, miners by the looks of them, stormed into the attic. The first was short and nearly bald and held a flaming torch in one hand. The second was the fattest man Tye had ever seen, with a belly the size of an ale barrel and arms as thick as tree trunks. He held a pickaxe before him in two meaty hands.

"You ain't Torr," the fat miner said.

Tye stood, stifling a moan. "Clearly."

"Who are you?" the bald one demanded. "And what in the Abyss is going on? What was that noise we just—?" The man's eyes shot wide. "Is that bloke dead?"

Tye skirted around the bed and limped over to where the sellsword lay on the floor. Ander stared blindly up at the rafters. Blood still oozed from the gaping hole in his throat. Tye bent down and his back flared with agony. He closed the sellsword's eyes.

Onya grunted and got up from the floor. "He's a shadowhunter," she told the miners, pointing at Tye. "And I'm his apprentice."

"A shadowhunter?" the fat man said, disbelief clear in his voice. "Truly?"

Tye nodded. "A valkar has been nesting in this house. We surprised it, and it killed our companion here. It nearly killed the girl. And me. I managed to stab it in the eye right before you fellows showed up." He gestured at the shattered window. "When it heard your voices it blasted out of here."

The fat man gasped and lowered his pickaxe.

The bald one shook his head. "Ryke's beard, it can't be. A valkar? Thought you shadowhunters killed them all."

"I thought so, too," Tye said.

"Torr's dead, then," the fat man muttered. "We ain't seen him in weeks. The valkar must have got him, poor bastard." He stared at Tye for a moment. "Looks like he got a bit of you, too."

Tye put a hand to the jagged hole where his eye had once been. His patch was gone, torn off in the scuffle. He could feel the valkar's blood still wet on his cheek, and he wiped it away.

Onya grunted. "Tye, you need to see this," she said. The girl had wandered to the doorway at the back of the room and was now staring through it, her nose wrinkled in an expression of unmistakable disgust.

Tye shuffled over. The pain in his back, thankfully, was starting to let up, and his feet were growing less numb. The two miners tromped after him.

The light from the bald man's torch fluttered through the doorway, revealing a large closet crammed with clutter. Against the back wall squatted several old barrels stuffed with scraps of clothing. A flock of mismatched boots were scattered across the floor. A moth-eaten blanket lay in a heap in the corner. And from the slanted rafters hung four strange, cocoon-like objects. They were slimy, bulbous, and reached near to the floor. And they were disturbingly man-shaped.

Tye knew exactly what they were. He wrenched a dagger out of a thigh-sheath. "Give me a hand," he ordered.

One by one, Tye cut down the cocoons, and the miners passed them to Onya, who laid them on the floor near the bed. Then Tye picked one at random and knelt beside it. Carefully, he sliced the tip of his dagger into the viscous material. He set the dagger aside, stuck his fingers into the slit, and ripped open the cocoon.

Inside was a young man.

The bald miner staggered into a corner and vomited. Onya got down next to Tye and the two of them tore away the rest of the cocoon.

The young man wasn't much older than Onya. He was garbed in a seaman's tunic and breeches and his eyes were closed. Brown hair matted his forehead. His skin was smooth and unmarked, save for a ring of red wounds that circled his face. He let out a soft whimper and opened his eyes.

"Ryke's beard!" the fat miner bellowed. He clapped a hand on Tye's shoulder. "He's alive!"

Tye leaned closer to the young sailor. "What's your name, son?" he asked.

"Ch-Ch-Chibb." The words were barely a whisper.

Tye smiled. "You're going to be fine, Chibb." He glanced over at Onya. "Fetch the Watch."

The girl nodded.

The bald miner stumbled over, wiping his chin

on his sleeve. "I'm going with her," he said.

*

Tye watched as the two men he had just freed began to regain consciousness. Each bore the same circle of wounds around the face. The first appeared to be a common peasant, dressed in a blood-stained tunic, tattered cloak, and a pair of torn, roughspun breeches. The other was a tiny, wrinkled, shell of a man who'd seen his share of summers. The huge miner had immediately identified him as Torr, the owner of the house.

The two men moaned and twitched on the floor as the young sailor, who was floundering about the room, rubbed furiously at his arms and legs. "It stings," he complained.

Tye knelt next to the last cocoon. "It'll pass," he assured him. "Or at least I think it will."

The fat miner sat down on the edge of the bed, and it sagged under his tremendous weight. He pointed a thick, shaking finger. "What are they?" he asked.

Tye took up his dagger and cut into the cocoon. "The valkar would store humans in their hives, for when they couldn't find fresh blood," he explained, setting the dagger on the floor. "They would hang them in these cocoons, which would keep them paralyzed. And somehow strangely preserved. There are those in the Brotherhood who believe an entire hive could feed on a single man for a hundred years, maybe more."

A look of revulsion crawled across the fat man's face, and he fell silent. Behind him, the young sailor continued to rub the feeling back into his limbs.

Tye turned to the last cocoon and went to work, tearing away the slimy matter piece by piece. Before long he found himself staring down at a woman.

She was a tad younger than Tye, in a tan tunic and black breeches that were modest but well-made. Her hair was a mass of auburn curls, and her cheekbones were high and smooth. And she was beautiful. Desperately beautiful, Tye thought, despite the angry, red wounds that ringed her face. Tye felt his heartbeat quicken, but then he remembered Ithicar. He remembered what he'd lost. What he had given up. His hand wandered to his ruined face. He was ugly, maimed, no longer a complete man. That life, that dream, was over. He was a shadowhunter now, nothing more.

The woman's eyes snapped open. They were dark green and filled with fear. "Who are you?" she murmured, her voice shaky and slurred.

"The creature's fled," Tye told her. "You're safe."

The woman rolled onto her side and tried to crawl away from Tye, but her arms wobbled like jelly, and she sprawled back to the floor. The valkar must have captured the woman recently, for it seemed the full effect of the cocoon's paralysis had not yet taken hold of her. Either that, or she was somehow able to recover faster than the others.

She tried to move again, and this time managed to squirm her way over to the two other victims who lay nearby, trembling and groaning as they fought their way to consciousness. The woman tugged at the front of her tunic, muttered something softly, and then stared straight at the ragged-looking peasant. She began rifling through his tattered clothes. Her hands jittered awkwardly as they fumbled at his cloak. She took a small wooden box from a pocket and tossed it aside. Then, with a cry, she grabbed the peasant's dirty hand and slid from his thumb a thick, golden ring.

Tye stared at the woman in amazement.

She scurried away from the peasant, leaned back against the wall, and closed her eyes. Her head drooped as if she were completely exhausted from the effort. In her struggle, a fine silver necklace had come free of her tunic. From it hung a shard of black flamite carved into the shape of a budding rose.

For the second time that night, Tye was slammed with shock.

*

"Your pickaxe," Tye hissed at the huge miner. "Now."

The miner raised a brow, but said nothing. He lifted his enormous bulk off the bed, which creaked in protest, and then handed him the axe. Tye moved to the woman and in one quick motion snatched the rose from her breast. He gave it a fierce yank and the silver chain snapped.

The woman's eyes shot open. She jerked herself to her feet and stumbled after Tye, hands outstretched, reaching for the necklace that now dangled from his fist.

"Give it to me!" she screamed.

Tye dropped the necklace to the floor. He stepped back, lifted the pickaxe, and brought it crashing down on the center of the black rose. There was a loud crack and a flash of red light. The rose shattered, and a thick, sulfurous odor slithered up from the broken shards.

Abruptly, the woman collapsed to her knees. She lowered her head and began to weep.

"What in the Abyss did you do that for?" the fat miner boomed.

Before Tye could answer there came a noise from below. Footfalls clomped hurriedly across the floor and then someone tromped up the stairs. "There were no watchmen in the Crags," Onya said as she stalked into the bedroom.

The fat miner scoffed. "Could have told you that." He looked behind her to the staircase. "Where's—?"

"Your friend went down to Southside to find a patrol," the girl informed him. "He should be back soon."

The fat man nodded and sat back down on the bed. Beside him on the floor, Torr and the peasant were still unconscious, shaking and moaning. The young sailor had slumped down against the far wall and was now trying to work the feeling back into his feet.

Tye turned to the woman, who was wiping her tears on her sleeve. He bent down and helped her to her feet. Abruptly, the woman threw the golden ring she'd taken from the peasant, and it smacked against the far wall.

"Never again," she said.

She looked at Tye and then threw her arms around him. As she squeezed him tight, he could feel her trembling. He felt his own heartbeat quicken, and again, his thoughts turned to Ithicar. Tye eased himself from her embrace.

"You saved me twice," the woman whispered.

Tye shook his head. "It was nothing."

The woman put a hand to Tye's face. It was soft and warm. She stared at him for a long moment, her green eyes brimming with tears. "It is everything," she said. Her fingers brushed against the ragged scar on his cheek.

Tye jerked his head away and the woman let her hand fall. She gave him a questioning look, and then her eyes widened. She laughed. "I see worse every time I walk through the city. Fell's Hollow is full of people who bear terrible scars. Ugly people, on the outside and on the inside."

The woman reached up and placed her hand back on Tye's cheek. "You are the most beautiful man I have ever met."

A surge of warmth coursed through Tye. It was something he hadn't felt in ages. He wanted to stand there forever, savoring it, but instead he forced himself to ignore the woman's touch. Those days, those dreams, were over.

"What next?" Onya asked.

Tye gently removed the woman's hand and turned to his apprentice. "The valkar's wounded," he told her. He pulled the velistone from his pocket. The skull was still warm, but its warmth was fading. "Find my sword. And grab our bows. We're going after it."

He turned to the fat miner.

"You stay with these people until the Watch arrives," he ordered.

*

The torch was nearly spent. Tye had dug it out of a miner's shack near the entrance to the Pass, and now the end of it was not much more than a shimmering hunk of ash. Its red glow spilled onto the ground before them. A path, old and worn and nearly indiscernible, headed straight through the tall grass.

Tye took a moment to catch his breath. He and Onya had struggled for hours to follow the valkar's trail. They had entered the crack in the cliff face and had clawed their way through the ravine, over rock and ledge and up steep stony inclines until they had finally made it out of the hidden cove to the top of the surrounding bluff. The trek had been hard on them, and their hands and knees were bloody and scraped. To the east the sky was beginning to lighten, and the smell of the sea hung heavy in the predawn air.

Tye rechecked the velistone. It was warm. Very warm. He held out the dying torch and gestured to the path. "This way," he said.

Onya followed close behind.

"What did you do to that woman?" his apprentice asked after they'd gone on for a while.

Tye's thoughts filled with a sudden vision of auburn curls and green eyes. Tempted as he was to dwell on the woman's beauty, he shut out the memory and then quickened his pace. "She was being controlled by someone against her will. Someone who must have sent her to find that ring," he said.

A quizzical expression came over the girl. "Controlled? How?" she asked.

Tye stopped and took out the velistone. The fanged skull gleamed black in the torch's ruddy glow. "This is not the only kind of amulet that the sorcerers of Cabyll crafted," he told her. "That woman was wearing a patristone. I recognized it the moment I saw it. A rose carved in flamite. It was once a common amulet, used by husbands to enslave their wives to their will. Unfortunately many of them are still around, though mostly in the Midlands." Tye shook his head. "Some say the patristone granted certain powers, powers that could be used to aid the women in serving their masters." He pocketed the velistone. "She was a slave, Onya."

"A slave?" The girl's voice dripped with disgust.

Tye shrugged. "Some things don't change. There will always be evil in the world."

Onya spat in disgust, and the two continued on in silence. The path skirted along the edge of the bluff. Despite the fog, Tye could make out a few lights sparkling in the city below. He wished it was a clear summer's day, wished he could see the city down there in the hidden cove, see the buildings in all their myriad shapes and sizes, the hills, the winding roads, the blue waters of the harbor and the docks and structures that ran out along its surface to where their ship waited at the wharf. He suspected the view would be nothing short of breathtaking.

Eventually the tall grass died out, and soon the torch's glow fell on nothing but bare dirt and rock. Onya tapped Tye's shoulder and they halted. "Look," she said.

It took a moment for Tye to see it. In the predawn darkness a hundred paces ahead loomed a large, tower-like shape. It had to be sixty, maybe seventy feet tall. Its peak was ragged and sharp, like the end of a spear that had been snapped in two. Huge blocks of shattered stone lay scattered about its base. Tye slipped the velistone from his pocket. It felt like it was on fire.

"It's here," he said.

Onya gazed out toward the east. "Daybreak is only an hour off. We should wait, force the valkar into the open. I know it won't burst into flames, but at least it'll be weaker."

Tye shook his head. "The sunlight might slow it down, or it might not. The fog is thick, maybe thick enough to protect it. I know I wounded the thing. Badly. It has to be in a lot of pain. If we attack it now, we're sure to have the advantage."

Onya shrugged and drew her sword. "Then let's go."

Tye buried the end of the torch in the dirt, then he unslung the bow from his back and nocked an arrow.

"Follow me," he told her.

*

The two crept closer, picking their way carefully through the broken rubble. The tower was about forty feet in diameter, tapering slightly as it jagged up into the night. Its rough-cut stones were weathered smooth by years of wind and rain, and patches of thick green moss had grown half way up one side. On the other side, an open doorway faced the bluff.

"Ready?" Tye whispered.

Onya gave him a nod. There was no fear in the girl's eyes, and Tye wondered how that could be possible. She had seen what the valkar was capable of. Indeed the thing had nearly killed her only a few hours ago. It was all he could do to settle his own nerves.

Tye gritted his teeth and slipped through the doorway. He found himself in a large, open room. There was no one there but the shadows. Shards of driftwood lay about a dirt floor. In the center sat a cold firepit, and high overhead stretched a ceiling of blackened timbers that had withstood the crush of time. A stone stair wound up the wall to an opening in the ceiling.

Tye eased the velistone from his pocket. It burned hotly in his hand. He gestured to Onya, and the two made their way slowly up the stair.

They came into another room similar to the one below. It was high-ceilinged and empty. The stair continued on, circling up the wall to another opening. Through it, Tye could make out the dark gray of the sky. This was it, he thought. One more climb and they'd reach the top of the tower. Where the valkar was waiting.

As the two circled up the stair, Tye felt his heartbeat quicken. His fingers tightened around his bow. The thing had to be up there. Perhaps they could surprise it, kill it before it knew what was happening. Or perhaps it had spotted them as they had approached, and it was lying in wait just beyond the opening.

He turned and put his mouth to Onya's ear. "Remember," he breathed. "Divide and conquer.

It will fear the arrow more than the sword. When it comes at me, you'll have one chance to attack it from behind. Make it quick, and make it count."

Onya nodded. Once more Tye took a moment to calm himself, and then he rushed up the last few stairs and out onto the top of the tower.

He was hit by a sudden blast of sea air that whipped his cloak behind him. Above, the sky stretched gray-black from horizon to horizon. He bent his bow and gazed down the arrowshaft, running his sight from right to left along the broken wall of the tower. The wall rose and fell, a ragged line as high as ten feet in places, as low as two in others. And there was the valkar. It sat perched on a section of wall like a giant white gull, wings outstretched, tentacles dangling from its chest like a tangle of vipers. One eye gleamed red in the dark. The other was a bloody splotch of shadow.

"Spread out," Tye commanded as he sidestepped to the left. Onya veered to the right, sword at the ready.

The valkar hissed and launched itself from the wall. It soared straight at Tye and then banked sharply toward Onya. The girl, caught in midstride, hesitated. The thing snatched her in its tentacles and battered her like a dirty dishrag against the wall. There was a crack and a cry, and Onya slumped to the floor.

Tye loosed his arrow. It flashed across the tower and sank into the valkar's back. The thing bellowed in pain and spun around to face him. Tye plucked another arrow from his quiver. The valkar charged, rage seared into its white face. In a single motion Tye nocked, drew, and released. The arrow struck the thing in the shoulder but did nothing to slow it down. It crashed into him.

Tye's bow flew from his hand, and the two slammed onto the floor. The thing landed on top of him, its weight knocking the wind from Tye's lungs. It grabbed his head in both hands and forced his chin back. Then it bared its teeth in a violent scowl and buried its face into his neck.

Tye shrieked as he felt the valkar's fangs pierce his throat. He tried to move, tried to twist free, but the thing held him fast. He felt a tentacle wind up each of his arms and then, roughly, the thing pinned his arms to the floor. Two more tentacles circled around his legs. He was trapped. Helpless. Tye howled.

And the thing fed. He could hear it, lapping, slurping, groaning in pleasure. Tye's neck burned fiercely, and then, bit by bit, he felt a cold numbness begin to settle over him. Black spots swam across his vision.

"Bastard!"

The valkar lifted its face from its feast, and its fangs were smeared in blood. There came a sound of steel thunking into flesh and bone. The valkar cried out, and at once its tentacles loosened their grip on Tye. There came another thunk, and a bat-like wing tumbled to the tower floor. Blood arched through the air.

The valkar let go of Tye and scurried away on all fours. Then it turned and stood. Its tentacles snapped and twitched before it. A single wing stretched from its back. Black blood ran in streams down its white skin.

"Humans," it hissed. "I with bathe in your entrails."

Tye forced himself to his feet. His legs trembled. Beside him stood Onya, her blood-drenched blade gripped in both hands, a look of fierce determination blazing in her eyes. He yanked his sword from its scabbard. The blade was heavy. Too heavy. It felt like it was made of stone. His hands shook. The valkar had weakened him. He would never defeat it now. But maybe he could save the girl, give her a chance to flee. "Onya," he said. "Run."

The girl raised her sword over her head and raced toward the valkar.

"No!" Tye cried.

The valkar drew back its tentacles, preparing to strike. Onya took three strides and hurled her sword at the thing. Shock crossed the valkar's face, but it recovered quickly. Tentacles flashed and the girl's blade went flying over the wall and into the night. But Onya didn't stop. She continued on, barreling straight at the thing. The valkar, realizing its mistake, tried to yank back its tentacles for another strike, but it was too late.

His apprentice slammed into it.

The thing staggered backward, and Onya kept going. Like a pit-wrestler, she wrapped her arms around it and drove it back, back, back, until they collided against a low section of wall.

The valkar teetered.

Onya heaved. She lifted the thing from its feet, gave a final surge, and the two tumbled over the wall. There was a long cry, and then nothing.

*

Tye stumbled out of the tower. Sorrow burned in his stomach as he staggered through the rubble. The girl had sacrificed herself, had given her life to slay the valkar. Who knows how many innocent victims she had just saved, how many people would now live because of her courage? A wave of guilt washed over Tye. He was the shadowhunter. It should have been him that had died.

He clambered over a section of broken stone, and there, not three paces away, was Onya. The girl was lying still, face down in a patch of dirt. Beside her, bent backwards over a chunk of jagged rock, was the valkar. Its tentacles were splayed in all directions, limp and motionless. Its pale body was twisted and ruined, its head an unrecognizable stew of brain and bone.

There came a moan, and his apprentice rolled onto her back.

"Onya!" Tye lurched to her side. "I thought you were dead," he gasped.

"Me too," she said with a grunt.

"How did you—?"

"I forced it beneath me as we fell. Landed right on top of the thing. Suppose that saved my life, but I think my leg's broken."

Tye was thunderstruck. Even as the girl was plummeting to her death, she'd kept her courage. She had ignored unimaginable fear and pain, pushed it all aside to do what had to be done. Tye doubted he could have done the same.

Onya Oker was a true shadowhunter.

Tye took out the velistone. The black skull was cool to the touch. He slipped it into Onya's pocket. "It's yours now," he told her.

The girl looked shocked. "Mine?"

Tye grinned. "You've earned it. You're already a better shadowhunter than I ever was."

Onya shook her head. "That's not true. Besides, you have to keep it. There are only twelve. You can't be a shadowhunter without one."

Tye placed a hand on her shoulder. "The velistone is yours, Onya. It's your destiny. Of that I have no doubt."

The girl frowned. "What about you? What will you do?"

Tye's thoughts turned to auburn curls and deep green eyes. This time he didn't push them away. He allowed himself a moment to dream, and he felt truly happy for the first time in a very long time.

"I think my destiny lies elsewhere," he told her at last. "It's time I learned to deal with my fear. And pain. It's time I learned to be bold in all things, not just in hunting shadowspawn."

Tye smiled.

"I'm staying here, Onya. In Fell's Hollow." He gave her shoulder a squeeze. "It's a beautiful city, don't you think?"

SCALES

"Injustice ever finds a way to balance."
Equipoise, *Act VII, Sc. 6*
—*Espare dae Kesh*

SHELVES UPON SHELVES were stuffed into the Sorsagorium. They were of varied construction and held objects of every conceivable sort. The newest, along the wall by the door, were tall and wide, built by the previous shopowner, and overflowed with trinkets of lesser value: a set of lockpicks from Alar, slightly worn boots, hats, miners' tools, a taffyl board carved out of a chunk of driftwood. Between the back windows ran a set of older, narrower shelves installed by a tin smith a half-century back. On

269

these were heaped items of greater worth: an assortment of steel and iron weapons, pieces of armor, Ukrian glassware, a Sindellan cittern with all but one of its strings. A mix of free-standing shelves were stacked back-to-back in the middle of the shop. They were staggered in height and sagged under the weight of old tomes and alchemical paraphernalia, scriveners' implements, several worn copies of the collected writings of Espare dae Kesh, each hand-bound in plum-red leather, and a thousand other oddities.

Over the years the objects on the shelves came and went. When one was sold, the empty space it left behind was soon filled by another, often of the same size and shape as the first, as if the shelves contained a magic about them that kept the Sorsagorium in a state of perpetually crammed equilibrium.

The shop's current owner, Rorham Nach, opened the doors to an antique curio that sat behind the front counter. It was the oldest item in the shop, an heirloom left behind by the original owner. On its glass shelves some of the shop's more exotic items were displayed: a gold armband from Kern, a spyglass, loose gemstones both cut and uncut, five Thalian blowguns lying on a black velvet cloth. Nach slid aside a solid brass balance he'd recently obtained from a Nyland trader and retrieved a crystal decanter from the bottom shelf.

He was shocked, and he needed a drink. Some

bastard had killed Ukko! How could that have happened? He poured a splash of amber-colored liquid into a glass and took a slug. The Molish fragrat burned his throat, and a welcome warmness spread through his belly. Nach set the glass on the counter and glared over at his wife.

The sight of her disgusted him. Her fat face, her wrinkled, pallid skin, her thinning, gray-streaked hair. The dress she wore made her look like a pig wrapped in silk. Though she'd been worth the bridal gift at the time, he'd had little use for her since. But he'd promised her father that he'd take care of her, and that was what he did. Fair was fair, after all.

"Go home, Yenga. I've business to attend to," he told her.

His wife's black eyes narrowed. "I need money," she complained, crossing her arms over her chest.

Nach scowled. "I've already given you your weekly allotment."

"I need more." Her voice was whiny. Sharp. Like a knife point jammed in his ear. "I've found a gorgeous silver bracelet at Jurrick's—"

Nach slammed a fist onto the counter. "Out! Or I'll have Sandar drag you back to the Heights by what's left of your hair."

Yenga shot a frightened glance at Sandar. Nach's bodyguard stood by the door, a mountain of corded muscle. He had cold gray eyes and a crooked nose that been broken more than once.

His greasy brown hair dropped straight to his shoulders. The big man gave her a smirk.

Yenga opened her mouth, then shut it suddenly. Her eyes narrowed even further as her gaze slid to the narrow staircase that led up to the second floor. "Of course," she said, sarcasm simmering in her voice. "Enjoy your whore, Rorham." She spun around and stormed out of the shop. A cluster of bells over the door jangled harshly.

Sandar cocked his head toward the staircase. "Can we talk?"

Normally Nach didn't like to discuss his other business ventures in the shop. Whores had ears, and he nearly always kept a whore or two in the small bedroom upstairs. He'd use them until he grew bored, then he'd get rid of them. But while they lived there, he needed to make sure they wouldn't talk, wouldn't repeat anything they might have accidently overheard. So he beat them. Regularly. Fear was a great persuader. Yet he could be kind as well. The ones that gave him particular pleasure he'd reward after their tears had dried. He'd offer some token, some favorite fancy. Cheap jewelry, snorts of opit, freshly cut lilacs, whatever they desired. But in the end he could never be sure they wouldn't sell him out to the Watch. And so he'd been forced to send quite a few to the bottom of the harbor.

"Yes," Nach told his bodyguard. "The slut hasn't moved back in yet. She's away on an errand." He moved from behind the counter and threw the bolt on the door, closing the shop for the evening. "Now, who in the Abyss killed Ukko?"

Sandar shrugged. "Nobody knows," he said. "Or nobody's saying."

Nach's anger surged. Whoever it was would pay. And pay dearly. No one crossed Rorham Nach. Ever. He now had a score to settle. But first he had to find someone to replace Ukko. Someone to keep the riff-raff, not to mention the Watch, out of his opit den on Buckler Street. Why did it have to be that one? he wondered. Why not the den in Oldtowne? Or the one in the Crags? Being in the center of Rogueswarde, where the Watch was less likely to bother customers looking for a fix, the Buckler Street den was his most profitable venture. And now it needed a new guardian. And fast. His revenge would have to wait.

"You want me to watch over it?" Sandar offered.

Nach considered that for a moment, but dismissed the idea with a wave of his hand. "No, I need you with me. I've made too many enemies in this city to walk around unprotected."

Sandar frowned. "Then what are we going to do?"

Nach walked back behind the counter. "Have you cleared the den?" he asked.

Sandar nodded. "We dragged out the last of

the dregs this morning."

"And the building's boarded up? No one can get in?" Nach didn't want to deal with squatters on top of everything else.

Sandar gave him another nod.

"Then get your cloak," Nach told him. "We're going out."

His bodyguard grabbed his sword belt from a hook by the door. "Where to?" he asked.

Nach returned the decanter to the curio and closed the cabinet.

"We're going to Fullers and Fangs," he announced.

*

A swarm of cityfolk were milling up and down the Run, their footfalls clomping on the dock planks, their chatter drifting into the fog-filled breeze that ran off the harbor. Many were dockhands, clerks, and other shopowners, heading back to their homes. Most of the establishments on the Run closed at sunset, except for the Hole, of course, and a couple of taverns and inns on the north end. Nach envied them. Their work day was ending. It seemed that, lately, his never did.

Over the bluff on the far side of the harbor, the sun had disappeared behind a gray haze. He hadn't seen the sun in weeks, not since the tempest had roared through the city leaving behind it an ocean of fog and mist. He could feel the dampness in his bones as he headed down the dock, Sandar striding beside him, quiet and brooding, eyes scanning the area for signs of danger. There were none, though Nach appreciated Sandar's diligence nonetheless. He had proven himself quite a capable companion over the years.

"Nach!" a deep voice bellowed behind him.

Sandar whipped around, his hand heading to his swordhilt. Nach turned to see a middle-aged man pushing toward him through the crowd. He wore the red and black tabard of a watchman, the gargoyle of Fell's Hollow embroidered on his chest. A gold commander's cord was at his shoulder. He had the look of someone who was not out for a pleasant stroll. His dark eyes were narrowed and held an angry gleam. His face was stony and his jaw was clenched, as were his fists. Nach recognized him immediately. "Commander Larron," he said. "How nice to see you."

Larron stuck a finger in his face. "You're going to hang for what you've done, Nach." He looked over at Sandar. "As will you."

Sandar stepped forward, and Nach put a hand on his bodyguard's massive shoulder. "There's no need for violence, Sandar. The man is simply doing his job. Even if he is mistaken about whatever crime he thinks we've committed. So tell me, Commander, what is it this time?"

Larron jabbed his finger into Nach's chest. "A friend of mine's daughter died in one of your dens."

"Dens?" Nach responded. He tried to make his voice sound calm, innocent.

"Don't play dumb with me, Nach," Larron spat. "I'm not in the mood. Your drugs are poisoning the city. Have you seen what opit does to a person? Or do you just sit in your shop while your thugs handle all the dirty work?"

"I—" Nach began, but Larron simply went on.

"Let me tell you what your poison does. It eats people alive, Nach. It consumes them, sucks every ounce of life from them, until they're nothing but skin and bones. And then they die. They die naked and alone, curled up in some cellar or back alley."

Nach gave him a forced smile. "I don't know what you're talking about, Commander. I do run several poorhouses about the city, but those are humble places where the homeless can find a bed and a bite to eat. My idea of giving something back, you might say."

Larron scoffed. "Your poorhouses are nothing more than a front for your drug business."

Sandar spat at Larron's feet. "We don't have to listen to this, boss." he said. "Let me—"

"Let you, what?" Larron challenged.

Sandar stepped toward Larron. "I'll kill you where you stand, watchman."

"Now, now, Sandar," Nach said, trying to calm the situation. Bloodshed was bad for business. "We've done nothing wrong. We don't need to threaten the Commander."

Sandar scowled, but didn't move.

"Are you arresting me, Commander?" Nach asked.

Larron stared at Sandar for several long, uncomfortable moments, then he turned to Nach. "No," he said. "At least, not yet. When I can prove what you two have been up to, I'll be back. And then you'll both answer to the Lord Mayor. And to the hangman." He pointed at Nach. "Mark my words. Good things sometimes come to the good, but bad always comes to the bad."

The Watch Commander turned, took a quick step, and collided straight into a petite, dark-haired woman who was making her way up the dock. "Pardon me," Larron apologized, bowing his head to the startled woman. He shot a final hate-filled glare back at Nach, and then disappeared into the crowd.

"That's quite—" the woman began, but Larron was already gone. She straightened her gray, ankle-length dress, offered a harrumph at Larron's back, and then continued on her way. There was something familiar about the woman, Nach thought. He could have sworn he'd heard that voice before.

"Someday, I'm gonna kill that guy," Sandar muttered.

"What?" Nach asked, returning his attention to the big man.

Sandar removed his hand from his swordhilt. "I said I'm going to kill him."

"Right," Nach agreed. "But first, we've got business to attend to."

*

Dusk was falling fast as Nach trudged through the mud of Buckler Street. It was a cramped road, hemmed in on both sides by tall buildings, and though it hadn't yet rained that day, the buildings had a bloated, waterlogged look about them. Their clapboards, porches, and shutters swelled with several weeks' worth of moisture.

"Have you weighed out the packets for tomorrow?" Nach asked Sandar, who was fiddling with the cowl of his cloak.

"Yeah," he confirmed. "I'll drop them off at the dens in the morning."

"Good." Sandar was efficient. Nach was growing fond of the man, at least as fond as he'd ever been of anyone.

They walked for a while in silence. Few people were out on this end of Buckler. It was the seedier end, the end where Nach made most of his money. His anger sparked as they passed an old, rundown building. If any paint had ever coated its sides, it was long gone now. The front steps were warped and rotted. Wide planks were nailed over its windows and across its open front doorway. The sight of the place infuriated him. He was losing money every day his den remained closed. He'd find the bastard who killed Ukko, he promised himself. And then he'd even the score. What was fair was fair, after all.

The two moved on. Up and down Buckler, the lamplighters were out, setting flame to wick. Further up the street, a throng of cityfolk teemed about. Many of them wore grim looks on their faces and greeted each other with nothing more than a wave or a nod as they passed into one establishment or another. They seemed nervous, and it was no wonder.

"Did you hear about Felgus?" Nach asked Sandar.

His bodyguard looked at him, then shook his head.

Nach smirked. "They say he's going to launch his fleet any day now."

Sandar let out a grunt. "That's good," the big man said. "Once this war is over, our ships can get back to business."

"Exactly," Nach agreed. "In fact, when Felgus has control of the city, I was thinking we should expand. They say he is much more forgiving to those in our line of work. Perhaps we should open a den in the Heights. Or in Southside."

Sandar pursed his lips as he mulled over the idea. "We would need more guardians," he pointed out.

That was true, Nach realized. Perhaps after he had found a replacement for Ukko, he'd start looking around for more. Which could take a while. Good men like Ukko and Sandar were hard to find.

They stopped at the corner of the Street of Seven Lamps where a crowd was swarming around the front of their destination. Fullers and Fangs, a large, four-story structure, was the best beast-baiting arena in the city. It featured only the finest pit-fighters and brought in only the most exotic, most terrifying beasts from as far away as Puret and Mol. Cityfolk flocked to Fullers and Fangs to bet on their favorite men, or on their favorite beasts. On any given night one never knew which would leave the arena alive, though Nach suspected certain events were rigged. A good man was an asset worth protecting, and yet more often than not a pit-fighter, even the most skilled, was dead within a month.

"So," Sandar said. "Why are we here?"

Nach grinned. "We're going to offer someone a safer line of work."

*

High above Nach's head, a wooden ceiling arched over the arena, and below him lay the pit, a wide, oval, sand-filled area surrounded by a high palisade wall. Doors of different sizes were set into the wall at intervals, some used by the pit-fighters to gain entrance from the waiting chambers, others to release the beasts from their cages. The top several feet of the wall doubled as a railing for the first gallery, a slanted section at ground level that circled the pit, where the poorer folk could stand for a copper chip's admittance. Above that hovered the second gallery. For a half-silver each, a thousand spectators could fill its benches on a good night. And above that ran the grand gallery, where several hundred wealthy patrons, patrons like Nach, could pay a gold troyal to enjoy their entertainment in comfort.

Nach shifted in his seat. He was anxious for the match to begin. It had been hawked all across Fell's Hollow for more than a week, the greatest Kernian pit-fighter in a decade to battle a strange new beast never before featured at Fullers and Fangs. A beast imported all the way from the uncharted lands beyond Thalia. The hawkers claimed it would be the match of the year, and, apparently, many in the city thought the same. The galleries were packed near to capacity. The din of the crowd was loud and raucous and pounded in Nach's ears.

A door opened in the pit wall, and a short, raven-haired man in a finely cut black tunic marched to the center of the pit. He clutched a silver-tipped walking stick in one fist and wore a wide, teeth-filled smile. The man raised his stick and the crowd quieted.

"My good people!" he cried. "Welcome to Fuller's and Fangs!"

The crowd cheered and whistled. The man let the applause continue for a moment, and then went on. "This evening we have a special treat! A spectacle beyond your wildest imaginations! An encounter that is sure to leave you breathless! It is my great pleasure to bring to you, Holdinar Freece and the grakkyn!"

The crowd erupted, and the man bowed with a flourish. He skipped back through the door just as another door opened and a well-muscled, bronze-skinned man stalked into the pit. He was bald, naked to the waist, and carried a thick-bladed broadsword.

Nach smiled. Holdinar Freece was perfect. He'd seen him twice before, and was impressed with the man's skill with a blade. He would make an ideal guardian if Nach could convince him to abandon the thrill of the pit. He would have to pay him handsomely, something he hated to do, but he couldn't lose the Buckler Street den. He needed Freece.

The pit-fighter thrust his broadsword into the air, and the crowd roared. The man was nearly as big as Sandar. One look at him would intimidate the most ardent of watchmen.

"He'd be good," Sandar yelled over the din. "No one would dare mess with him."

Nach's smile broadened. The crowd quieted slightly. Then another door opened, and a winged, lizard-like beast charged into the pit. The crowd gasped. The grakkyn was enormous, easily twice the size of a good draft horse. Black scales glittered along its serpentine body. It roared, dug its claws into the sand, and skidded to a stop. It shook its head, apparently confused by its new surroundings. From an iron manacle clamped around one of its ankles, a length of chain stretched back into its cage.

Again, the beast bellowed in fury. Then it spotted Freece and streaked straight at him. Freece stood fast, broadsword at the ready. Nach was impressed. Most men would have pissed themselves by now.

Two paces from Freece the beast's chain snapped taut, and the creature was flipped onto its back. The pit-fighter shot forward and drove the point of his broadsword into the soft side of its belly. The grakkyn screeched. It twisted, thrashed, and then, righting itself, scurried backward, blood dripping from its wound. The crowd cheered wildly.

"Brave," Sandar shouted. "He didn't even flinch."

Nach nodded. Brave indeed, he thought.

Freece took a few steps toward the grakkyn. The beast crouched, roared, and charged again. The pit-fighter dove backwards, rolled, and came up in a low stance. The grakkyn's chain snapped once more and the beast wrenched to a halt. Freece took advantage of its confusion and lunged. The tip of his blade sunk into the grakkyn's snout. Blood spurted into the air and the beast bellowed in pain. Freece yanked back his sword and recovered to the edge of the pit. The Kernian laughed and raised his bloody blade to the crowd as they roared their approval.

"Fast, isn't he?" Nach yelled.

"Very," Sandar agreed.

The beast backed away, snarling. Blood smeared its snout, and it moved awkwardly, favoring its wounded side. It stretched its wings and roared.

Freece moved forward, slowly, his broadsword pointed at the grakkyn. This time the beast didn't charge. It slunk away from the pit-fighter, snarling and hissing and snapping its fangs. Freece stopped. The grakkyn stopped. They stared at each other, two mortal enemies.

Nach elbowed Sandar. "Watch this," he told him. "I've seen Freece do this before."

Abruptly, the pit-fighter turned his back on the grakkyn. He let his sword dangle in his hand and slowly walked away. Instantly, the beast reacted. It dug its claws into the sand and launched itself at the pit-fighter. In one smooth movement, Freece spun, swinging his broadsword like an axe.

The grakkyn, realizing its mistake, tried to stop, but was too late. Freece's blade cut into the side of its neck. Blood spouted. The beast wailed, a long, mournful howl that filled the gallery. It collapsed to the sand, and Freece again stepped out of its range.

The Kernian warrior thrust his blade into the air, once, twice, three times. The crowd thundered around Nach as he stared down at the pit-fighter. The man was a born killer. Nach didn't care what it cost. By the end of the evening, Freece would be working for him.

"It's all over!" Sandar shouted, gesturing at the beast. The grakkyn had crawled back some distance and now lay shaking, its head lolled to one side. A thick tongue, purple and forked, stuck out between its fangs. Blood soaked its black scales. It twitched, let out another cry, and lay still.

The crowd rose to its feet, and Freece returned his attention to the beast. It was time for the killing blow. Nach stood and watched in awe. The pit-fighter eased toward his prey. He held his blade in one hand, and blood ran down its edge. He moved closer, cautiously, studying the creature. Nach clenched his fists in anticipation. Freece took another step. And then another. The crowd was in a frenzy. Even Sandar, who never showed emotion, was cheering wildly.

When Freece reached the side of the beast, he leaned forward and smacked it with the flat of his blade. The grakkyn didn't move. Satisfied, the Kernian gripped his sword in both hands and raised it over his head. He hesitated, turning to look up to the galleries. The crowd exploded. Nach smiled. Freece was wonderful, he thought.

And then the grakkyn struck.

It shot up from the sand, its bloody snout split wide open. With an audible crunch, it clamped its fangs around Freece's head. The beast jerked its jaws from side to side. Blood splattered the sand.

Freece's broadsword dropped from his quivering hands. The grakkyn whipped its head back and with a final tug tore Freece's head from his body. A fountain of blood sprayed up from the stump of the pit-fighter's neck. Then his body thunked to the ground.

The beast spat out the Kernian's head, stretched its wings, and leaped into the air. Behind it, its chain snapped like a piece of rotted string. The crowd screamed in panic as the grakkyn flew straight up, roared, and crashed through the center of the ceiling. Shards of wood rained down into the pit. The grakkyn roared once more and disappeared out into the night.

*

Nach opened the decanter and filled his glass. A candle burned on the counter, sending golden shards of light reflecting through the liquid.

Sandar shut the door to the Sorsagorium. Bells jangled. The bodyguard leaned against the shelves and grunted. "What now?" he asked.

Nach was stunned. He didn't know what to think, or what his next step would be. He had been so sure of Freece. "I don't know," he admitted.

"We could bribe a watchman," Sandar suggested.

"Don't be absurd," Nach snapped. "Larron will have warned his men about me already. All he needs is one excuse, and he'll send me to the gallows."

"Sellswords?" Sandar asked.

Nach shrugged. "I thought of that. No, those killers have no loyalty. They'd sell me out for a copper chip."

Sandar grunted in frustration. "Then who? This city is full of thugs. There's got to be one or two we could trust."

Nach took a long swallow of the fragrat, felt it turn to fire in his gut. Who? he thought. Yes, that was the question. Who could Nach hire to handle the den on Buckler Street? There had to be someone. But he didn't think he could trust anyone. Ukko had been a rare breed, as loyal as he was ruthless. There were few like him. Few like Sandar. No, Nach realized. There was no one. He would have to force someone's loyalty.

Blackmail, then? That might work. Perhaps he could use a watchman, after all. If he could find one that had something to hide. Something he could exploit. Or perhaps there was another way. Maybe he could get the Watch to ignore his dens completely. He heard Larron had a son. A son he was reputed to be very fond of. Maybe that was the answer.

Nach emptied his glass and poured another. The fragrat burned. More than usual. His stomach smoldered, as if he'd swallowed a bucket of hot ashes. His nerves were getting the better of him. He needed to settle down. He needed to relax.

His eyes moved to the staircase. He didn't expect his whore back for a while. Pity. He could use a distraction. But he had sent her to hunt down a family heirloom that some bastard had stolen from him. Just another problem he'd been forced to deal with. Maybe Sandar could go back to Rogueswarde, he thought. He could find him something delectable, some other whore to play with for the evening.

Nach's stomach burned hotter. And then he felt it. A sudden tightening in his throat. Something was wrong.

"Boss?" Sandar said. "You okay? You don't look so good."

Nach tried to draw a breath, and failed. His windpipe had closed.

"Boss?"

Nach's eyes shot to the glass on the counter. Poison! His lungs began to ache. His stomach roared like a furnace as a pulse of fear surged through his veins. He opened his mouth, tried to suck in air. It felt like someone had clamped his throat in a vice. Darts of light danced in front of his eyes. Nach's knees buckled, and he fell to the floor.

"Boss!"

Nach strained to breathe. He tried with every bit of strength he possessed, but failed. His heart hammered in his chest, and he squeezed his eyes shut. This wasn't fair at all! He wasn't supposed to die! Who did this to him? He'd find the bastard, rip his heart out with his bare hands!

He heard Sandar move behind the counter and felt him kneel down on the floor next to him. "What's wrong?" Sandar cried, panic lacing his voice.

Nach opened his eyes. He stared into the curio, at the crystal decanter sitting on the bottom shelf, at the amber liquid that had poisoned him. His vision started to blur. His lungs spasmed. He felt something rupture, and molten fire flowed through his gut. And then he saw it. On the bronze balance, an old sprig of lilac rested on one side. Its purple petals had withered nearly to black, and the weight of it pushed the pan to the shelf.

Lilac?

"Boss!"

Sandar grabbed his shoulders and shook him. "Talk to me!"

Nach's lungs spasmed again and went still. His heart slowed. The pain in his gut lessened as a cold numbness soaked into his body. Lilac? A memory tugged at his dying brain. He tried frantically to retrieve it. Then darkness swept his sight away and Sandar's screams faded into silence. His heart thunked one last time, and then stopped.

BENEATH THE SAVAGE POET

"O Evil, that master of disguise,
Will change its cloak for every eye."
The Chameleon, *29-30*
—*Flenter dae Chode*

T HE NEWS SWEPT THROUGH the city like a
sweet scent on the wind. The fog that had
been smothering Fell's Hollow for nearly a
month had finally lifted, and a small private
trading ship, the first the city had seen since the
arrival of the great storm, had arrived at sunset
with word of a stunning event: King Felgus of
Nyland had been assassinated, and all of Bosk
was in flames. As Felgus had sired no heir and
had neglected to designate one, Bosk was now a

battlefield. Several factions were fighting for control of the capital city, and thus Nyland no longer posed a threat to Fell's Hollow.

There would be no war.

Within minutes the news had blown down the Stonewharf and into every establishment on the Run. Within an hour it had whipped through the rest of the Warren and out into the other wardes. Cityfolk high and low spread it amongst each other without thought to class or station. Wealthy merchants passed it to peasants and peasants passed it to the Watch and the Watch passed it to everyone as they walked the streets on patrol.

By the time the evening sky was emblazoned with a hundred stars, the wondrous news had gusted into the Yards, Stockwarde, and Oldtowne. From there it wasted no time, rushing through the cramped and muddy streets of Rogueswarde, over Temple Hill, and up into the Heights and Faettewarde. It even reached the sparsely populated mining community up in the Crags. And then, just as a midnight moon was rising over the city, it made it to Southside, where it burst through the door of the Savage Poet on the lips of an out-of-breath silversmith.

The silversmith, an older, heavy-set man with curly white hair and wide, gray-green eyes, regaled the startled patrons with the good tidings between snorts and gasps and wheezes. Then he turned and left as abruptly as he'd arrived.

Emma Ellystun stared down into her half-empty tankard. Though the folk about the common room were slapping each other on the back and cheering loudly, the news did nothing to raise her spirits. A shadowhunter had arrived at Fell's Hollow a few days ago, and Watch Commander Rhandellar Larron had hired her brother to accompany the hunter on some kind of mission. Larron had said he only wanted Ander's sword, not hers, and Ander had told her to wait for him at their boarding house in Stockwarde. But he had never returned.

Ander and the shadowhunter had tracked something up into the Crags. Half the rumors said it was a madman. The other half claimed it had been a valkar, a creature of a predatory race that had preyed on humans for a hundred ages. Emma didn't believe that nonsense. The valkar were a myth, invented to scare children into finishing their gruel. Regardless of what it had been, madman or monster, the shadowhunter had killed it, but not before it had slain her brother.

Emma downed the rest of her ale in a single slug and gestured to Balinoch Crend, the spindly little innkeep, for another. With the death of Ander, her future had been thrown into chaos. Though her true passion had always been for the beauty of verse, she had never been able to succeed as a playwright. She had some skill with words, quite a bit of skill if she believed some, but she lacked a truly unique story to set her work apart. She had therefore earned her keep as a sellsword alongside her brother, but it was her brother's skill with a blade that had gotten them work, no matter what Ander liked to say. It was Ander who had earned a living for the both of them. She had just been a tagalong.

Emma glanced over at two rough-looking men playing taffyl at the bar, each in a dirty, oilcloth cloak, each with a longsword scabbarded at the hip. They would have no trouble finding work in Fell's Hollow, together or apart. No one was going to hire her for anything.

Crend skittered over to her table and set down a tankard. Foam ran over its rim. She slid the innkeep a few copper chips and snatched up the ale. *To Ander*, she thought, and took a deep swallow. Wiping her lips, she turned her attention to a book that lay open on the table before her.

She had come to the Savage Poet to risk her entire future on this book. It was hand-bound in plum-red leather, a complete edition of the works of Espare dae Kesh, the greatest poet and playwright of the ages. Several days ago she had noticed something strange in the text, and last night, in an attempt to distract herself from her grief, she had finally discovered what had caught her eye.

Emma opened the book and turned to *My Wellspring of Genius*. It was said to have been the last poem dae Kesh had written before his death. She had been reading it, pondering its meaning, when she realized the last letter in each line of the opening stanza, when put together, spelled out the word *beneath*. At the time she had thought it nothing more than coincidence. Last night she had transposed the last letter of each line of the entire poem into the margin of the book and had been shocked at what she'd discovered.

It was a message from Espare dae Kesh himself.

Someone in the crowd shouted a cheer and the rest joined in, tankards clunking together in celebration. Emma ignored them as she read dae Kesh's message again.

Beneath the Savage Poet lies my wellspring of genius, the secret that gave birth to all my work. I leave it to some future poet with the courage to continue what I have begun. Seek the black stone in the corner of the innkeep's quarters and fare thee well.

She had heard that dae Kesh had traveled over the Great Waste several times, from the Midlands into the Nine Kingdoms, but no one had ever known where he had gone, or what had drawn him on such a perilous journey time and time again. Now Emma knew. Or at least she hoped she knew.

How many inns in the Nine Kingdoms were called the Savage Poet? She guessed only one. This one. It had been around for at least four, maybe five hundred years. It had been here during dae Kesh's time. The poet had come to Fell's Hollow and left behind a secret hidden beneath this very place. The secret to his genius.

Emma needed that secret.

She studied the common room. The place was busy, but not as busy as it would be in an hour or so as word of Felgus's death spread throughout the warde. Crend was stalking about, clearing empty tankards from tables. Emma's gaze slipped past the innkeep to a small door at the end of a hall that led to a second common room at the back of the inn. That door, everyone knew, opened into Crend's own room.

Was that the room dae Kesh was referring to? Had every innkeep over the centuries used that same room for their personal quarters? She had to assume that was the case. She prayed to Ryke that was the case. She would only have one chance. If she was caught, she would be banned from the inn at best, arrested by the Watch at worst.

Since childhood she'd aspired to be a great playwright. She had dreamed of becoming Espare dae Kesh reborn. He was the last true master of the craft. Since dae Kesh, there had been only simulacrums, unworthy imitators. Skythe was mediocre. Phemorel was juvenile. And Bonnost hadn't written a word worth reading since *The Magister*. She didn't want to be like them. She wanted to be a true master of the craft, else why bother? And now, after discovering dae Kesh's message, she had a chance to do just that.

One of the rough-looking men at the bar stood and tossed a gold troyal at Crend. "Ale for everyone!" he shouted. Crend bit the coin and then skipped behind the bar. Cheers followed him.

Emma took another swallow of ale. Life as she knew it was over. Her brother was dead, her sellsword days were done. It was either take this chance and discover dae Kesh's secret, or find another way to earn a living.

*

The door to the inn opened, and a half-dozen more cityfolk crammed inside. Beyond the door, the moon hung shimmering in the night sky. Both common rooms of the Savage Poet were now full to bursting. The crowd was boisterous, laughing and shouting and toasting Felgus's death and their own good fortune. They had been spared a Nyland invasion, and they were happy. For them, life had returned to normal.

Crend was nowhere to be seen, most likely in the back room passing out ales as fast as he could draw them. The crowd was not likely to get much larger, or more celebratory. They were as distracted as they were going to be. It was time to act.

Emma pushed back her chair. Feigning a yawn, she took a candle from her table and edged her way through the crowd to stand before the door to Crend's quarters. She raked her eyes through the common room. No one appeared to be watching. Taking a deep breath, she opened the door, slipped inside, and closed it behind her. She turned, and stopped short.

"Ryke's beard," she gasped.

The flickering light of the candle fell upon an utter mess. An unmade bed was shoved into a corner, a rumpled blanket balled up on its hay-stuffed mattress. A chest of drawers stood against one wall, several drawers half open, spilling wrinkled and greasy shirts onto the stone floor. Atop a chair and table that footed the bed, unwashed plates and tankards teetered in stacks. The rest of the room was littered with old crates, casks of ale both opened and unopened, and dozens of copies of the *Gargoyle*, Zoltin Maark's gossip-filled broadside, crumpled and tossed about like trash.

Her thought turned back to dae Kesh's message. *Seek the black stone in the corner of the innkeep's quarters and fare thee well.* Three of the room's corners were relatively free of debris. She would start with those.

*

Anxious, Emma angled toward the bed. She had searched the three corners thoroughly and found nothing. She had to move fast. Crend might walk in on her at any moment. Wrinkling her nose, she eased the mussed-up bed away from the wall and skirted around it for a closer look.

Dust balls the size of rats flittered in the breeze along the floor. She brushed them away and bent over to examine the corner. The floor was set with large, close-fitting flagstones. The walls were of gray, rough-cut carterock, mined out of the Crags most likely, and held together with lines of flaking mortar. And there, right in the bottom corner of the room, one black stone stood out from the rest.

A jolt of excitement shot through Emma. She knelt and placed the candle on the floor. Holding her breath, she slipped a dagger from a sheath at her waist and knocked at the black stone with the pommel. There came a solid clack of metal on rock. The stone was set firmly into the wall.

She took the tip of her dagger and stuck it into the mortar surrounding the stone. The point sunk to about the depth of her fingernail. It was not mortar at all, she realized. It was simply packed dirt. Emma quickly scraped it away and gripped the stone with her fingertips. She wiggled the stone back and forth, back and forth, back and forth, until it began to loosen. She worked at it some more and then, finally, the stone slipped out of the wall, revealing a dark hole behind it.

She set the stone aside and reached a trembling hand into the hole. Her fingers closed around something small and dry, like a curled up leaf. Heart beating like a hundred Thalian war drums, she pulled out the object. It was a piece of parchment, rolled and tied with a length of string. And it was heavy. There was something inside it.

She cut the string and carefully, slowly,

unrolled the parchment. An old rusted iron key fell from the parchment and landed in her lap. A key? A key to what? She held the parchment closer to the candle and read a single line of script that ran across it, written in a thin, elegant hand. The ink had long since faded to a dull gray.

Your destiny lies beneath the flagstone upon which you kneel.

Emma's heart nearly leaped out of her chest. She was holding a scrap of parchment that the great Espare dae Kesh had once held in his very hands. And she was reading his words, words that she knew he had been meant only for her. Goosebumps broke out on her arms. She slid over a bit and examined the flagstone beneath her knees. It was considerably old, seemingly set into place when the inn was originally constructed. It looked as if it had never been disturbed.

Once more, Emma took her dagger and stuck it into the mortar surrounding the stone. And again, the tip sunk into a line of compacted dirt. She brushed a strand of hair from her face and set to work, scraping and digging. Sweat broke out on her brow, and she wiped it away with the back of a hand. She was close. Close to discovering the secret that would set her on the path to greatness. The notion sent a chill racing down her spine.

After a final scrape, she wedged the point of her dagger under the edge of the flagstone and pried. The stone eased up a fraction. She twisted her dagger, driving it deeper beneath the stone. The stone lifted a tad more, and she was able to get a hand under it. She dropped the dagger, slipped both hands beneath the stone, and heaved. The flagstone flipped over and thunked noisily onto the floor. She froze. Had someone heard? She waited for a long moment, silent, listening. On the other side of the door, the raucous crowd continued with their celebration.

Emma let out a long, slow breath and returned her attention to the floor. Before her gaped the opening to a narrow shaft that descended straight down into darkness. The shaft was hewn from solid rock, and rusted iron rungs were driven into it at intervals. Her fingertips tingled with excitement. Where did it lead? What secret had dae Kesh gone to such great lengths to hide?

She sheathed her dagger and grabbed the candle. The yellow light danced wildly down the shaft. Emma paused to settle her nerves. What was waiting for her down in the dark?

"I guess there's only one way to find out," she whispered.

*

She let go of the last rung and placed her foot on solid ground. The shaft had taken her down a hundred feet or more. It had terminated at the end of a tunnel, also cut from the rock, that headed off in a westerly direction. The tunnel was so low she had to stoop to enter it, and so narrow her arms brushed against both sides. The air was cool and damp, and it was as silent as the inside of a Davacre tomb.

She held the candle before her and started down the tunnel. It sloped slightly and steadily downward as she shuffled on. After only a short distance, her legs began to cramp. She could almost feel the crushing weight of the rock overhead. She pushed on and on until, at the edge of the candle's light, she spotted something. Bars, a wall of rusted iron bars. The tunnel had been sealed off.

Emma scuffled closer. The bars were close-set and flaking with age. Two huge hinges stuck out on one side of the iron wall, and a crude lock hung from a handle on the other. She was wrong, she realized. The tunnel hadn't been walled off at all. This was some kind of door, and she knew in an instant who had the key.

She held the candle up to the bars. Behind the door the tunnel continued on for a short distance, and then ended abruptly at a wall of dark stone. It was hard to tell, though, as the light didn't quite reach that far. And there was something else, a darker shape against the stone. Perhaps it was the entrance to another even narrower passageway. The shape was odd. It almost looked like a person standing there in the dark.

The shape moved, and Emma's stomach jumped into her throat.

There came a clank of metal, like a chain being

dragged across an anvil. The sound echoed loudly down the tunnel. Emma leaped back and snatched out her dagger.

The shape spoke. "Put down the light." Its voice sounded odd, more like a hiss than a voice, and it had a strange accent, as if it had a hard time forming the words.

"Who are you?" Emma demanded, trying to keep the fear out of her own voice.

There came a long sigh. "I have not had a visitor in quite some time."

"Who are you?" Emma repeated.

"Have you come for a tale?" the shape asked.

Was this dae Kesh's secret? Who in the Abyss was this? *What* in the Abyss was this? No one could have survived down here, for it had been centuries since dae Kesh's death. Perhaps it was some kind of sorcery. That thought came with a shock of fear.

"Well?" the shape urged. "Are you here for a tale or not?"

"Yes," Emma said. She didn't know what else to say.

The shape shifted its position, and again Emma heard the clanking of a chain. "Unlock the door," the shape told her. "Come and sit with me. Leave the candle out there. I cannot bear the light."

This is madness, Emma thought. What was this thing? Was it even human? She didn't think so. Her fear threatened to crush her. Could she bring herself to open the door? And then realization thundered down on her. Was this what dae Kesh had meant by having courage? *I leave it to some future artist with the courage to continue what I have begun.* He hadn't meant the courage to become an artist like him. He'd meant the courage to face this creature! Did she have the courage? Could she face this unknown thing, alone, in the dark, all for the gift of dae Kesh's genius?

"What are you waiting for?" the shape hissed. It was definitely not a human voice, yet there was a slightly feminine quality to it.

Emma hardened her resolve. She set the candle on the tunnel floor and took out dae Kesh's key. It felt cold in her hand as she slid it into the crude lock and gave it a turn. There came a crunch and a sharp crack. She yanked down on the lock and it snapped into pieces, bits of rust raining down on her hand. She pushed open the door. The hinges shrieked in protest, echoing madly down the tunnel. Emma clutched her dagger tightly in one hand and moved toward the creature.

It wasn't human. The thing had strangely shaped shoulders and ears that came to points. And it was gaunt. Very gaunt. Almost skeletal. An iron manacle encircled one of its boney ankles. A heavy chain snaked from the manacle to a thick rung set into the tunnel wall. What in the Abyss was this thing? Emma took a step closer. "How long have you been here?" she asked.

"Far too long," it said.

"Who are you? What are you?" Emma wasn't sure she wanted to know the answer.

"That is not important," the creature said. "You have come for a tale, yes?"

"I have."

"And what will you give in return?"

Emma hadn't thought of that. There was a price for the tale? A price for dae Kesh's genius? She had come this far, and there was no turning back now. She had no choice but to pay it, whatever it was.

"What do you want?" Emma asked.

"I want freedom," the creature hissed. It shifted its position again, settling its back against the wall, and then it continued. "I have been chained here for more years than I can remember. I was captured by a shadowhunter and sold to a bard in Cabyll. The bard brought me here. He treated me most foully. Left me with only one leechet to feed upon." The thing gestured to something in the corner Emma hadn't noticed before. There was another shape. This one seemed to be hanging from the ceiling, like the husk of some giant cocoon that had dried up and shriveled over the ages.

"The bard returned many times," the creature went on, "always promising my freedom in exchange for another story of my people that he could twist and corrupt for his own purposes.

And then, after many years, he left and never returned. And I've been alone here ever since."

Emma shook her head. That was impossible. Espare dae Kesh was a great man. He would never have done such a thing. What this creature was suggesting was beyond belief. She tried to get a better look at the thing. Her eyes, now more adjusted to the darkness, took in more details. The creature's skin seemed pale, almost white. It had no hair, and it was nearly naked, save for a strip of rotted cloth over its loins. Something stuck out from its chest, like a handful of stumps. Behind it, leather-like folds of flesh stuck up over its shoulders. Were those wings?

"What are you?" Emma asked.

"What am I?" The creature let out a laugh that sounded like a stewpot boiling over. "I am misunderstood, I and my kind. Though I doubt there are any of my race still alive. You humans have destroyed us all."

And then Emma knew. "You are a valkar."

"I was," the thing admitted. "But I can hardly be called that anymore. Now I am nothing but a broken beast, chained forever in the dark."

Emma squeezed the hilt of her dagger. The rumors were true. This was one of the creatures that had killed her brother. "You are evil," Emma told it.

"Evil?" the valkar croaked, its voice hissing wildly. "Look at me. The bard sliced off my tentares, leaving me here to feed with nothing but my teeth. I am old and maimed and pitiful. How am I evil and he was not? How are the valkar evil and humans not?"

Despite her anger, Emma felt a twinge of sympathy for the poor thing. It was wretched, she realized. And if it spoke the truth, dae Kesh was nothing like Emma had imagined. He was no great man, no genius, no hero to be worshipped. The valkar had to be lying.

"Will you grant me my freedom?" it asked.

"You wish me to set you free? Your kind feed on humans." Emma glanced over at the husk hanging in the corner, and she shuddered. She did not want to think about what that might be. She shook her head. "I could never release you."

The valkar sighed. "You misunderstand me, human. I am not asking to be released from my prison. I am asking to be released from this life. I will give you your tale, but in return you must slay me. I am weary beyond reckoning. And yet, I cannot do the deed myself. I have no means other than starvation. And that I have tried. Many times. But each time the thirst takes hold, I crawl to my leechet and sink my worn and cracked teeth into its withered flesh. If you want your tale, you must promise to end my torment."

Stunned, Emma leaned back against the wall of the tunnel. She now knew exactly what dae Kesh had meant when he'd talked about courage. It wasn't that she would need courage to be an artist like him, or the courage to face the valkar alone in the dark. If she wanted to become the greatest playwright of her age, she would have to summon the courage to continue what he'd started. She would have to prolong the suffering of this thing. She would have to promise the valkar she would end its life, and then, when she'd received her tale, she would have to betray it. She'd have to leave it unharmed, only to return again and again for more tales, more stories from the valkar's history that she could set into verse. Those tales would make Emma the greatest playwright of her age, she had no doubt. As long as she had the courage to torture this thing that stood before her.

The valkar stirred. "Well?" it hissed.

Emma frowned. Could she do it? Could she torture an evil creature for her own gain? And now that she thought on it, were the valkar truly evil? Were they really that different from her own race? They fed on mankind to survive. That was part of their nature. And mankind had destroyed them. That was part of mankind's nature. So, were humans any less evil? It all came down to that, really. If she believed an entire race could be inherently evil, then she could follow in dae Kesh's footsteps. Easily. But if she thought evil was something else, a choice to act contrary to one's own nature, then her future lay elsewhere.

"Have you decided, human?" The valkar shifted its position and its chain clanked.

Emma slid down the side of the wall, crossed

her legs, and tried to make herself comfortable.
"What is your name?" she asked it.

The valkar hesitated for a moment, and then
spoke. "I have been called the White Death and
the Scourge of the Sands. The Mesurites referred
to me as Blooddrinker. I've had other names over
the ages, names I can no longer remember. But
amongst my own kind I was known as
Tuzsheset."

"Well, then, Tuzsheset, tell me a tale," Emma
said. "Tell me *your* tale."

*

Emma pushed the flagstone back in place and
brushed the dirt into the seam around it,
removing any sign that she'd been there at all. She
stood, eased the innkeep's bed back into place,
and wiped away the tears that streamed down her
cheeks. She had never heard such a tragic story in
all her life. Chode's *Rhailiffaeben*, Trenee's *Lament*,
even dae Kesh's masterpiece *Har and Iva*, none of
them came even close.

She moved to the door and opened it a crack.
Beyond it, the common room had settled down.
It was late. Only a few persistent customers
milled about, still celebrating the news from
Nyland. Crend had his spindly back to her,
cleaning off a table by the front window.

She slipped quietly out of the innkeep's
quarters. No one noticed. Emma felt a rush of
confidence, the same rush she used to feel after

she and Ander had finished a job. She frowned at the memory of her brother. He was gone, and so was that part of her life. She blew out her candle, set it on the bar, and exited quietly out of the inn.

The night was bright and clear. The moon was shining happily in the west, and a thousand stars glittered against the black sky. The fog that had suffocated the city for nearly a month was gone, and with its absence, Fell's Hollow seemed to breathe easier.

Emma inhaled deeply and tried to calm her nerves. Once she put the valkar's tale to verse, she could well become the most famous playwright in the city. Perhaps in all the Nine Kingdoms. She smiled and started off toward Oldtowne. She needed parchment and ink. Lots of it. Arryn's bookshop was closed at this hour, but she'd wake the old storekeep and beg him to sell her what she needed. She had work to do.

As she walked, she put a hand to the empty sheath at her waist. She had left her dagger with Tuzsheset so that she could do what Emma could not. For good or for evil, that was the price she had paid.

ABOUT THE AUTHOR

A. J. "Jim" Abbiati lives and works in historic Mystic, Connecticut. He holds an MFA in Creative Writing, a BA in English, and a BS in Computer Science. When not writing, Jim works for a major software engineering firm. He is currently at work on his second novel and is considering doctoral programs in either creative writing or narratology.

Jim loves to hear from fans and fellow writers. Contact him at: http://ajabbiati.com

A BONUS *FELL'S HOLLOW* STORY — FREE!

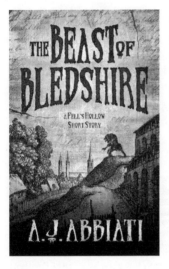

In this exclusive short story, you'll meet Kretch, the anger-plagued strong-arm at the Hole. When a stranger comes to the famous tavern in search of a fellow Ukrian, Kretch fears his secret will be revealed, a secret that has kept him on the run for more than thirty years. A secret so terrible, if discovered, it could get Kretch hung by the Watch, or worse, unleash a bloody slaughter upon the city…

HOW TO GET YOUR FREE COPY:

To receive your free copy of *The Beast of Bledshire*, post a short review of *Fell's Hollow* on Amazon, Audible, or Goodreads.
Send a link to your review to beast@ajabbiati.com

Include in your email your preferred format:
- Kindle Ebook
- PDF
- Audio
- Signed Print (will include a small fee to cover print cost, shipping, and handling).

Once the review has been verified, you will be sent *The Beast of Bledshire* for free!

THE [NORTAV] METHOD for WRITERS

The Secret to Constructing Prose Like the Pros

A.J. ABBIATI

"A fascinating way to look at prose...I highly recommend this book."
—VICTORINE LIESKE, Bestselling author of *Not What She Seems*

This work of fiction was created using *The NORTAV Method for Writers*. For more information visit:
http://thenortavmethod.com

LAK Publishing
http://lakpublishing.info

Made in the USA
Charleston, SC
03 February 2014